USA TODAY BESTSELLING AUTHOR
# DALE MAYER

# Toes in up the Tulips

Lovely Lethal Gardens 20

TOES UP IN THE TULIPS: LOVELY LETHAL GARDENS, BOOK 20
Beverly Dale Mayer
Valley Publishing Ltd.

ISBN-13: 978-1-773367-59-0
Print Edition

# Books in This Series

# About This Book

A new cozy mystery series from *USA Today* best-selling author Dale Mayer. Follow gardener and amateur sleuth Doreen Montgomery—and her amusing and mostly lovable cat, dog, and parrot—as they catch murderers and solve crimes in lovely Kelowna, British Columbia.

**Riches to rags. ... Time heals all wounds, ... but old deeds still haunt, ... even for the innocent!**
After helping the captain solve his long overdue case, Doreen's reputation is well and truly cemented in Kelowna. That's proven out when a young woman is murdered in her own apartment, and the police start looking at the boyfriend. With the town on edge, this young man seeks out Doreen's help to prove his innocence.

Corporal Mack Moreau is back to light duty work—mostly keeping an eye on Doreen, if the captain has any say in it. It's hardly a hardship, as he loves being around her, when she's not dipping her toes in his active cases. And yet somehow she manages to find old cases that dovetail with his ongoing ones, giving her an exaggerated opinion of where her boundaries are.

What seems simple on the surface goes back into history to a case that was done and dusted, with the killer now out free, looking for revenge. But, of course, it's not that simple or that easy; and, by the time Doreen and her animal crew are done, the world has shifted for more than just one person in this case.

**Sign up to be notified of all Dale's releases here!**
https://geni.us/DaleNews

# Chapter 1

*Thursday Evening, Not Quite a Week Later ...*

A LMOST A WEEK later, she sat outside, her face up to the sun, just enjoying having nothing to do—no killers to run down, no crazies to go after, just finding some semblance of normality in her world. The captain had been more than profuse in his thanks, and, as she had filled everybody in afterward, there had been several news announcements about the case being cracked finally.

As a lot of people already knew Doreen had been on the case, she had already received a lot of cheers and well-wishing.

She was due to head down to Nan's soon, and Mack was coming with her for a postponed celebration. They were supposed to have the celebration a while ago, but then Mack had been shot. Since then they hadn't been able to set it up—until tonight. So, in about ten minutes, Mack would be here. She got up, brushed the grass off her dress, and slowly moved toward the house. She wandered through to the front door and found Mack standing outside on the front step by the hydrangeas.

He said, "Wow, I don't think I've seen you in a dress

before."

She looked down, smiled, and replied, "I haven't had a whole lot of reason for wearing one."

He asked, "Are you ready to walk down to Rosemoor?"

"Yep. Are you?"

And, with his nod, they locked up the house and slowly moved toward the creek, all the animals coming as well. She had insisted because it wasn't fair to have a private celebration for Mack and Doreen in solving all these cold cases, when the animals were as much to thank for everything that she'd done anyway. And the Rosemoor management had finally agreed.

As she walked with Mack at her side, she noted, "It has been a crazy-busy summer."

"You think?" he quipped. "But the captain is chortling because of the cold cases you've closed, even though we had to open a couple new ones due to you," he added, with an eye roll.

"I think it is only fair to the families to explain their loved ones didn't die by accident and that we have the murderer behind bars."

"Absolutely," he agreed, squeezing her hand.

"Ha," Thaddeus cawed in her ear. He'd been riding on her shoulder, humming gently as they strolled along. But now he poked his head through her hair and turned a gimlet eye on Mugs.

Recognizing the signs, she hurriedly warned him, "Don't you dare. You be good. Mugs is being good, you can be good too."

That gimlet eye turned her way. Doreen quickly picked up the pace.

"Problems," Mack asked as he kept pace. He looked at

Thaddeus curiously. "He's behaving nicely."

"So far – but not for long. He's got that look in his eye."

In a master move, Thaddeus sniffed his disdain and quickly shifted to Mack's shoulder. He then proceeded to cry out, "Hehehe."

She glared at him but ignored him. As long as he didn't ride Mugs or chase Goliath they might get past the creek without a catastrophe.

As they walked closer to Rosemoor, she looked at the houses on the opposite side of the creek. "Some really beautiful places are here."

"They truly are," he agreed.

"And I did finally connect with Scott at the auction house."

"Oh, good. Anything coming?"

She looked up at him. "Yeah, a pretty hefty check for the books. I haven't even told Nan."

"Is it enough to keep you in style for a little while? At least in pizza?" he asked, with a grin. When she told him how much, he stopped in his tracks. "Good God, you can almost buy a house in Kelowna for that."

She shook her head. "I wouldn't want to."

"Why not?" he asked. "Are you not planning on staying?"

"Oh, I'm planning on staying, but I'm partial to Nan's house."

He smiled, tucked her hand up close to him, and said, "At least now I won't have to worry about you not being able to feed yourself anymore."

She nodded. "*As long as I'm smart with it*, people keep telling me. I guess I'm not exactly sure what that'll mean though."

"And you will learn," Mack stated. "You're a smart woman."

She laughed. "Again there's that cheerleader."

"Nothing wrong with being a cheerleader." He gave her a hard glance. "Particularly when it comes from somebody who means it."

"I'm doing much better though, handling my money," she said, with a nod. "Never thought it would come to this, but really I am doing much better."

"You're doing fantastic—never meant to imply anything other than that."

"Good, because it's been a long hard summer in many ways, but it's also been very fulfilling."

"It has, indeed," he murmured. "For me too. ... And I talked to my brother today."

"Oh, right. How's that move of his coming?"

"He said that he's tried to call you a couple times today."

She frowned, pulled out her phone, and winced. "Yeah, I saw that earlier, and I just thought it was the one call."

"Are you avoiding him again?"

"No, not so much again," she admitted, "but I know my divorce settlement is going back and forth between him and my ex's attorney."

"They reached a settlement," Mack noted.

"They did?" She stopped to look at Mack. "Nick didn't tell me."

Mack gave her a wry look. "You'd have to answer your phone for that."

She winced. "Okay, good." She hesitated, then asked, "Did he tell you the details?"

Mack shook his head. "It's not for me to know. He's your lawyer, and you have to deal with that."

"Do you think it'll keep my ex-husband off my back now?"

"I hope so," Mack said. "The question really is, if it'll be something that makes him feel threatened."

"Oh no, meaning that if my lawyer's happy, then my ex-husband won't be?"

"It's always a possibility," Mack noted. "Anyway, promise me tomorrow that you'll get in touch with Nick."

"I will," she said. He looked her straight in the eye. "I promise."

As they walked up to Nan's, she asked, "Have you got any new cases?"

"Meaning, *You don't give me enough cases*, right?"

"I don't know about that. However, the last one was *Silenced in the Sunflowers*, and that was a week ago."

"So, what does that mean?" he asked. "You must have a *T* case now?"

"Yes, that's what I was thinking, but I don't know what it would be. I mean, what murder would involve a word beginning with *T*?" He came up with several words. She laughed at some of them. "I think *toes*," she suggested, nodding. "Toes in …" She stopped, saw headless tulips off to the side that hadn't been cut back, and said, "*Toes up in the Tulips*."

"And yet," Mack noted, "I don't have a case even similar to that."

"You didn't find any dead bodies recently?" she asked, with interest.

He stared at her and sighed. "Yes, … a young woman."

"Oh, I'm so sorry about that," Doreen said, sobering instantly. "It's always sad when it's a young person."

"I agree." And then he stopped and cursed.

"What's the matter?" Doreen asked.

He glared at her. "She was found in a garden."

She beamed. "Please, please, please, tell me that it was a garden with tulips."

"But tulips don't flower this time of year," he noted, shaking his head.

Her face fell.

"Except for the fact"—he stared at her, obviously with a terrible realization—"it wasn't really a garden. Flowers were thrown across her body. *Plastic* flowers."

She stared, her eyes wide. "And?"

He nodded slowly. "They were tulips."

She crowed. "Yes, *Toes up in the Tulips*, my next case."

He stopped, pulled her up close, put a hand on either side of her face, and murmured, "*My* next case is *Toes up in the Tulips*."

She reached up, kissed him hard and fast, seeing a glint rise in his gaze before stepping away quickly. "My case," she said. "*Mine*." And, with that, she started to laugh and ran toward Nan.

Nan stood on her patio, and, when she saw the two of them, she opened her arms wide and called out, "There you are. At least you're here, and the party can begin."

# Chapter 2

*Thursday Night, Second Week of September ...*

NAN HAD FINALLY discovered a good time for her rescheduled celebration of Doreen's and Mack's hard work in closing all these cold cases. Not only that, it was also a celebration of life for Paul, the captain's cousin, killed some forty years earlier, as well as others who celebrated getting some closure from all these solved cold cases.

Nan had pulled it together rather quickly, and it turned out lovely.

Plus it gave everybody a chance to say goodbye to Chrissy, one of the Rosemoor residents and Nan's friend, who had already passed, yet not by her own hand. The former cook here at Rosemoor, Peggy, had poisoned Chrissy. Her nephew, who was in Chrissy's will, Peter Riley, had even come by after the murder had come to light and had thanked Doreen for finding the truth about Chrissy's death. Doreen had made a trip up to Rutland to tell Chrissy's disowned daughter, Cassandra, who had shown up tonight too. It had been both a joyous occasion and a sad one because a Rosemoor resident and friend had been murdered, and nobody had realized it—until Doreen had started digging around.

At this point her reputation had been cemented, and it would be hard to get away from any of the talk that she overheard from the attendees, like, *She should do this professionally*, and *She should look into Great-Grandma Jo's death.*

Doreen crept away from most of those conversations as quickly as she could. She kept an eye on her brood, let loose in this contained room where the celebration was staged, making sure they were up to no mischief. She smiled as she saw Thaddeus hopping from person to person, chatting up each one. The seniors here loved that he could talk to them. Some of these poor people had outlived their family and didn't get much in the way of visitors.

With a frown, Doreen tried to spot Mugs and Goliath. *There.* Mugs was in his element, rubbing legs with so many people, who were happy to give him a pat on his head or to scratch behind his ears. *But where is Goliath?* Doreen was a little worried that he would jump onto the food table. Maybe she should have kept him in his harness and leash and tied him up, away from any temptations.

Then she spotted her huge Maine coon, happily sitting at the foot of one of the residents, who was feeding him off his plate of goodies. Doreen smirked and shook her head. Maybe that will hold Goliath in good stead for a couple hours. She'd check on all of them throughout the celebration this evening.

She was happy to see both Darren and the captain had shown up, to represent the local authorities, as well as family members who had lost loved ones. The captain had smiled at Doreen, making her realize they were on much better terms now. After all, she'd also helped to solve the decades old murder of his cousin that had plagued the captain all his life. Several times he had taken her aside tonight to repeatedly say thanks to her.

She'd smiled at him. "It's all good," she replied gently. "You can put your own demons to rest."

He nodded slowly. "And yet, in some ways, I want to keep them alive. More people are out there with cases that haven't been solved."

"Absolutely," she agreed. "I'm sure a lot of them. At the same time, there is a limit to how much any one of us can handle at one time."

He quirked a grin at her and teased, "What? Even you?"

She laughed. "Especially me," she declared, eyeing him intently. "Some days you think you can do it all, and then some days you wake up and realize that you shouldn't get out of bed."

He chuckled. "Hey, that is our world all the time."

She paused, then asked, "So what's this I hear about a dead young woman?"

He raised his eyebrows. "Mack hasn't told you?"

She winced. "Mack's being Mack," she announced. She looked over where he stood, beside a group of elderly citizens.

The captain noted, "If I had thought a celebration of Paul's life would have touched so many people as have come here tonight, I would have considered holding one of my own. So thank you again for this, and I'll give my thanks to Nan too," he murmured. "I know closure is huge for a lot of people, and it is something I've spoken about to Sarah, Paul's mother, a couple times."

Doreen nodded. "Sometimes maybe it's better to just let things lie, as long as people don't forget who Paul was and what was important in his life. He was a child, so … it's hard to know what to do."

"I've left it in his mother's hands, and, if Sarah wants to do something more, then I am more than willing to support her."

Doreen smiled. "You're a good man."

The captain winced. "I'd feel better about your saying that if I'd been the one to solve Paul's case."

She chuckled. "In a way you did."

"How do you figure that?" he asked, staring at her in confusion.

Mack came up behind them. "That's her version of logic, so I can't wait to hear this."

She glared at Mack. "I'm not talking to you. Remember?"

He just rolled his eyes. The captain looked even more confused. Mack patted him on the shoulder. "It's all right. Don't even try to figure it out."

"Why's she mad at you?" the captain asked Mack.

"Because I won't tell her anything about the new case we have," he replied, with a sigh.

At that, Doreen glared at him. "I can help you. As I have demonstrated time and time again that I can."

"Yes, you have," Mack agreed gently. "In the meantime, why don't you explain to the captain how it is that he had a hand in solving this murder."

"You asked me to look into it, so, therefore, you did have a hand in it."

The captain blinked, and then he started to chuckle. "I'm thankful that you have such a positive attitude and that you'll give me credit, but it's really not due."

"Absolutely it is," she disagreed, grabbing his elbow gently. "You kept Paul's memory alive, and you kept that whole scenario alive for these people in town, and it just took the right circumstances for it to all come together."

"The right circumstances that *you* pulled together," he pointed out, with another chuckle. "You wove those threads, all by yourself."

"Sure." She shrugged. "I'm just the instrument. You got it this far."

He did look quite a bit happier hearing that, and, when somebody called him, he made his excuses and headed over to deal with a couple older ladies, who appeared to be arguing over something.

Mack stepped up beside her and whispered, "That was a good thing you did."

She looked up at him. "What did I do?"

He studied her intently for a moment and then smiled. "You see? That's one of the reasons everybody likes you. You do things like that, and you don't even realize what you did."

"But he did do something very special," she argued.

"Yes, the captain did, but he wouldn't have seen that on his own. He only saw his guilt and battered himself over not being able to put it all together," Mack explained.

She frowned. "So I helped him to see it from a different perspective. It was hardly anything."

Mack smiled at her. "And yet, for a lot of people, it's a lot of things."

She sighed. "Doesn't seem like it. Didn't seem like much at all. Wish I could do more."

At that, he burst out laughing. "You can't be *that* bored already," he declared. "Certainly you can do lots around your place."

"Sure," she admitted, then groaned. "I mean, there's

weeding, shoveling, ... some gardening stuff to be done. And to my dismay, always a house to be cleaned." She gave him an eye roll. "And down the road, when I get some money, if and when I get some money," she corrected, "some renovations to consider."

"Will you do some?" he asked her curiously.

"I don't know." She pondered that a moment. "I know some things need updating."

"Like what?" he asked.

She looked over at him and shrugged. "I know I don't use it as much as you, but I was thinking the kitchen."

He nodded. "That would be a really good idea."

"I know the floors are showing a lot of wear and need sanding down and resealing. I don't know what else. I should speak to Nan first, get a list made, let her point out which ones to do in order of importance. Then I'll have to talk to a couple contractors." She added, "Yet all that is not today's issue."

"Would you ever sell your place?" he asked her curiously.

She shook her head. "I don't think so. It's a pretty special place. I love being at the river. I mean, obviously I haven't gone through any flooding, and, with any luck, I won't have to. However, at this point, I don't think I could sell Nan's place."

"Good," Mack agreed. "You're right. It is pretty special, and you can always expand the house a little bit, if you wanted more space. You could even do a full-on reno to update the whole structure. It would cost a lot, be expensive, but, if you get all that money just on the old books, not even counting all of Nan's antiques, you could certainly do a nice job of it."

"I wonder." Then she lowered her voice and added, "If I

were to do anything like sell Nan's place and move—although I can't see it happening right now—it wouldn't be until after Nan ..." Doreen couldn't bring herself to say those words.

Mack nodded slowly. "I can see that, and it makes total sense too."

"A lot of the house I wouldn't know what to do with—like the basement and the cold room—but the bathrooms could use an update," she mused.

"Honestly," Mack added, "all of it needs an update, especially the basics, like the plumbing, the electrical." He tilted his head. "A lot of money would be spent to bring it up to snuff."

"Well then, it's just perfectly fine as it is for now," she declared.

He grinned at her. "Yep, but just imagine that your plumbing didn't crackle all the time, when you flushed the toilet, and you didn't have breakers that kept going on and off, tripping right and left because you turned on two appliances at the same time? Consider things like that. Up until now, I've been the one around to fix the minor irritations that happen, but you might want to have those resolved completely by a licensed plumber and electrician."

"I'll see. Definitely not today's issue, not until I get paid from Scott."

"But you have Christie's catalog now," he noted.

"I do." And she grinned. "Everything looks so wonderful," she murmured. "It just makes me a little more worried about what money I might or might not get."

"It's the *might not* part that's hard," he agreed. "I mean, there's always hope that you could get more than you actually do or fear that you'll get less than you expect.

"And yet, at the same time, it's hard not to think about the possibility of riches."

"Of course it's hard, after doing without so much. However, you have a lot on your plate right now, so just take some time and relax."

She sighed. "You're still trying to keep me out of your case."

He burst out laughing. "I am. I absolutely am," he admitted. "Remember. It's not a cold case."

"But it is my *Toes Up in the Tulips* case," she muttered.

He glared at her. "No, it's not."

"Fine." She shrugged, but, in her heart of hearts, she knew exactly what she would call it. "I just have to find another cold case that's connected to it."

"How about we don't find anything connected to it?" He groaned. "We have enough work on our plate."

She just waggled her eyebrows, as if to say, *How about you get some extra help?*

He shook his head. "We can't. The minute we start getting all these amateurs, interrupting and butting into police business ..."

"Has the DA mentioned anything about my involvement yet?"

"We're trying to keep your name out of it, as much as possible," he shared. "You're not an easy element to explain. A civilian popping up all over the case tends to make things messy."

"*Concerned citizen* is all he needs to know," she stated.

He chuckled at that. "So you *will* call my brother?"

"I said I would tomorrow, but I already did. I promised and I did. Although it was quick one as he was busy."

"Good. What did he say?"

She contemplated not telling him, just because he was being difficult about the one case he had. And then decided that Nick would probably tell him anyway. "Well, it looks like they're down to just the nitty-gritty details. Mathew's agreed on the bigger parts of the settlement. Nick asked me if I wanted to know exactly how much, and I told him no. I think I shocked him with that answer," she added, frowning at the afterthought, yet chuckling on the inside.

"Yeah, I imagine you did." Mack smiled at her.

"I don't know," she replied. "It doesn't feel real, and I don't want to sit here thinking about a big chunk of his money coming my way because it, … because Mathew is not an ordinary person, and the thought of crossing him scares me."

At that, the smile fell off Mack's face. "You still think he'll do something?"

"Again, I didn't ask how much money, so if it's just a small amount, then I think Mathew would probably be okay with it. I just don't know what a small amount is to Nick."

"I don't think Nick's into small amounts," Mack noted, taking a casual tone, as if not to alarm her. "And, in this case, I agree with him. Mathew pulled an awful lot of illegal stunts to rob you of any divorce settlement, plus whatever else Mathew has done to remove you from Robin's will totally. So Mathew doesn't deserve to get a break."

"Maybe not, but, if it makes my life easier, I'm good with it." She then admitted, "I am sure any money would really help me."

"*Uh-huh.*" Mack grimaced. "In the short-term. But, in the long-term, you need some money so that you are taken care of."

"I still have that reward money from Bernard," she reminded Mack.

"Which you shared half of with Esther. Still, knowing you, that five grand will last you a very long time. However"—he pointed a finger at her—"it won't last forever. Let's be realistic. Since moving here this year, your nan helped you out a lot. So, once you begin to pay for all that on your own, you'll find that five thousand doesn't go very far."

"Yeah." She winced. "I've already been thinking about that. Some of the items on my list to get done are a little bit more money than I was thinking. At least that's what Nan and Richie tell me."

"Like what?"

She shrugged. "Just a few things, like, maybe getting new toilets."

He frowned. "You mean, the one that's got the cracked seat?"

She nodded.

"You can also just replace the seat too."

"They don't come as a single unit?" she asked. He managed to hold back a laugh, but she caught it anyway. "Why didn't you say that beforehand?" she cried out. "We could have done that earlier."

"Sure," he agreed, "but it'll still take some money, and, up until now, you haven't had any."

"Oh, that's true." She immediately worried. "How much is *some* money?"

"So just to replace the seat or the whole toilet?" he asked.

She frowned at that. "I don't know what's needed, but, I guess, we should probably do it right."

"I like that attitude," he replied. "I'll come by, and we'll take a closer look. Chances are, it's pretty old. So you might get a better water-saving one, and that'll help you with the water bills too, when it is all done and dusted. A little more money spent today could save you more tomorrow."

"That wouldn't hurt either," she said, with an eye roll.

Just then his cell phone went off.

"Probably that same case, *huh*?" Doreen asked.

"No, not likely," he muttered. He checked his phone and frowned, looking over to see the Captain staring at his phone too. The two men lifted their heads at the same time, and their gazes met over the crowd, both of them towering over all the other guests. Then Mack turned to look for Darren, who was already making his way over to him.

"I guess duty calls," she noted, with a sigh.

He stopped for a minute and asked her, "Do you mind if I leave?"

She shook her head. "No, not at all. That'll never be me."

"What'll never be you?" he asked, still studying her face.

"Somebody who hates it when you get called away to work," she replied. "What I'll hate is, when you don't share." And, with that, she gave him a wave of her hand. "Go. You have work to do. I'll see if I can find something to get into trouble with here."

He glared at her, and she grinned. "Now I'm happy."

He raised an eyebrow. "You could, for once, try to *not* get into any trouble." He dragged out the word *not*, and a scowl marred his handsome face.

"I could try," she noted, "but I don't know what kind of success I'll have."

"You won't know unless you try," he stated instantly, glaring at her.

The captain came up beside them. "We have to leave."

Mack nodded. "I'm trying to convince her to stay out of

trouble."

At that, the captain gave a boisterous laugh. "That's a lost cause. You should probably just warn her to be safe. That will probably go over better with her." And, with that, he walked out of the retirement home toward his vehicle without a backward glance.

Mack sighed. "I suppose he's got a point." He leaned down, kissed Doreen gently, and added, "So stay safe." And, with that, he was gone.

She looked over to see Nan and Richie, nodding at her. "What's that look for?" she asked, as she approached them.

"You and Mack," Richie said. "*We* like it." And there was that stress on *we*.

Doreen groaned. "That's nice, but we'll get there in our own time."

Richie rolled his eyes at that. "That's only because you're young." He chuckled, as he winked at Nan. "Those of us who don't have quite as much time, we like to get to things a little faster."

Doreen felt the heat running up her cheeks. Desperate to change the subject, she said, "I wish I knew more about his current case."

"What case is that?" Maisie asked, as she stepped forward, looking at Nan a little sideways.

Nan stiffened but didn't say anything.

"I don't know," Doreen replied. "Something about a young woman who's recently died."

"That's Annabelle," Maisie noted.

Doreen asked Maisie, "Who's Annabelle?"

Nan piped up to answer. "She was killed in her home. She was doing up those big displays of flowers, those everlasting cut flowers that people put all those chemicals into to keep them preserved. She was doing up some big displays for one of the local events in town here, only she didn't show up for work. Last thing I heard was, they went into her apartment and found her among all the flowers."

Doreen stared at her, fascinated. "It never ceases to amaze me how Rosemoor always has information so much earlier than anybody else."

At that, Nan gave her a knowing look.

"*Right*," Doreen said, with casual sarcasm. "I didn't know anything about the case, and Mack won't tell me. How can I get that information, when I am on the outs from no one else but Mack, of all people."

"That's because you keep getting into his face," Maisie stated in her typical blunt way.

Doreen just stared at her, and Maisie tittered. "Her name is Annabelle Hopkins. Now you can go find out everything you need to know on your own." And, with that, Maisie sallied off.

Nan turned to Doreen. "At least she had something to offer this time. Most of the time she's ..." Nan lifted her finger and did a swirling motion around her ear.

Doreen grabbed Nan's hand, pulled it down, and whispered, "Don't do that. You know how much it upsets people."

Nan went into gales laughter. "Are you kidding? They say the same thing about me."

"Oh, maybe in that case," Doreen teased, adding a sigh, "I guess they're right."

At that, Nan stopped to glare, then chuckled. "You're getting somewhat good at that joking thing."

"Am I?" Doreen wasn't so sure. "Still feels like I don't have a whole lot to joke about."

"And that," Nan declared, "is because you haven't gotten rid of that no-good ex of yours, and, you need to move forward with Mack in your life."

"We're getting there," she replied, trying to hold off Nan. "Besides, we want to do things our way."

"That's fine and dandy," Nan agreed, "only if you get there and do it somewhat quicker than the speed you're going right now." Nan gave her granddaughter an eye roll.

At that, Richie chuckled and then changed the subject. "I might have something about the Hopkins's scenario."

"Oh, yeah? What's that?" Doreen asked.

He leaned over and whispered, "I think Darren may have told me something. He didn't mean to."

Doreen eyed him hopefully. "Like what?"

"The woman had all these contracts for projects in town here. She was quite well-liked, and apparently her live-in boyfriend didn't like the work she was doing. From the sounds of it, they're looking at him as the suspect."

"Interesting," Doreen noted. "They always look to the family first."

"I don't think he did it," Richie replied. "I know he's pretty worried that the cops are looking at him."

"Why is that though? If he didn't do it, he's in the clear."

"Maybe, but ..." Then he hesitated.

"Go on, Richie," Nan said, encouraging him. "If you know something, you better spit it out before you die."

"The boyfriend was going to ask Annabelle to marry him." Richie shot Nan a look. "So I don't think he killed her, not if he's crying this much."

"Yes, but we also know that relationships can go south rather quickly," Doreen added. "What is his name?"

"Yep. Relationships can be tough. His name is Joseph Moody."

"Well, I'm sure Mack will sort it out. If there was anything connected to a different case, a *cold* case," she noted, her gaze going from one to the other, "that would be a different story, and I could get involved. But, if there isn't, I have a bunch of things to tie up at home."

"Like what?"

"I might take another look at Solomon's file, specifically the Bob Small research—but so much is there that it'll really be something I have to take in little bites."

At that, Nan nodded slowly. "Honestly you'll have to do an awful lot of small bites when it comes to that file, what with him being a serial killer."

"I'm also thinking about running down and checking on Wendy."

They nodded at that. "Probably not a bad idea," Nan agreed.

"Maybe take a few days off," Richie suggested in a low tone. "Just in case this current case breaks wide open, and then we'll need you to be ready."

Doreen noted the conspiratorial glint in his gaze and nodded slowly. "Good point," she replied, studying them closely, wondering what was going on inside those two minds.

She reached over, kissed Nan on the cheek, and said, "Thank you for putting together this party. You did a wonderful job. Now, if you don't mind, I'll sneak away too and talk to you later." And, with that, she quickly rounded up her crew and made her escape.

# Chapter 3

OUTSIDE DOREEN TOOK several deep breaths. She'd met Mack at her house and now she just wanted to have a cup of tea and sit in the peace and quiet by the river. And, with that thought settling, she walked her animals slowly toward home.

As she turned to walk up the path in her backyard, a man called out to her from her side yard. "Hello?"

She turned on the steps to her deck and saw a young man standing there by Richard's fence, waiting for her nervously. She smiled at him. "Hi. What can I do for you?" She was happy to have her animals with her, and none of them seemed deeply alarmed by this stranger's presence.

She stepped up onto the deck and unlocked the rear kitchen door, so the animals could get a drink a water, if needed. Instead they greeted her visitor a bit crossly, before wandering off, apparently to do something in the bushes and to enjoy their freedom outside in the cool evening.

The young man took a deep breath. "My name ..." he began, his voice sounding broken, "is Joseph Moody."

Her eyebrows popped up. "Ah."

"I see you've already heard of me," he stated in a grim

voice.

"Unfortunately, yes. I'm so sorry for your loss." She thought she saw a glint of tears in his eyes.

He nodded. "Thank you. So few people even understand what it's like to lose somebody."

"And, at the same time, be considered as a murder suspect," she noted.

"Right?" he cried out. "How is that even a thing? I've already got enough to deal with, without having the cops all over me."

"That may be," she agreed, "but they will get to the truth eventually, and, if it has nothing to do with you, then you have nothing to worry about. They will find out who is involved."

"Maybe." He shook his head. "Yet it seems like they're determined to ruin my life in the meantime."

She winced at that because he wasn't the only person to have made that comment in the past. "I'm sure that's hard too. What can I do for you? Besides, how did you know where I lived?"

"A friend of a friend of a friend," he replied vaguely, with a wave of his hand. "You're starting to get a reputation."

"Maybe." She walked to the outdoor table and sat down, not comfortable letting him into her house. "That still doesn't explain what you're doing here."

He shifted nervously, his hands opening, then clenching, just to open them again. "Do you mind if I sit?"

"Absolutely, be my guest."

And he pulled out one of the chairs at the table. "I was hoping you could help me."

"Help with what?"

"Help me find whoever did this. So that I can get the police off my back. I need you to help me clear my name."

"Ah." She nodded, staring at him. "Generally I have been warned to keep out of active police investigations," she explained. "I don't have a license, and I'm not a cop, and they don't like it when I interfere."

He nodded. "I've heard that too. At the same time, I've also heard that you don't always listen."

She winced at that. "Wow, I really do have a bad reputation, don't I?"

He almost smiled. "I don't think the cops are looking at anybody else," he stated. "For me, that's even more distressing."

"Of course it is," she said. "The last thing you want is for anybody else to assume that you're guilty."

"Especially when I didn't do anything," he cried out. "It's hard enough to lose the woman I loved, but to know that everybody suspects me of having killed her? Well, it just doesn't …" He stopped. "I don't know how to get out of this, and, to top it off, I don't even have any money to pay you."

She winced internally but tried to keep her face devoid of emotion. Not that it worked; she was an open book. "That's pretty normal," she replied, with a sigh. "Almost everybody I know doesn't have any money."

He nodded. "Right? I mean, it's not an easy thing to make an honest living these days."

She pondered that, but it was hard to argue. With her methodology, it was certainly not something she wanted to tout as being a good way to make a living. If it weren't for Nan and Mack, Doreen probably would have starved to death by now. "I don't know that there's anything I can do to help," she admitted. "Have you been totally honest with the police?"

He nodded. "Yes, I have. Then there's my brother. He's studying to become a lawyer, and he wants to help, but he's also in school. He can just point me in a direction, but that's it."

"Is he in school here?"

"He goes to the university in Vancouver. He is gone most of the time but flies back and forth to visit."

"Well, if he does that very much, it can't be too cheap."

"No, I know. I don't really understand how he affords it, to be honest. But I know that his girlfriend's very wealthy, and she does a lot for him."

Doreen smiled. "In that case he's lucky."

"He's very lucky," Joseph agreed. "I also know he really cares."

"Do you have any idea why somebody would kill Annabelle?"

He shook his head, tears coming to his eyes. "No, and that's part of the problem. I really don't understand why anybody would have done that. She was just one of those really bright, bubbly girls, and everybody loved her."

"Everybody but one," Doreen clarified.

He winced at that. "No, you're right, everybody but one," he repeated, with a certain amount of bitterness. "And how the heck we're supposed to figure out who that would be, I don't know."

"That's where the challenge comes in," she admitted, with half a smile, "because somebody out there didn't like her or liked her too much."

He stared at Doreen in confusion, and then, as if a revelation struck, he appeared more shocked than anything.

"You think she had another partner?" he asked hesitantly.

"No, I'm not saying that at all, but what are the chances that somebody wanted to be with her? Even more than you?"

"But then wouldn't they kill me?" he asked.

"No, not always," she replied. "Emotional impulses are hard to control, be it from rejection or twisted obsessions, and then the resulting actions become their fault."

He blinked and then shrugged. "Still I don't see how that is even relevant."

"Meaning?"

"She didn't have anybody else in her life. It was just me."

"Which is also why the cops are so interested in you, I presume."

"Of course," he muttered. "Yet I was at work at the time of her mu ... murder."

"At the time of the murder?" Doreen repeated.

Joseph nodded. "The cops told me that they had a three-hour window, and I was at work during that time, yes."

"Where do you work?"

"At one of the pubs downtown." He gave her the name, but it wasn't one she knew.

"Okay, so, therefore, you have lots of people to give you an alibi."

He nodded. "But that didn't seem to make much of a difference to the cop who I spoke to."

"Ah."

"He ... He was ..." Joseph hesitated. "He was scary."

"Was he big?" she asked.

"Yeah, really big, like ..." And he held up his hands way over his head.

"Yeah, that's Corporal Mack Moreau," she said, rubbing her temples. "He won't really like it if I interfere."

At that, the young looked crestfallen. "Please, I don't know what to do."

Doreen sighed. "Come up with as much information as you can that has anything to do with her life, your life, your life together. I want you to be thorough and to list people in her life, so that the police can investigate them too," she explained. "We never really understand just what is important in situations like this, so you have to really think about it and pull up everything that may or may not be important."

"And yet how?" he asked. "They asked a whole pile of questions. I gave them a whole pile of answers."

"The fact is, you have an alibi, so that'll play into this pretty quickly."

"Maybe," he replied. "But whether they think I'm a suspect or not, I really do want to find out what happened. I want to find the person who did this."

"Good. Hold on to that purpose, and don't let out-of-control emotions rule you," she noted. "Now wait a moment. Let me grab a pen and piece of paper."

He waited, as she entered her house and then walked back out. "Does this mean you'll help me?"

"I'll help you, but it doesn't mean that I won't share this information with the police too," she admitted. "Sometimes helping you means helping them."

"But they don't seem to care," he said.

"I think you'd be surprised who and what they care about," she noted. "It just doesn't always *look* like they care."

"No, I don't think they do care," he argued, and his tone took a more hysterical turn.

"Do you know if anything else happened in regard to the case tonight?" she asked.

He shook his head. "I don't know." He shrugged. "I don't know anything. Nobody's telling me anything."

"No, that's par for the course too," she stated, pondering that. "Okay, so let's go over this. Let's see if we can add to what you told the police. Even like her favorite coffee shop and other habits like that."

Joseph just shook his head.

So Doreen began. "Annabelle was at home, working?"

"Yes, she had promised to do up a bunch of bouquets for an event happening in town. I think a baby sex reveal party or something like that," he said in bewilderment. "I don't get it. I mean, it used to just be you, like, … you waited until the child was born. Then you found out whether you had a boy or a girl, but now? Now they go all out. Like a photo shoot on the beach when they're pregnant and another photo shoot on the beach when they're ready to pop," he rambled, unable to stick to the topic here. "These reveal parties are so over-the-top." He just struggled with it all.

"I get it. It's not your thing," Doreen told him. "However, I think nowadays it's a big thing for a lot of women."

"I guess." Joseph shrugged, not convinced. "Anyway, Annabelle was pretty happy because she had thousands of dollars worth of orders ahead of her and was at the point of considering a storefront versus working from home."

"I guess that event has already come and gone then."

"Yeah, and they were pretty upset. Not that they were just upset about their order, which obviously they were, but they also knew Annabelle. They liked her."

"Right. So who were they?" she asked. "I'll have to talk to them too."

He looked at her in surprise and asked, "Why?"

"When it comes to stuff like this," she replied, "we ask

anyone and everyone to get the answers that we need, but they sometimes sure can come from very far-flung places."

He just shrugged. "Whatever." And he quickly gave her the names of Larry and Sylvie Halstead. "They live down on Bernard. This is their first baby, so it had to be *special*," he said, with an eye roll.

"Yeah, I get it." Doreen really did. She wasn't sure that she would go through a big deal like that, but, knowing Nan and everybody else at Rosemoor, they would all want something in terms of a celebration, so who knows what Doreen would end up doing. At that, she stopped because *wow*. Here she was, wondering if she would have her own baby reveal party—and more than that. She was casually thinking about if she ever got pregnant.

"You okay?" Joseph Moody's voice pulled Doreen from her thoughts.

When she asked about the murder scene, Joseph quickly went over the events as he saw them. "I was at work. I came home from work late and found her there." He swallowed, looking up at her. "And there just didn't seem to be any sign of anybody else. I didn't know what to say."

"How was she killed?"

He paused, swallowed again, and then replied, "She was shot."

Doreen stared at him. "So somebody had gotten hold of a gun.'

"Which isn't that hard," Joseph noted, with a hard glance at her. "Almost everybody knows how to get a gun."

"Maybe," she replied, "but getting a gun—or at least knowing how to get a gun and then following through with getting it—and then going to shoot somebody with it, all that takes an awful lot of premeditation."

"Right," he said. "And that's another problem."

Now she had to wonder where this was going because Joseph's demeanor had changed. "What's that?"

"I have a gun. She was shot with my gun."

Here she thought that this would be a simple matter.

# Chapter 4

DOREEN STARED AT Joseph in shock. "That's just another nail in your coffin then."

"Exactly," he noted morosely.

"So were you two living together full-time?"

He nodded, as he grimaced.

"So your gun was at her house on any given day? Would she have pulled that gun if somebody had tried to break into your place?"

He straightened up. "Yes, she would have. … That must have been what happened."

"It's certainly one scenario," she noted cautiously. "However, we're a long way away from getting to the bottom of this." Yet he looked remarkably more cheerful. She was glad she could do that much for him. "Did you have a license for the gun?"

"No," he admitted. "So another black mark."

"Why was Annabelle's death considered a murder? Is it not possible that she committed suicide?"

He shook his head. "No. At least I don't think so." He frowned at that, as if thinking about it.

"I'm not authorized to see any crime scene photos, so I

don't know how she was found," she stated. "Can you go through it for me?"

"She was lying on her back, fully dressed, arms out, as if she'd just fallen backward. A bullet hole was between, ... was in her forehead," he got out, his voice getting thick. "The flowers had been dumped, or she was holding them, and they fell all over her."

"Right," she murmured. "What was she wearing?"

"Blue T-shirt, blue jeans, white socks," he replied.

She frowned at these details.

"She usually wore that outfit," he explained, "unless we were going out somewhere. She was very much a jeans and T-shirt gal."

"Which is all good," Doreen replied. "I can't say that I wear much else myself."

He nodded. "Especially every day, right?"

"Exactly." She hesitated and then added, "Okay, I need a list of anybody she worked with—suppliers, clients, even repairmen, that kind of a thing."

"She spoke of her business growing. And, with my working nights, I made myself scarce during the daytime, whenever she had a client show up. And it's not as if she had one big client who gave her massive amounts of business—not that she told me about anyway. So, in my mind, she got random jobs from random people. Some of it was done strictly on the phone or via email. You'd have to look at her invoices to track her clientele," he suggested.

"Did she work anywhere else?"

He shook his head at that. "She used to work at the grocery store. Just one of the small farm-to-table ones, off Spall, and that was years ago. They're not likely involved in ... this."

"No, maybe not, but it would help to get an idea of what she was like as a person."

He stared at Doreen, nonplussed.

"You have one opinion," she explained. "That doesn't mean anybody else has the same opinion."

"They should have," he stated bluntly. "She was a beautiful woman, inside and out."

"What was the nature of your relationship?"

He stared at her in confusion. "What do you mean?"

Richie had told Doreen that Joseph had been prepared to ask Annabelle to marry him. "Were you planning on marrying her, or was this just a for-now type relationship?" she asked, struggling to find the words that would explain what she was asking.

"I don't know," he said. "We never got that far."

"How long were you two together?"

"Three years." She stared at him, and he flushed. "Okay, so maybe we had that discussion every once in a while, but I wasn't quite ready to commit."

"That," she replied, "at least is a more truthful answer and will get you a whole lot better response than telling the cops anything different."

He nodded. "Right? I … I just… It's one of those emotional questions that I don't handle really well."

She smiled. "You're not the only one. So what else?"

He shrugged. "I do think I can find a list of her clients at home. I remember Annabelle had mentioned a spreadsheet."

"Good, send that to me," she stated. "What about girlfriends?"

He nodded. "Rosa and Linda."

She wrote them down and added, "I'll need phone numbers."

He winced. "They're on her phone, and the cops collected it as evidence."

"Of course they did." She pondered that. "You're sure you don't have any physical phone book or anything else?"

"She did everything on her phone or her laptop," he noted.

"Last names?" He quickly gave them to her, and Doreen nodded. "I might be able to track them down."

He hesitated, as if wanting to say something. She looked over at him and waited. "They may not be all that beneficial for me."

"Why? Did they not like you?" she asked, without looking up at him, at least not overtly. She wanted to see what his reaction was to all these questions.

"As you just mentioned, I hadn't brought up making our relationship permanent, and I think her friends were on her case about it."

"Right," Doreen agreed. "Everybody wants to see everybody married."

"Yeah, but we're not always sure about the best time of life to get married."

And then again she studied him. "Often you don't get another chance." He stared at her, and his face just crumpled. "Hey, I didn't mean it quite that way."

"Yeah, you did," he muttered, oozing sorrow. "And you're right. I won't get that chance now." He got up to his feet slowly, like an old man. "If you can do anything to help …"

"I need your phone number too, and then I will see if there's anything I can find," she said.

He nodded slowly, and, after giving her his cell number, he turned and walked away.

With that done, she went into the house and watched as he went out to the front yard and got into an old car. Small, silver, but she had no idea what it was, and he drove off. As soon as the car was out of sight, she phoned Mack.

"Hey, I'm a little busy right now," he told her. "Can I call you back?"

"Yeah," she replied, then hesitated. "You got something connected to that poor woman's death?"

"No, not necessarily. I really have to go." And, with that, he hung up.

And she knew that he did probably have to go. Still it seemed like such a shame that she couldn't talk to him right then and there. On the other hand, this gave her a reason to get in his face a little bit more. Not that he would want that at all. And, when he found out who had come to visit her, she was pretty sure Mack would be livid as it was.

Regardless she wasn't even certain what to do now. She added water to her electric kettle, and, with that now simmering, she got out a pretty teapot and brewed some tea to take down to the river. It's what she'd been planning on doing since she got home, but now? Now things had changed. She wasn't sure how much they'd changed because she still couldn't get into Mack's case. However, she did want to talk to him about this. It seemed, well, … important.

As she sat on her riverside bench and used her phone to get as much information as she could come up with—which wasn't a whole lot, considering it was a new case, and the police hadn't released very much—Mack called her back.

"Hey," he greeted her. "Sorry, I was talking to a few people."

"That's okay," she said. "We can talk tomorrow. I know

you're tired."

"It depends. What is this about?" When she hesitated, he immediately groaned. "*Uh-oh.* I'm coming right over."

"No, no, no, no, that's not necessary."

But it was too late, as he'd already disconnected and was gone. She groaned as she looked over at the animals. "How is it that he always knows when something like this is going on?" she muttered.

She hadn't been very good at giving him different signals; that wasn't something she was good at, ever. She stared at her phone, noting she'd missed another phone call. She quickly hit Redial on the number that she didn't recognize, so had no idea who had called. When a familiar man answered on the other end, she froze.

"You finally got back to me," her soon-to-be ex-husband declared in a hard voice.

"Sorry," she replied, without thinking, instantly regretting it afterward. Old habits and all that. "We were down at Nan's for a celebration of life this evening, and I stayed a little later than I thought."

"It would be nice if you could at least get your lawyer off my back now."

"I don't know anything about it. I haven't even asked for details."

After a moment of shocked silence on the other end, Mathew burst out laughing. "Oh, that's rich, that is. You obviously don't need to because he's looking out for you all that much more."

"Why are you even calling me? Now I'll have to tell him that I accidentally phoned you back."

At that, he burst out laughing again. "Good, I should get you into trouble for getting me into trouble."

"I haven't got you into any trouble," she protested.

He groaned. "Your lovely lawyer wants to discuss a few other issues."

"Yeah? What's that?"

"The jewelry I gave you for your birthday?"

"Yeah, that's an interesting one, isn't it?" she stated. "Apparently you didn't really give it to me. You just wanted to *lend* it to me, so I could wear it. You know? Like your dressed-up arm candy."

More silence came on the other end. "That's part of the problem. The real problem is, they were given to you," he admitted grudgingly. "I guess I'm checking to make sure you really want them."

She stared down at her phone. "Were you really planning on giving them to another woman?"

"No, I'm not," he said. "I was just thinking I would take them back to the jewelers and sell them."

"Wow. I would really like to keep my gifts, so thank you."

His voice turned warm and persuasive. "I can deliver them in person."

She frowned at that, not sure where he was going with this. "I think all that stuff has to go through my lawyer," she noted.

"Why don't we just keep our lawyers out of this," he snapped. "Especially yours, as he's become a pain in my backside."

"Maybe, but you've also become a pain in mine too." And, with that, she hung up the phone.

# Chapter 5

DOREEN QUICKLY PHONED Nick and told him what she'd done. "Could you please stop answering the phone—unless it's me calling?" He groaned.

"Yeah, wouldn't that be nice? I didn't recognize the number. It didn't come up on my screen," she began, and then she explained what Mathew wanted.

"I hope you told him that you wanted the jewelry."

"I did, and he wanted to come up and deliver it himself." At that came a surprised silence on the other end. "I told him that I think that had to go through the lawyers."

"Good," Nick replied. "That is very good."

"He told me to try and keep my pain-in-the-backside lawyer out of his ... away from us. He told me how you were becoming quite a pain in his backside."

At that, Nick laughed. "Yeah, we're not done yet either," he replied cheerfully. "If he calls again, just hang up. I will now send him an email requesting all the jewelry. You did give me quite a list."

"Yeah, a lot of birthdays happened during that marriage," she noted. "I know this probably sounds like I'm being really, really greedy, and I'm not trying to be, but ..."

"What?" he asked curiously.

"He had fakes made of all of them."

At that, he started to laugh. "Don't tell me. That's what you got to wear in public?"

"Exactly. I highly suspect that's what he'll try and hand over to you."

"Oh no, he won't. Now that you've told me that, we'll make sure that we get the originals."

She smiled. "I'm really not a vengeful person, but, at this moment, just the thought of you being a thorn in his side is making me so happy."

"Good to hear. I'll let you know what he says."

And, with that, they disconnected, and she turned around to see Mack standing there, glaring at her.

"Who was that?"

"That was your brother." She glared at him right back. "Why are you in such an ugly mood?"

"What are you up to now?" He frowned.

"I didn't think I was up to anything right now, although earlier, … I called you to talk, but you were busy. Then Mathew just called me, and I made the mistake of calling him back because I didn't recognize the number."

At that, Mack glared at her again.

She raised both hands. "It wasn't the usual number, people. What am I supposed to do?"

"How about you don't answer unknown numbers?" He sighed. "At least you called Nick."

"Yeah." And she explained what her ex-husband was after. "And then I told Nick how Mathew always kept fakes of everything."

Mack laughed. "So presumably he's trying to give you the fakes."

"I wouldn't be at all surprised. I think he was hoping I didn't want any of it, that I hated him so much."

"I'm surprised you do." Mack eyed her closely. "Sentimental value?"

"No, he pissed me off," she declared. And then she tapped her temple. "Do you really think Nan isn't rattling around inside my head, saying, *Take it. Take it. We can always sell it.*"

At that, Mack burst out laughing. "She's right. I don't know exactly where one would sell something like that, but I'm sure, with all the connections that you're slowly building, somebody could tell you."

She smiled. "That's what I was wondering."

As he walked toward her, he yawned and said, "And now I can't stay. I'm on my way home, and I need to grab some sleep." He rubbed his face. "Haven't had a whole lot of that lately."

She stared at him in consternation. "I wouldn't have added to your day, if I'd known you'd had a bad time of it."

He snorted. "Yes, you would have."

She glared at him. "You don't know that."

He just gave her an eye roll. "So get to it."

She opened her mouth and then snapped it shut, not sure how to start.

"*Uh-oh.*" He took two more steps toward her. "When you act like that, you worry me."

"No reason to be worried," she replied.

"Did you interfere in my case?" he snapped. Her shoulders hunched. "Oh no, please not. What did I tell you?"

"I didn't have a choice," she replied, holding up her hands. "This guy came to me."

"What guy?" he asked in confusion.

"Joseph Moody."

Mack closed his eyes and swore under his breath.

In a low tone and trying to not make it sound like she was guilty, Doreen explained what Joseph wanted.

Mack sat down beside her, with a hard *thunk*. "Even when I try to keep you out," he noted, with a headshake.

"I didn't do anything," she repeated.

He nodded glumly. "The problem is, at this point in time, you've become a force of your own."

"Not really," she argued. "I mean, I couldn't tell him anything because I don't know anything. I did tell him that I would talk to you guys." He shook his head, and she shrugged. "It seemed like the best thing I could do."

"Oh, absolutely." Mack sighed. "And believe me. I appreciate your doing that much."

She winced. "You sound like you're pretty fed-up."

"It's hard when everybody decides that an amateur detective"—he gave her an eye roll—"would give them a better shake than us."

"I think when people get into this situation, they react purely in fear."

"Sure," he agreed. "But fear of what?"

"I know he's probably your best suspect, just because of his relationship to the victim."

"Yet he does have an alibi," Mack acknowledged.

"I know, and he did tell me that," she shared. "Have you checked with his coworkers?"

He nodded. "Yep, we have."

"So technically he shouldn't really be on your list."

"Of course he's on the list," he replied. "Just doesn't mean that he's super high on the list."

"Right. But, if you don't have anything to go on, then

I'm not hurting anything," she said cautiously. "And, if I give you whatever information I come up with ..." He just glared at her. She raised her hands again. "What would you have me tell him?" she asked. "Obviously I tried hard to let him know that he should give you guys all the information and that you would give him a fair shake and that sometimes it looked like the police weren't looking at anybody else, but they were."

"Is that what you told him?" he asked in astonishment.

She nodded. "Something like that. Don't quote me on it," she muttered. "I'm already very tired."

"You and me both." He sighed again. "Didn't really need this tonight."

"Of course not." And then she smiled at him. "You didn't need it any night."

He grinned at her. "True enough. We'll see what comes out of this. Just please be careful."

"I will. I will."

And, with that, he got back up, but this time he looked even shakier and older than before.

She asked, "You sure you don't want to stay, have a cup of tea?"

He looked down at her and shook his head. "A cup of tea was *not* on my mind. Sitting at the river with a glass of whiskey? Yeah, that sounds better. However, I need to get home now, before I don't have the energy to get there."

And, with that, he turned and headed—or maybe she should say *stumbled*—toward the kitchen. She hopped up and walked with him, more concerned than she'd been in a long time. He looked really tired. She waited until he got in his vehicle and drove off. Then she quickly messaged Nick.

**Mack looks pretty rough tonight, really tired.**

Instead of texting her back, he phoned. "What's going on?" he asked curiously.

"I'm not sure. I mean, I did … Well, I did get into one of his cases, so he's not really happy with me, but, when he left just now, he looked exhausted."

"Ha. Maybe it's the work. I'll give him a phone call and see how he's doing."

"It wouldn't hurt," Doreen noted. "I don't know if it's just a *sick of the criminal life* thing or maybe he just isn't sleeping. He wouldn't talk about it very much."

"It's all good," Nick replied. "Thanks for the heads-up." And, with that, he hung up on her, presumably to call his brother.

She wondered if she'd done the right thing. And it stayed on her mind right through the night, but she managed to get some much-needed sleep.

# Chapter 6

*Friday Morning ...*

D OREEN WOKE UP the next morning, surrounded by all her animals. After giving each a cuddle, she showered and dressed. Going downstairs, she had Mack on her mind yet again. She sent him a text, just saying, **Good morning.** She got a happy face right back. She smiled at that, not sure exactly what was going on with him, but wanting him to know that he wasn't alone. At that, she stopped and thought about it.

Wasn't that something to consider that she'd gotten this far?

She pondered the changes in her world—some happening so fast—and yet here she was, still trying to get rid of her ex. She oscillated between calling him her *ex* and calling him her *husband* because legally he still was. And yet how wrong was that? She didn't like anything about him, and the sooner this was all dealt with, the better for her sanity and for her peace of mind. When her phone rang, she thought it would be Mack, but instead it was Nick.

"Hey, Nick. How was Mack last night?"

"Exhausted," he replied bluntly. "I'm hoping that he

takes my advice and enjoys a few days off. I don't think he has quite fully recovered from his wound."

"I know," she agreed. "And yet not a whole lot I can ever say to him to get him to stop."

He laughed at that. "Is there anything he can say to get *you* to stop?"

She winced. "I guess we're a hell of a pair, aren't we?"

"Yeah, you got that right." He chuckled. "Now you should put him out of his misery and let him know that."

"He knows it," she said, her voice soft. "Even if we haven't discussed all the details."

"Are you sure?"

"I am. I just … This divorce. Mathew …"

"Oh, I understand. It's one of the reasons Mack's looking forward to my getting your divorce finalized," he noted.

"I won't move the relationship forward until I'm free."

A seemingly surprised silence came from the other end. Nick replied, "That's definitely some encouragement to get it going forward. You know that most people don't have that compunction."

"I'm not most people," she stated. "Besides, you guys don't really understand how dangerous Mathew is. The last thing I want is him coming after Mack."

"Oh, good Lord," Nick said. "Do you really think that's something Mathew will do?"

"I don't know, but he's not …" She hesitated and added, "I … I don't know what to say. I just know that he's not normal. He's not like everybody else in this world, and so even saying that you've come to an agreement makes me very suspicious."

"He sounded pretty fed up with the whole process."

"Maybe, but I'm not sure I trust that either," she murmured. "He hasn't mentioned Robin's will at all, has he?"

"Not to me. He wouldn't ask me—outside of trying to figure out who is handling it."

"He can't stop me from getting anything, can he?"

"I wouldn't think so. I can check in with the lawyer, if you want."

"Yeah, maybe you should do that," she agreed. "Hey, could you also get a time frame on the inheritance? It'll all be a pain in the butt for me, until I get some money."

He laughed. "You won't let my brother help either, will you?"

"Nope, that I won't. He already does a ton for me. Do you have any idea how many groceries that guy picks up?"

"Yeah, but just think about it. You and I both know how much groceries he eats. And this way you're saving him from having to eat alone." And, with that, Nick rang off to start his day.

Sitting outside with her cup of coffee, she pondered his words. When Nan phoned a few minutes later, Doreen was uncharacteristically quiet.

"What's going on?" Nan asked. "You sound off."

"I'm fine," she murmured. "Just a little tired."

"Tired maybe," Nan agreed, "but that sounds like more of a contemplative type of tired."

Doreen burst out laughing. "I don't even know what that means."

"And that's fine," Nan stated, "as long as everything's okay."

"Yep, it is. Do you know anything about Joseph Moody?"

"Nope, but I'll ask around. That's why I was calling," Nan shared. "One of the women here knows one of her clients."

"You mean, one of Annabelle's clients?"

"Yes." Nan sighed, as if Doreen should have figured that out already.

"Okay, and?"

"I think you should talk to her."

"Is there any particular reason?"

"It's important that we talk to everybody."

"Is this person at Rosemoor?"

"No, no, no. You need to head over to the client." Nan hesitated. "You really do sound tired today."

"I'm fine, Nan. I was just trying to follow the conversation."

"That's what I mean though," Nan replied in an odd tone. "And it does sound like you're having trouble doing that, dear."

Doreen laughed. "I'm fine, Nan."

"Good, glad to hear it," she noted in exasperation. "So you'll get over there today?"

Still trying to get a handle on the conversation, Doreen asked, "Have you got the details?"

"Absolutely." And Nan rattled off the person's name and address.

"Do you have a phone number?"

"No, I don't," she said. "You'll have to go by her house."

"Great." Doreen yawned.

Almost immediately Nan snapped back and suggested, "Or maybe you should go back to bed."

"I'm fine. I'm fine. I'm fine," Doreen replied. "I'm just not fully awake yet."

"I don't know how you can sleep that deep anyway," she muttered. "I mean, there's only so many hours in a day.

You've got things to do."

Nan always seemed to have that instant energy popping out from nowhere. Doreen smiled. Not really sure what else she could do to satisfy Nan, she replied, "I'll contact her today."

"Good." With that, this time Nan rang off.

But Doreen wasn't done. Even as she got her second cup of coffee, her phone rang again. She snatched up her notepad and stepped outside as she said, "Hello."

It was Joseph Moody. "Hey, I have good news."

"What's that?"

"I'm no longer a suspect," he stated in a jubilant tone.

"That's good to know." She smiled. "I gather they checked out your alibi."

"Yes," he replied, "thank God for that."

"That's wonderful. Now let them do the rest of their job."

He hesitated. "Would you mind still looking into it?"

"I'll see what I can come up with but no promises."

"No, no, that's okay. Now that the police are a little bit more on track," he noted, "it should be fine."

"So are you sure you want me to look into it?"

"Why not?" He sounded puzzled.

"Nothing," she replied.

"Yes, I do," he confirmed. "I want to, … I want to make sure that whoever did this is caught. So I would appreciate it if you can still look into it."

"Okay." With that agreed on, she hung up. And then realized that he hadn't given her all the other information that she had requested from him yesterday, but it was enough to go on for a while. Plus Doreen had that client to contact that Nan gave her this morning.

Didn't matter whether Doreen was tired or not, she knew for a fact that both Nan and Richie would be on her if she didn't follow up with this client lead. With half a smile she looked up the name and found a phone number, and, when she dialed the number, an older woman answered.

"This is Claire. Who's this?"

"This is Doreen. I understand you were a customer of Annabelle's."

"Oh yes, yes, yes. Oh yes, dear. I heard that your grandmother was looking for Annabelle's clients for you to talk to."

"Yes, to a certain extent," Doreen noted. "We're just trying to trace her last days. And see if anybody knew of anything that would get that poor woman killed."

"Oh, isn't that terrible," Claire replied. "She was the sweetest thing. 'Course that boyfriend of hers was no-good, but, hey, it seems to be that way a lot."

Doreen paused at that. "Was the boyfriend really a louse?"

"He's one of those lazy kinds, you know? Annabelle was all about dreams and having her own company and working hard to get to it somehow, and he was all about *Why bother? This is good enough. I've got a job. We're good.*" Claire added, "I mean nothing is wrong with that, but it wasn't the best match for her, if you ask me."

"I guess the question then is, was she happy?"

"I think she was," Claire muttered. "I mean, amazingly I do think she was."

"Well then, that's what really counts, isn't it?" Doreen asked. "As much as we think that somebody might be better off with someone else, it doesn't mean that they are."

"No, no, I hear you there," Claire agreed.

"So what can you tell me about Annabelle? How often did you use her services?"

"Since she's a local gal, we've known her for a long time. This was the first time for me to use her business. My daughter is pregnant, and we were doing a reveal for her."

"I guess it didn't go off because you didn't get the final product."

"We ended up having it yesterday anyway. I baked a cake," she added, with a wry tone, "instead of the flowers, after poor Annabelle's death."

"How did you hear about it?"

"I snooped around her apartment, and the neighbor told me," Claire shared. "When I didn't get Annabelle on the phone, I started to get really worried. So I went to her apartment, and there was no answer. That's when the neighbor came out and told me that Annabelle was dead. It was such a shock."

"Which neighbor was this?"

"She lived on the same floor, across from her door though. I think she is one of those nosy women."

"Right." Doreen had met many of those. "Maybe I'll go speak to her myself."

"Oh, I'm sure she'd love that," Claire replied, with a wry tone. "Anyway I don't know of anybody who would have killed that beautiful young woman. Every time I spoke to her, she was professional. She was upfront, and she wasn't very expensive. It was just a fun way to make this happen for my daughter. It came to naught anyway. But that wasn't that poor girl's fault."

"No, it certainly wasn't. I'm not sure who's making arrangements for her body," Doreen noted. "Do you know if she has any other family around?"

"I think they're all back East," she replied. "That detective of yours can tell you."

Doreen winced at that because everybody knew about Mack. "I can ask him," she said in a calm voice. "I'm sure he's had to deliver the next-of-kin notification."

The other woman gasped. "That has got to be the worst job in the world."

"I would think so," Doreen agreed. "Thankfully I haven't had to deal with any of that."

"No, and you wouldn't want to. That poor girl." And Claire went off on another round of how beautiful and likable that poor girl was.

"Do you know what school she went to?"

"The one downtown," she replied. "Kelowna Secondary or something, and then she was in college, but I'm not sure what she was taking. She wasn't very old either. I think she was like twenty-three."

"Right." Doreen took down notes. "As far as you know, she had no problems, no other ... no ex-boyfriends, nothing like that?"

"Well, she had a beau from way back when," Claire said. "I thought that he was probably a better match for her than the current one, but it's too late now."

Nothing Doreen could say to that because it was definitely too late now. "Do you know what his name was?"

"*Hmm*, I want to say something like Brent, but I don't know about a last name."

"Okay."

"Besides, it was probably a long time ago. I think so. ... I don't think anybody's been in her life, except for Joseph, for quite a while."

"Any idea where they met?"

"No, probably at that bar where Joseph worked," Claire guessed.

Doreen asked, "Did Annabelle have a drinking problem or anything like that?"

"Oh my, I wouldn't know," Claire said, "but she certainly didn't seem like the type to."

"Right. Did Joseph have a drinking problem?"

"I don't know about that either. Yet, working at a bar, I would imagine that he did drink."

Even long after the phone call with Claire was over, Doreen thought about what the woman's *type* had to do with having a drinking problem. Because, as far as Doreen knew, there wasn't so much a type as much as people who got into a habit of drinking, and then it became a crutch, and then it became an addiction.

She could almost see Joseph having that kind of a problem. He looked a little shaky when he was here. But that didn't mean that grief wasn't a great motivator for getting that bottle back into your hands. And, for a lot of people, it was a great way to forget everything. She hoped that Joseph had some support too because it didn't look as if the town would look on his participation in this event with any compassion. But it was early days yet.

With that, she picked up the phone and started making more calls. She needed to stay ahead of the information.

# Chapter 7

A FTER LUNCH DOREEN noted her animals seemed a bit on edge. "How about we go for a walk?"

Mugs looked up at her and woofed. It wasn't all that far to the apartment where Annabelle and Joseph had lived. It was close to the college, in fact, and that meant about a forty-minute walk for her. Or she could drive partway and then could walk the rest of the way. Lots of nice areas were there, perfect for a routine walk in a new neighborhood.

And, with that, she loaded up the animals, headed to the parking lot of the college, deciding to stroll around it first, and then, if they wanted to later, they could walk down to the beach.

With two of her pets on leashes, Thaddeus on her shoulder, she crossed the road and headed to the apartment building she was looking for. She found it within minutes. She walked up to the second floor, not sure whether Joseph was allowed in or not.

Her money was on *probably not*, considering that his girlfriend had been killed here. As she went up to the apartment, she knocked, trying to get an excuse formulated in her head as to why she was here. If Joseph was here, she would just tell him that she needed to see the crime scene. But, as she knocked again and still got no answer, a door across the hallway opened up, and an older lady with spiky hair poked her head out.

When she saw Doreen and all the animals, she gasped. "Oh, I don't think you're allowed to bring animals in here, dear."

Doreen looked down at them and frowned. "Sorry."

"That's all right. Were you looking for poor Annabelle?"

"I was looking for Joseph," she replied.

"Poor Joseph," she said, with a sigh. "But then you know about poor Annabelle? That's the worst part."

"I did hear," Doreen admitted. "I wasn't sure whether he was allowed back into the apartment or not."

The woman looked at her curiously. "I suppose they won't let him in for a while, will they?"

Doreen shrugged. "I don't know. If he's not here, then I can't ask him any questions."

"What questions?"

"I like to do a little bit of this detective stuff," Doreen shared, with an eye roll. "And I was talking to Joseph about Annabelle yesterday, and I just had a few more questions."

"Is he helping you?" she asked. "He's not been the most pleasant neighbor to have."

"No? What about Annabelle?"

"Annabelle was a sweetheart," the nosy neighbor replied. "Joseph's just … I think he's very lucky that he hooked up with her, but I'm not so sure that she's lucky she hooked up with him."

"Oh, that's interesting," Doreen replied. "I did hear from a few people that maybe he wasn't all that motivated to do much in life."

She snorted. "Nope, my father would have called him a ne'er-do-well."

Doreen held back a grin at that because she knew the phrase well. Her husband wouldn't have used it so much, but she certainly understood it from Mathew's disparagement for people who weren't out there actively trying to be a success in life. "Interesting. I gather he was happy working at the pub."

"Maybe, but that's not exactly long-term work, so I don't understand how he could be happy or working much either."

Doreen didn't say anything. It was definitely long-term work for a lot of people who worked at pubs, and supposedly the tips were great, so that was an interesting comment from the neighbor. "Did Annabelle work at the pub too?"

"No, I don't think so. She was doing pretty well with her business, and she wanted to expand it to have a full-time flower shop, but that'll never happen now." She sent a sad look toward the apartment.

"No, I'm sorry to hear that too," Doreen murmured. "Sounds like Annabelle needed a few more people looking out for her. Did you hear anything on the day that the shooting happened?"

"I heard the shot," she declared, with a nod. "I mean, I didn't know that it was that shot, and I told the police I didn't know it was a shot, but there was this hard *pop*, you know? I didn't look out. I didn't ... I didn't even think of something being wrong, and believe me. That's something I'll have to live with." She stood at Annabelle's front door, and her bottom lip trembled.

Doreen grimaced. "I'm pretty sure that, even if you had called the police at the time, it wouldn't have made any difference."

"That's what the police told me too," she relayed. "But you always wonder, if you had heard the one shot, ... maybe a little bit more then, just maybe that beautiful girl would still be alive."

She couldn't reassure her about that because Doreen had absolutely no way to know whether what this woman was afraid of was true or not. "Did you get along well with them?" Doreen asked the neighbor.

"I got along absolutely marvelously with Annabelle. Him? Not so much."

Doreen nodded. "Did you see anybody come to visit that day?"

"No, I didn't, and that's why I was so surprised at the shot. I did wonder ..." She hesitated. "I did wonder if maybe Annabelle had done something to herself."

"I don't think the police are looking at it as a suicide," Doreen offered. "I mean, I could be wrong because we haven't got the autopsy results yet."

At that, the other woman winced. "That's a nasty thing, that is."

"Maybe, but, if it helps solve some of these cases, we need to do them."

"Maybe," the older woman hedged, "but I don't want anybody cutting into my flesh."

"I don't think you'll be feeling it, if it does happen."

The other woman shuddered. "Maybe not, but I'll be upstairs looking down, and I won't be taking it very kindly if somebody does that to me."

"Let's hope you don't get into a situation where it needs to happen then," Doreen said gently.

"Not for many, many more years—at least I hope not."

She sighed. "Annabelle was such a sweetheart."

"So you didn't hear anybody, and you didn't see anybody, yet you did hear a shot, but you didn't contact the police."

"No, not until another lady was banging on the door, looking for Annabelle, and I talked to her and told her the news. Her boyfriend found her, you know?"

Doreen checked her notes, as if not sure about that, and then nodded. "You're right. He did."

The other woman just nodded. "I'm sure he was a mess at the time. I mean, it's the one time I was sympathetic for him."

"That had to have been a pretty rough thing to come home to."

"Exactly, and it was late. So, by the time the police got here, the kerfuffle got me out of bed too," she murmured.

"Sorry about that. I'm sure Annabelle wouldn't have wanted you disturbed."

The other woman shook her head. "Annabelle was a sweetheart," she repeated.

Doreen felt like she had heard a broken record.

"Annabelle wouldn't have disturbed anybody. I'm just so sad that I didn't see anybody before."

"Did they have an alarm on their place, do you know?"

She frowned. "I don't think so. If they did, I've never heard it go off."

"I just wonder how anybody got into the apartment."

"She must have let them in," she guessed. "I don't think the police thought that the door was jimmied or anything. I know they asked me if I had heard anybody trying to break in, but I was in bed. Nobody seems to understand that." Now upset, she folded her arms across her body. "I didn't hear anything."

"That's all right," Doreen said. "The police will figure it out."

The neighbor's shoulders slumped. "I hope so. I can't see … I have to admit that I'm not sleeping all that well myself now."

"Are you afraid of a break-in?"

"I just don't know what I'm afraid of," she admitted. "That's part of the problem. I mean, what if it was somebody who's coming back?"

"I don't think that would be the case either," Doreen noted cautiously. "I mean, why would they? They already found who they wanted."

"But what if it was random?" she asked, arguing the point that had played around in her head.

"If random, then they won't come back here. I mean, why would they?" Doreen asked. "They already caused all kinds of chaos, and now the police are looking at anybody who was here at any recent point. So, to come back will just make them look even more suspicious. Bring more scrutiny."

The woman frowned. "Maybe." Yet she didn't sound at all convinced.

"Just keep your door locked, if that's the case," Doreen suggested. "Meanwhile, let the police do their thing, and hopefully stay out of trouble yourself."

"Well, that's the hope," the woman declared. She went to enter her apartment and close the door, and then she opened it again. "Do the police know you're here?"

Doreen nodded. "Absolutely they do." She smiled at the nosy neighbor. "I'll be talking to Corporal Mack Moreau afterward, as soon as I am done here."

"Oh, good. Otherwise I'd have to report you too."

At that, it took a moment for Doreen to register what the neighbor lady had said. "Report me *too*?"

"Yes, I'm reporting anybody who has been here," she stated rather hotly.

"I see. Who else did you report so far?"

"I probably shouldn't tell you."

"It would help if you did tell me, and that would save me some legwork."

She frowned at that. "Well, Joseph tried to come back."

"Of course he did. All his stuff's here, including a change of clothes. Plus I'm sure he needed his work stuff and all that ..." But, looking at the woman's face, Doreen had missed something.

The other woman nodded. "I didn't think of that. I did tell the police that he came back though."

"Did anybody else come by?"

"Just the woman looking for her flowers. ... Other than that, it's been pretty quiet."

"Nobody else? Nobody even maybe coming back to just look around?" Just something here didn't feel quite right to Doreen.

"Nobody that I saw. I mean, the superintendent came up with the police, and he came back one other time, looking to see if the apartment was locked up. But, other than that, nothing."

Doreen nodded. "Thank you for that."

And, with that, the woman gave a nervous look around and quickly went back inside her apartment and closed her front door.

# Chapter 8

D OREEN SLOWLY WALKED back outside and stopped to smell the fresh air. Mugs sat down, not too worried about walking. She looked down at him and smiled. "Hey, buddy, we need to keep in shape."

At that, a man called out to her, "No animals in the buildings."

She looked up to see him glaring at her. She nodded. "Somebody just told me that. I am so sorry, but now we are outside."

He sniffed. "People are forever breaking the rules here. I always have to remind people when they're looking to move in here, no animals are allowed."

"That would exactly be one of the reasons why I wouldn't move in."

He continued to glare at her. "Have you applied?"

"Nope, don't need to. I have a home."

"So what are you doing here?" he asked her suspiciously.

"I was looking for Joseph," she replied.

His face closed up. "Well, he ain't here. Not allowed back in."

"I assumed that the police would have already cleared

the apartment and let him back in again."

He shrugged. "I don't know when that'll happen. And they're behind on their rent, so I'm not sure what I'm supposed to do about that either."

"Ouch, that'll be tough."

"Annabelle was supposed to pay the day after she was killed," he noted, raising his hands. "And, if I say anything, it makes me sound like I'm a terrible person."

Doreen privately thought that he was, but, hey, he had a job to do too. "That can't be easy, but I'm sure, for Annabelle, she would have cheerfully paid her rent, rather than be where she is right now."

"I know, right?" He shook his head. "She was the nice one in that couple."

"Joseph wasn't?"

"*Naw*, he was okay. I mean, ... he was all about being at the bar and doing his thing, but she was a darling. That's too bad because she's also the one who dealt with the rent."

"I don't think you can even evict him over something like this, can you?"

"I don't know," he said, "but I'll have to try soon. If they don't pay their rent, what are my choices?"

"Were they really that broke all the time?" she asked. "I thought Annabelle was doing okay with her business."

"I don't know about that." He shrugged. "She certainly didn't have the money to pay the rent—or at least she told me that she didn't." He hesitated at that. "I sure don't want to find out now that she was stringing me along."

"I doubt it," she murmured. "Everybody seems to believe in Annabelle."

"It was easy to believe in her," he admitted. "Joseph was a different story. He worked at the pub and often came home more than a few sheets to the wind."

"I think that would also be an occupational hazard," she noted.

He nodded. "That it is. However, they still have to pay the rent."

He seemed to be pretty hung up on the rent not being paid. "How much longer until you had to evict them?"

"Well, if she'd paid tomorrow, it would have been good for another month," he shared, "but, because she didn't pay, it's a problem."

"Right," she murmured. "So he needs to come up with that rent money fast."

"Yeah, really fast. It's still a process though, and that's the problem. So even if I try to evict him, it'll take time."

"And, if he gets the money to you, will you give him another chance?"

He shrugged. "Can't say I want to. I've been up against this wall too many times with him, but, if he pays the rent, then that's just what it is. It'll go again, until they don't pay again. Or *he* doesn't pay again." The man frowned, as he looked back at the building.

She shook her head. "He's in a pretty rough spot right now."

"Yeah, I know he is. And my heart goes out to him, but my heart goes out more to her." And, with that, he turned and stormed off.

"So that was obviously the superintendent," she muttered to Mugs. He woofed at her.

Almost on cue, the guy called back, "Remember. No dogs."

"Thank you," she replied, trying for a nice tone. "I guess animals are not allowed to visit then either, are they?"

He hesitated and then nodded. "Yes, as long as you clean up behind them."

"I always do," she said cheerfully.

He just glared at her again.

She didn't think there was very much cheerful in his world at all. He seemed to be all about grumpiness. She looked down at Mugs. "We don't have any reason to stay here anyway. Let's go down to the beach."

And, with that, they turned and headed toward the car. Once she got everybody loaded back up again, she picked up a coffee at a nearby drive-through and then headed to the beach.

When she arrived, she realized that no dogs were allowed here either. She stared at the sign and frowned. She was allowed to take them on the sidewalk, but she couldn't bring them along the sandy beach, where Mugs really wanted to go.

She sighed. "Well, this is disappointing too." She walked along the sidewalk, struggling to restrain both Goliath and Mugs, who both wanted to head down to the much more interesting sandy areas.

Finally she gave up. "Okay, we're going home. I can't have a tug of war and argue with you the whole time here."

At that, a man called out. "Are you certain? Man, they sure look like they want to go to the water."

She nodded. "They do, but no dogs allowed." She pointed at the signs.

He rolled his eyes. "Of course. Anything that's fun in this town is obviously not allowed."

She considered him curiously. He wasn't all that old, maybe thirty.

He walked over to Mugs, who was quite happy to have

some attention and to not fight with her over trying to get down to the beach. The stranger smiled and said, "He's a beautiful dog."

"Yeah, he is. Come on, Mugs. Let's go back."

"What does *back* mean to you?" he asked curiously.

"I'll take them home, and we'll go play in the river, instead of arguing about the sign," she said.

"You see? That's the problem. The beach should be for everybody."

"I agree. Yet they've made it pretty clear that I can't take them off the leash, and Mugs won't cooperate if he can't get down to the water."

"All dogs love water," the man noted. "I know a couple dog parks are around here." He turned and frowned, as if he could see them within his sight.

"I should have looked it up before I came," she told him. "I was in the area and thought I'd come for a walk, but obviously that wasn't a good idea."

"I think it's a great idea," he said. "Just this town isn't terribly generous to dogs."

She wasn't sure that that was true either. She'd had quite a bit of decency and good treatment from everybody. "It's fine." She waved goodbye to him and tugged Mugs to her. "Come on, buddy. That's enough now." He got to his feet, but he wasn't happy about it. "I know. I know. When we get home, we'll go down to the river."

"Where's home?" he called out.

She pretended to ignore him because the last thing she wanted was to deal with a stranger showing up at her doorstep. When he called out again, Mugs stopped and gave her a *woof* and a hard look. "No, no, and no," she muttered. "Come on. Let's go home." And she continued to argue with him all the way back to her car.

She finally wrestled him inside, with Goliath pouting and Thaddeus tucked up still against her neck. "I don't know what's got into you, Mugs. I'm sorry that the beach was out of bounds. And. yeah, it looked like it would have been a great place to go, but we weren't welcome, and you couldn't go off a leash there." When she realized she was sitting here in her car, trying to explain life to a dog, she groaned.

As she turned on the car and pulled out, the same guy stood nearby, staring at her. She gave him half a smile and quickly pulled out of the parking lot. She didn't know why he made her uneasy but he did, and maybe it was just the fact that he was asking personal questions that she wasn't prepared to answer, and she didn't seem to have any ready-made replies. Maybe he was interested in her socially? Well, she had never been comfortable dating either.

At this point in time, Mugs was being very noncoopera-tive, which was also very unusual. She glared at him, as she drove home. "What was that?" she asked. "That wasn't like you at all."

He woofed at her again and then slumped down into the front footwell and dropped his head onto his paws.

"Now you're making me feel bad, and I'm so sorry, but I have to follow *some* of the rules. Otherwise we get into trouble too."

It was one thing for her to get into trouble; it was anoth-er thing to get into trouble with the animals. So far everybody loved having her animals around, and most people were generous and tolerant. But she couldn't start getting fines because her money would not get her very far in that case.

"How about we go and see Nan?" she suggested, hoping

that would cure Mugs's depression and disappointment.

He pricked up his ears. While she was driving, she contemplated it, and then, as soon as she pulled up into her driveway, she decided. "Let's go on foot. We'll head down to the river, and then we'll see Nan."

Just about as she reached the river and was considering sitting here for a little bit, Nan called. "Hey," Doreen answered. "I was thinking about coming down and visiting you."

"That's why I'm calling. You should come down."

"Why?" she asked, frowning.

"We might have some information for you."

Closing her eyes, she replied, "Fine. Mugs is disappointed because I couldn't take him to the beach earlier. All those signs down on the big beaches state No Dogs Allowed."

At that, Nan replied, "Isn't that silly? All that space, all that beautiful beach, and they won't let the dogs have any fun."

"It's frustrating, and Mugs is quite out of sorts with me."

"Then bring him down," Nan said. "I'll get him back into a good mood." And she hung up.

# Chapter 9

DOREEN WAS ALMOST at Nan's, with Mugs still acting off. She wasn't sure what was going on with him, but he didn't seem to be terribly happy with her right now. By the time she'd turned the corner, and he could see Rosemoor right in front of him, he picked up speed and started dragging her along. "Hey, hey, hey," she cried out. "Let's not get too crazy."

But, just like before, he wasn't listening. He raced toward Nan and even jumped over the little patio barrier to greet her.

"He's been acting weird all morning," Doreen noted finally, when she came to a stop. "I don't know what's the matter with him."

"He saw something he really wanted, and he couldn't have it," Nan stated. "They're just like children. Everybody gets disappointed when they can't have what they want."

Doreen thought about it and shrugged. "It's possible. He did seem to really want to go into that water at the beach."

"You may have to take him down to a doggie park, where he can be off the leash and just paddle around."

"In which case," Doreen added, "I might as well stay at

73

the river. There he can paddle in the water just fine. He does it all the time."

Nan laughed. "That makes the most sense so far because you're right. Why take him someplace where he'll get in trouble, when he can have his own space right there. Still a change of scenery might have a positive impact."

"He would have been fine. It's just … I didn't even give him time to play on the way down," Doreen explained. "So he's even more upset with me."

"Well, that's not easy on anybody." Nan reached down and cuddled Mugs. "What's the matter, big guy?"

He woofed at her several times, as if trying to tell her a tale of woe, and then finally collapsed at her feet and looked up at her adoringly.

Doreen sat down at Nan's patio table. "Well, he certainly seems to be feeling better, now that he's here."

"Of course he is," Nan declared in that bracing tone. "What's not to be feeling better about? I mean, this is home for him."

"Well, it's one of many at least, that's for sure," she said, as she smiled at her grandmother. "Now what's this I hear about you having information?"

"We do and we don't," she replied. "I was hoping to get you down here so we could talk about it."

"I'm here now. So what's up?"

Nan looked around several times to ensure nobody was listening in.

At that, Doreen raised an eyebrow. "Do you really expect to be overheard?"

"You never know around here," Nan noted almost crossly. "We do have an awful lot of people with big ears."

Doreen waited for Nan to go through the motions of

making tea and then bringing out the pot and finally sitting down with her. Doreen wondered if maybe her grandmother's attitude was because she was lonely. Which would go along with Mugs's attitude of the day too.

Finally Nan spoke. "I think something's wrong with Mack."

Doreen's jaw dropped. "What?"

Nan shrugged. "Darren mentioned that Mack is looking at taking some time off."

She frowned at her. "What are you talking about?"

"I just think that he's tired, worn out, and he probably should take some days off. But I don't think you knew that Mack was taking time off, did you, dear?"

She slowly shook her head. "No, he hasn't told me anything about that."

"Right, I think you need to talk to him."

Doreen slowly rubbed her temples. "I think, if something were wrong, he'd have told me," she replied hesitantly.

"Maybe, and maybe … he just needs some attention."

Doreen rolled her eyes at that. "He's hardly your garden-variety schoolboy."

At that, Nan raised one eyebrow. "You know, dear? You do say the darndest things."

She sighed. "I know. I know. It's just Mack is Mack," Doreen said, with another sigh.

Nan shook her head. "I don't think you quite appreciate what he's going through."

"No, I probably don't," Doreen admitted, looking at her grandmother. "He's always been very self-sufficient, put together, and independent, so it's hard to gauge what he's going through."

"Exactly," Nan agreed.

"How would Darren know?" Doreen asked.

"Like I said, Darren found out that Mack was looking at taking some time off."

"Well, he did go back to work awfully fast after the shooting," she reminded her.

Nan nodded. "I think you need to do more for Mack."

Doreen winced at that. "Do you now?"

Nan nodded. "Yep, I do, and so does Richie."

Doreen groaned. "You two just couldn't leave us to work it out on our own, could you?"

"Well, you're doing a terrible job of it," Nan muttered.

She stared at her grandmother. It wasn't something that she expected to hear from her. In her defence Doreen replied, "He's got a lot of cases. Especially right now, he's got a couple that are causing him trouble. However, I don't think, outside of being tired, there's a problem."

"I think you're wrong," Nan stated.

"Okay, so what do you think is wrong?"

"Well, I don't know the core of it. That's for you to figure out. It's just … you need to do it faster. Sooner rather than later."

Not exactly sure where this was going and what was happening, Doreen replied, "Possibly, but I mean … Okay, I can talk to Mack and see what's going on."

"So you should. Sooner rather than later."

At that repeated warning, Doreen realized that Nan was really worried. "What do you think is the problem?" Doreen asked her grandmother.

"I'm not sure, but something is … Something's bothering Mack, and you need to figure it out."

"Oh, do I now?" Doreen asked. "I didn't really see that there was a problem."

"No, *you* didn't, but we do."

Doreen gave in. "Fine, I'll talk to Mack after, ... when he's off work today."

At that, Nan studied Doreen's expression to see if she was sincere and then nodded. "Okay, that's probably enough."

"Enough what?"

"*Just enough* to ease my worries," Nan stated, "but you must do it fast because I don't really know what's going on."

"Nan, I don't really want you to get panicky about this."

"Too late for that," Nan snapped. "We have noticed a change in Mack, and, to me, it's obvious something is wrong."

"Okay, so maybe something is wrong in Mack's life," Doreen answered carefully, "but I don't think it is anything terribly major."

"That's because you're not seeing what we're seeing," Nan declared.

Frowning at that and not liking where the conversation was going, Doreen said, "Fine, I'll talk to Mack tonight."

"Good." And, with that, Nan changed the conversation. "Now how's your investigation going?"

"Not very well," Doreen admitted. "Everybody I have talked to so far didn't think that the boyfriend was worthy of Annabelle. Nobody really likes him. I haven't gone to the pub and talked to any of the people in his world yet. I talked to one of her clients, talked to the neighbor, talked to the superintendent. Everybody's got good things to say about Annabelle, and nobody really has anything good to say about Joseph, nothing that amounts to much."

"Of course not," Nan noted. "That's so often the way."

Unfortunately it was. Often the hardworking women

were well-loved, and, according to everybody else in their world, they needed somebody better suited as a partner. "We still don't have any motive though. And they were behind on the rent, so money was definitely an issue."

At that, Nan tsked-tsked. "I guess money is the root of all evil in these cases, isn't it?" She looked over at Doreen. "Mack wouldn't have any money problems, would he?"

Doreen stared at her in surprise and then slowly shook her head. "No, he doesn't have any money problems."

"Good." Then Nan came back to the conversation at hand, only to revert back to Mack again a few minutes later.

"Look, Nan," Doreen said in exasperation. "I already told you that I'd talk to him, and I will. This worrying isn't helping."

At that, Nan thrummed her fingers on the table. "I just want to make sure that everything's okay," she declared crossly. "I like Mack. I don't want anything to happen to him."

"And you're really thinking that something is seriously wrong?"

"Yes," she snapped, with a definitive head nod. "Something is definitely wrong."

"Okay, fine," Doreen said. "I'll talk to him later tonight. I think we should leave it at that for now."

Finally Nan seemed to calm down.

They talked some more, but after Nan's worried declarations, an odd atmosphere took over their conversation, as if Nan were getting stressed about Mack again. So Doreen stood. "I'll take the animals home, and we'll sit out at the river and relax."

Nan nodded. "That's a good idea. Maybe call Mack over to do the same thing."

Trying not to commit to anything, Doreen just gave a noncommittal nod. "That might work."

Doreen, with her animals in tow, slowly headed home. She wasn't sure what the heck was going on, but somebody, somewhere, had her grandmother really worried about Mack. And now that her grandmother had started that, it was hard for Doreen not to be worried about Mack too. She phoned Nick.

"Wow, two phone calls so close together," he teased. "I'm honored."

He was humoring her. She snorted. "Not likely."

"Are you in trouble?" he asked curiously.

"Nope, I'm sure not, but my grandmother's got a bee in her bonnet that something is wrong with Mack."

"In what way?" he asked cautiously.

"I don't know that there's any way to describe it, but she's in quite a tizzy about it."

"I did talk to him earlier. He told me that he was just tired."

"Darren, the other cop that we see at the retirement home all the time, mentioned that Mack's looking at taking some time off."

At that, Nick made an odd sound. "I highly doubt that's the case. Mack does have vacation days coming though, and he does have to take those because you can only do so many continuous hours on the job."

"So maybe that's what it's all about," she said, with relief.

"Maybe," Nick replied, "but I don't think that's enough to cause anybody to get worried."

"You don't know my nan." Doreen chuckled. "She is unbelievable, but her heart is in the right place. So I'll see what Mack's like when I talk to him next."

"Yeah, you do that," Nick agreed. "You guys are pretty serious, *huh?*"

"I don't know what we are," she answered cautiously. "I can tell you that we are … *both* not too open about discussing whatever this is between us. … So we haven't talked much about it."

At that, Nick burst out laughing. "Is that a hint?"

"I don't know whether it is or not," she admitted. "It seems like, just as I get one thing sorted out, something else comes down the pipeline to confuse everything."

"I don't think anything's all that confusing about my brother and you," Nick stated. "But I know it would make him feel better if you two had your relationship more settled."

She winced at that. "You're not the first person to remind me about that either. I definitely don't want to think about that right now."

"No, I'm sure you don't, not with the divorce still pending," Nick agreed, "and I understand that you don't need any pressure from me."

"Good. I've got enough going on."

"Yeah, are you involved in another case?" he asked curiously.

"Yes, and unfortunately it's literally Mack's case."

"I thought you weren't allowed to touch those," he said in alarm.

"Yeah, but what do I do when one of the main suspects comes to me and asks me to help clear his name?"

"Did he?" he asked in dismay.

"Yeah, he did. So now I don't know what to do."

"I imagine that doesn't sound very good at all to Mack.

On the other hand, it's smart on the suspect's part."

"Smart in what way?" she asked.

"Well, because doing what he's doing … throws suspicion off him. Anyway, I gotta go." And, with that, he hung up.

She was left staring at her phone, wondering exactly what Nick was trying to say. When her phone rang again, she was almost determined to not answer. But seeing that it was Mack, she did. "Hello."

"Wow, that's a tired hello."

"Is it? I'm feeling a little bit peopled out at the moment."

An odd sound came from his end of the call. "Is that a message for me?"

"No," she replied crossly. "You're the one person I'm okay to see. But everybody else? … They seem to have their wires crossed. I feel like I am running off-road today. Either it's that or it's me, in which case I just need a break."

"Ah, got it. Did you tell my brother that I wasn't doing so well?"

"Yeah, I did," she admitted. "I just got off the phone with him now because I'm getting inundated with calls and concerns from Nan, who seems to think that something is wrong with you."

A moment of silence followed. "Seriously?"

"Yes," she snapped. "So just in case you have any plans to run out of town or do something completely crazy, wild and wacky, or stupid, you should realize that a lot of people in Kelowna apparently are affected by everything you do and how you do it."

"Oh, good Lord." Mack started to laugh.

Something was so infectious about that sound that it

DALE MAYER

brought a smile on her face. "See? That makes me feel better already. You don't sound quite so exhausted as you were earlier."

"I didn't get any sleep last night," he told her, still chuckling.

"What's this about you taking time off?"

"Time off?" he asked, mystified.

"Yeah, and you're not allowed to get mad at him, but supposedly Darren said something about you taking time off, so Richie went to Nan, and Nan came to me. Or, in this case, I went to her, ... when she called me, so you get the idea. And everybody's got the wild hair that you're either broken-hearted or exhausted or went back to work too fast after getting shot, which we all know is quite true, but you won't acknowledge it," she said, with a groan. "Who knows what else they're dreaming up."

At that, Mack burst out into great loud guffaws. "That's funny. I didn't realize that anyone cared."

"Most of the time I'd say they absolutely do care and then some, but sometimes I'm just wondering if they're not bored."

And that made him laugh again. "Oh, I needed that. It's just been an off day."

"Yeah, for me too." She explained about going down to Annabelle's place and how Mugs had been so upset about the beach. "So I'll take him to the river and just chill and let him bounce around in the water. And I don't want to do or to think of anything. I swear, Mugs is still mad at me. The way he looks at me ..."

"Oh, he will come around," Mack stated. "Now I would suggest that I come for dinner but sounds like you've already got plans."

"My plans could include you, particularly if you need some destressing time," she added. "The river's really great for that, you know?"

"You're right. The river is excellent for that. ... And, if you're okay with it, maybe I'll do just that—as soon as I'm done for the day."

"I'm up for that. I don't have a whole lot for dinner though."

He chuckled. "I'm sure we can make something."

"Okay, as long as you're prepared to eat whatever's here," she warned.

"As always," he murmured. "I'll see you in about an hour." And, with that, he hung up.

With that handled, and a smile on her face, she headed down to the river, waiting for him. It was the very first good thing of her day, and she was definitely looking forward to that.

# Chapter 10

*Saturday Morning ...*

T HE NEXT MORNING dawned bright and clear. She got up, made coffee, and, instead of sitting on the deck, headed right to the river. There, she sat down and just relaxed. She was still tired, still sleepy even. While the animals did their usual morning exploration around her, she just tried to get her brain to wake up. She wasn't even sure what was on tap for today. She didn't feel good about getting into Mack's way because that was their unspoken agreement.

Although he did hound her about it, and she did tease him about it, she understood full well that Annabelle's death was an active police investigation. And now that the one guy suspected of her murder, Joseph Moody, was off the hook, then really Doreen had no right to get involved in any way. Yet it still ... Honestly it felt wrong. She pondered the vagaries of all these cases coming across her path.

In this case, she knew it would be a while before she could let it go. She had gotten involved, and that seemed to be one of the problems. Once she got her mind caught up in something, how was she supposed to ever just walk away from it? Yet she had no reason to continue her investigation.

Even though Joseph had asked her to keep on it, this was not an optimal path to take. That was also the part that would be extremely hard on her, and she sighed at that.

When Nan phoned her a few minutes later, Doreen asked her, "Hey, what are you up to today?"

"Oh, I'm not too sure," Nan replied, "I was just checking in on you. And Mack."

"I'm fine," she replied. "And Mack was amused that people cared to find out that he was just fine. So you can stop worrying about him now. As for Annabelle's murder case, the one suspect was cleared yesterday. Now that Joseph has been taken off the suspect list, I guess I don't really have any reason to work on his case anymore."

"Yet shouldn't you? Just to make sure that he doesn't get put back on again?"

"Nan, it's Mack's case. It's hardly a cold case."

"True, but what if"—Nan's tone was nothing but cryptic—"I told you that Annabelle's brother was murdered years ago."

At that, Doreen's back stiffened. "Was he now?"

"Yes," Nan declared, almost a smug tone to her voice.

"How come I didn't hear about that?"

"Because it was quite a while ago. I guess in the minds of the cops, it's a solved case, not a cold case."

"Meaning that they found who did it?"

"Yes."

"Well, that may have happened," Doreen acknowledged, "yet it doesn't mean it has anything to do with the here and now."

"No." Nan chuckled. "However, it does give you an invitation to look into this, doesn't it?"

She smiled at that, knowing what Nan was trying to do.

She knew that Doreen taking a step back would be killing her, so Nan had found Doreen a loophole. "Do you have any details?"

"We're getting some of the details," she said. "If you want to come down a little bit later, we should have enough of it for you to take it off our hands and to lead with it."

After making plans for midmorning, Doreen hung up. Feeling that she owed it to Mack, she called him at work. When he answered, she began, "Did you know that your victim's brother was murdered too?"

A moment of silence came at the other end. "You found that out, *huh*?"

She snorted. "Were you trying to keep that from me?"

"Imagine that," he quipped in a dry tone. "I was trying to keep something about my case away from you."

"Yep, *imagine that*," she repeated, with a laugh. "Besides, that gives me a little wiggle room to look into the case."

"Well, hardly. It's not a cold case."

"Are you sure?"

"Yeah. Pretty sure that somebody was convicted of the crime. He confessed."

"Oh," she said, flummoxed.

"Yeah, so you'll have to look elsewhere for your next caper."

She laughed at that. "Do people still use words like that?"

He chuckled. "I have no idea. It just seemed to fit."

"I get it. So is the guy still in jail?"

"I don't know," Mack admitted, "but that much I can probably look up. Give me a minute." And he hung up.

She sat here by the river, waiting for him to call back.

When he did, he said, "He got out about six months

ago."

"Interesting timing. Don't you think?"

"Yep, we're on it. I don't need to tell you to stay away from this guy, right?"

"Well, if I happen to see him and to ask him a little bit about what happened to him, then surely you can't get upset at me for that." She had stated it so innocently that, despite likely being sick with worry, Mack had to chuckle.

"You don't know what this guy's like. He murdered a young boy."

"What were the circumstances though?"

"I don't have his file in front of me, but I know that he went down for manslaughter."

"Ah, so it could have been a hit-and-run car accident, a drug deal gone bad, could have been all kinds of things."

He sighed. "And again I don't have the details, so I can't tell you one way or the other."

"That's okay. I'll get the details just so I can write it off."

"I guess I can't talk you out of it, can I?"

"No, probably not. And considering it's really not connected to your case, I should be safe." With that being out there, she added, "Have a great day," and just hung up.

She wasn't at all sure that he was terribly happy about her hanging up on him, but, hey, sometimes it was just better to not let him get too complacent.

When it was time to meet her grandmother, she called her animals and said, "Let's go see Nan."

Thaddeus cried out, "Nan, Nan, Nan," and strutted toward the creek already. Not to be outdone, Goliath, noting where the group was going, raced ahead and then lay down in the pathway for them to catch up to him. She marveled at his ability to look so bored and yet be the first one in trouble all the time. Mugs was just happy to go for a walk, as he sauntered down the pathway, stopping to smell rocks and bushes, lifting his legs a couple times, along their way to Nan.

As Doreen approached the patio, she looked around for any sign of the Rosemoor gardener. It appeared she was free and clear, so she made a quick dash over the lawn and hopped onto Nan's patio. She called out, "Nan, are you here?"

"I'm here," she replied from inside. "Just making tea."

For Nan, tea was the answer to everything; whereas for Doreen, it was usually coffee. And a lot of people very much preferred alcohol, but whatever worked for everybody in their own scenario wasn't a concern for Doreen—as long as nobody was harmed or unless it turned out to be a mystery. Enough things went on out in the world that didn't require someone criticizing another's choice.

Mugs raced inside the apartment to greet Nan. Goliath took up his usual position on one of the big flower boxes. And Doreen, Thaddeus now on her shoulder, sat down at one of the chairs to Nan's little bistro table.

Nan came out a minute later, with a beaming smile. "There you are." She chuckled. "I figured you wouldn't be late."

"Of course not—at least not if I can help it."

Nan just gave her a bigger smile and brought out the teapot and then went back in for cups, cream, and the sugar bowl. Ever since hearing about Peggy and the sugar bowl, leading to Chrissy's murder, Doreen always kept well away from any sugar bowls. It was foolish to think it would ever happen a second time here at Rosemoor, but once warned and all that.

When Nan finally made her last trip, Doreen watched curiously, as Nan brought a basket, probably full of treats. She raised an eyebrow. "Have you been raiding the kitchen again?"

"Nope, not at all." Nan chuckled. "However, if they allow us to take stuff back to our room, who am I to argue?"

Doreen winced. "I don't want them thinking that I'm stealing your food." Yet she looked at the basket and smiled. "But now that you have them, it's not as if I can send them back."

Nan smirked. "No, you absolutely cannot send them back, so you might as well help yourself."

"I do worry they'll get mad at you though."

"Oh, they won't get mad at me. We caught a murderer, working right here in Rosemoor, because of you, my dear. So nobody here will begrudge you a few treats when you come to visit. You make them safe, and it is worth everything to them."

"Yes, but I'm not paying for them," she murmured.

"They didn't pay you to solve a murder either," she reminded Doreen. "So just relax and enjoy."

Not a whole lot Doreen could say to that, so she reached over, flicked back the tea towel, and smiled at crumpets and something else, maybe scones. She smiled at Nan. "Of course you brought a couple different kinds."

Nan gave her a fat grin. "It is nice to have a choice."

Shaking her head, Doreen reached for one of each.

And Nan grabbed up one herself. "I had breakfast earlier, but I'm certainly not going to say no to these. They just came out of the oven. I don't understand why the kitchen does that. They have us all eat, and then they bring out something special like this, and you're stuck trying to find room for it."

"Or you're supposed to have it later," Doreen suggested.

At that, Nan nodded. "I am having it later." She looked at her watch. "It is quite a bit later. I had breakfast early this morning. I'm more than ready for a snack now."

"You got a busy day planned?"

"I do, a lawn bowling tournament again." She sighed. "Now if only we could win this one."

"I'm sure it's a lot of fun even if you don't."

"It is, but I'm still unfortunately rather competitive, as you might have noticed."

Doreen just nodded because she already knew how competitive Nan was. And it constantly amazed her when she saw her grandmother in action. "Hopefully today is a good day for winning."

"Hopefully. If not, there'll be other days."

"Exactly." And, with that, Doreen quickly broke the scone in half and took some of the fresh butter that Nan had provided and buttered it up. As she sniffed it, she smiled. "I miss things like this," she murmured.

"No need to miss them at all," Nan noted. "They aren't hard to make, and they are certainly not all that expensive to buy as a treat."

"Maybe," she hedged, "but, until I'm a little more stable for money, I do feel that things like this are off the table."

"And that's a good thing you come here then, isn't it?" Nan noted, with a beaming smile. "Because they're on the table here."

Doreen chuckled at that. "Thanks to you."

"And who else will do it for you?" Nan asked. "You have to look after yourself in this world, what with everybody else out to get you."

It was such an unusual way for Nan to think that Doreen frowned. "You don't really believe that, do you?" she asked.

"Sometimes you have to wonder. It just seems like so much is going on in life that it's not always fun and games."

"No, I'm sure it isn't," Doreen agreed. "Besides, we've seen an awful lot happen here in town that has been much less than pleasant," she murmured.

About ten minutes later Nan looked up at her and said, "You're really calm about this case."

Doreen chuckled. "Not so much that I'm calm, just that I'm not sure that I can do very much with it." She explained the little Mack had shared.

"I think you should at least call the man who murdered Annabelle's brother."

At that, Doreen lifted her head. "So you know that he's out of jail, *huh*?"

Nan nodded. "Yep, I do. According to …" She stopped, frowned, looked into her apartment. "I can't remember who told me originally, but they did say at breakfast this morning that he was out of jail and had been out for about six months."

"Anybody have his contact information?"

"Nope. We just have his name."

"That would be?"

"Nathan Landry."

"Okay, maybe I'll find him. I'm not sure." At that, Doreen went back to eating.

Nan looked at her in surprise. "You really don't seem to be bothered."

"It's not about whether I'm bothered or not," she stated. "I just don't have any reason to connect these two murders.

And Mack does know about this Nathan guy, so Mack's on it too. And there goes my chance to work on this Annabelle case."

"As long as Mack's on it, you can't be?"

Doreen winced. "I hate to say it, but that's pretty much it."

Nan sighed. "It's really sad when we get hamstrung by the law," she announced.

Doreen burst out chuckling. "That's one way to look at it." She gave Nan a beaming smile. "But it doesn't have to be quite that way."

"That's what I was hoping you would say," Nan noted, looking at her oddly. "Yet you do seem off."

"No, I just know that, if Mack is looking into it, not a whole lot I can do about it." And Doreen resumed eating.

Nan shook her head. "Now your saying that ... just seems so strange to me."

"If it were a cold case though, but it's not. ... I know that Nathan did the time, and he did the crime, and it was a manslaughter charge. I still don't know any of the other details. I'll hit the library after this." Doreen motioned at her treat in front of her.

"Ah," Nan said, settling back. "That makes more sense. I couldn't figure out why you seem to be completely blasé about it."

"Oh, I'm not blasé about it, but I'm just more determined to enjoy my treats." She chuckled. "Then I'll hit the library, and we'll see what else happens."

"Okay, good enough." Nan nodded. "I guess that's just as important."

"It is." Doreen smiled. "And again, it's still Mack's case."

"Right." Nan scowled. "We'll have to do something so

Mack has to share."

At that, Doreen burst out laughing. "I really don't think he's into sharing."

Nan gave her a fat wink. "Nope, he isn't, especially when it comes to his cases. So, if this isn't a case, then you'll go back to the Bob Small stuff?"

"I might. I'm not sure why that one is a more daunting task."

"Because there's so much of it, considering it's a possible serial killer case," Nan noted.

"And it'll take a lot to solve that many cases."

"Sure," she murmured. "However, I am rather certain that you're up for it, dear."

"I feel that these cold cases, so far, are almost *practice cases*," she said, looking at Nan with half a smile. "Leading me up to that big one."

Nan crowed in delight. "Oh, that's a good way to look at it. Can you imagine how notorious you'll be if you solved that?"

She winced. "Not exactly what I was looking for in terms of making a name of myself."

"Well, you should," Nan stated, with a bright smile. "Not all that many people out there can say that they have solved as many crimes as you have."

"Maybe not," she agreed, then groaned. "You know that I didn't start out to do this, right?"

"And that's what makes it even more special," Nan declared. "You didn't start out to do it, but, when the calling came, you answered. That is what this work is all about."

# Chapter 11

D OREEN PONDERED THAT comment as she walked home from Nan's. She wasn't sure about the *answering the call* stuff, but she certainly wasn't anybody who would normally not help, and she'd certainly answered the call in terms of helping people here, time and time again.

Even the captain, after her last cold case, had said that a lot too. She considered that for the next while, and, when she got home, she locked up the animals and headed to the library. If nothing else, she needed to get to the bottom of the Nathan Landry case and fast.

Once there, she looked at the information on this Nathan guy and found what, in terms of articles, wasn't a whole lot. It was a manslaughter charge, and apparently he had gotten into a fight, leading to a gun discharge, and the scuffle had killed Annabelle's brother. It hadn't been targeted. It hadn't been deliberate. It had been a pretty simple case of a horrible accident in which an innocent life had paid the price.

She was saddened to read the newspaper articles because there are just so many things in life she didn't need to hear about, and something like that death was one of them. Still, it did give her a better idea of who this guy was and what he'd done and whether he felt he'd gotten a fair shake from the law on it. And most of the time people didn't feel they'd gotten a fair shake, but, in this case, she wondered. She checked the local phone book but found no name for Nathan. There was, however, a John Landry.

Hesitating, then deciding that she'd started down this pathway, so she might as well figure out what she could do to get to the bottom of it. With that thought, she drove home. As soon as she was inside, she dialed the number. And when a man's voice answered, it sounded creaky and old. She winced. "Hi, I was looking for Nathan Landry."

Then came silence. "What do you want him for?" he asked, and a wealth of disgust filled his voice, as if Doreen was after something that he didn't want Nathan to deal with.

"I'm Doreen. I was asked to look into this matter, regarding Nathan's shooting victim that he already did time for."

At that, the older man started to swear.

"Sir, please calm down. I'm not looking at him for this recent crime," she explained.

"Then why are you calling?" he snapped at her, his tone turning ugly. "That boy of mine's already suffered plenty."

"I'm sure, considering what had happened, you'd be fully justified in saying that," she agreed. "It was a loss of life that is sad for everybody."

"Nathan doesn't even know for sure that he did it," the man said, "but he was there at the time, and they said it was his gun."

"Did he have a gun with him?"

"Sure, but it wasn't just him there. Several others were around as well. And Nathan tried to explain that to the cops, tried to tell them that he'd been the one holding the gun, but others had been around at the time."

"Ah, so Nathan got into a fight, and the gun discharged, and, because he was the one holding the gun, and the shot killed the little boy, then Nathan was charged with manslaughter?"

"Yes, something like that." Then, with an age-old weariness that she really could understand, he added, "Just leave my boy alone. He's trying to rebuild his life."

"I get that, Mr. Landry," she said, "and hopefully everybody will leave him alone after Annabelle Hopkins's murder is solved."

At that, he stopped. "Really? That family lost another child?"

"Yes, the sister was murdered a few days ago," Doreen replied.

"How did she die?"

"Gunshot. She was shot."

"*Great*," Mr. Landry muttered. "Just in time for my boy to get out of the jail and to get pinned for this."

"I'm not sure anybody's even looking at him," she noted, "but that doesn't mean that they won't."

"Of course not," he grumbled. "Any ex-cons with a connection to this family will get a hard look."

"And, if Nathan wasn't anywhere around them, and he didn't have anything to do with them, then that, ... that's not even an issue."

"I do know that he contacted her because he wanted to apologize for what happened."

She stopped and stared down at her phone. "I guess I can understand his point, and I hope it was a long time ago."

"No, it wasn't," he stated bitterly. "Now I really wish

that I had never suggested it."

"It was your suggestion?"

"Yeah, it was eating him up. Nathan used to know Annabelle because they'd all been friends at one time," he explained, "but Nathan knew her father better."

"Right, so let me get this straight. How old was Annabelle's brother when he died?"

"Eight, and my son was fifteen. Now he's twenty-three."

"Same age as Annabelle."

"Right."

"So she would have been fifteen too at the time."

"Exactly."

"That would have been very tough for the family," she noted.

"It was," Mr. Landry agreed. "It was terrible for all of us. I know my boy regretted it every day of his life. He paid for the guilt with eight years in jail, and he is still not free and clear of his conscience."

"Of course," she murmured. "I mean, that's even harder to deal with when it was such an accident."

"But he shouldn't have been carrying that gun, and I told him that at the time, but he was fifteen, and we were all young and stupid once," Mr. Landry stated.

"No, I understand," she murmured. "Was Annabelle witness to any of this?"

"Yeah, she had seen the shooting, the whole thing. She's the one who tried to pull her brother away to get him farther from the fight, but, as it was, it pulled him into the trajectory of the bullet. Bottom line is, my son shouldn't have carried a gun." Mr. Landry's tone was weary of it all.

"I am so sorry for that," she replied. "Seems like sometimes the stupidest decisions are the ones that we can never get past."

"In this case, how is he ever supposed to get past it?" he asked. "If people know that he's back in town, they'll be all over him."

"That's possible too," she admitted, her tone sad, as she thought about it. "Is he working? Is he doing anything to, … to—I want to say, *rehabilitate* himself, but I know that's not quite the right word."

"He does construction, works with one of the paving companies. It's hard physical work, and it helps him get the demons out and get back to life," Mr. Landry told her. "However, it won't help at all if any of this comes out."

"I'm sure his company hired him knowing he has a record, right?"

"Yes, his boss is an old family friend. At the same time, for him to lose that job would be brutal."

"Well, I don't see any reason for that to happen," Doreen noted. "It would help if I could talk to him though."

"What good would that do?" he snapped.

"I just want to make sure that nobody else was around, that nobody else was involved in her brother's death, who might blame Annabelle somehow."

He stopped, thought about it, and said, "I'll talk to my son. No guarantees though."

"No, that's fine," she agreed. She quickly gave him her phone number. "And, if we can keep Nathan out of this current murder, then that would be good. However, I do know that the cops are already aware that Nathan is out of jail. So they'll come around looking for him."

"Of course they will," Mr. Landry groused, his tone bitter. "What is your connection to this case?"

"Annabelle's boyfriend asked me to look into it."

"Are you like a private detective or something?" he asked curiously.

She frowned at that, as she was getting asked this question more and more often. "I'm not a licensed PI by any means," she shared. "Although sometimes it makes me wonder if I should pursue that, but it's not really what I was thinking I would do with my life. So call it a hobby, if you must."

"You that amateur detective in town?" he asked, his voice rising.

"Yeah, I guess I am."

He snorted at that. "Most of the time people don't *guess* that that's what they are."

"Well, sometimes you get tossed into things in life, and you're not exactly sure how you're supposed to get out of them," she explained. "So this is where I ended up."

He thought about that. "Kind of like my son. He made a decision to help out somebody, and this is what happened."

"Who was he helping out? Do you know?"

"Not my story," Mr. Landry declared. "You can ask him, but no guarantee that he'll tell you."

"Good enough." She knew that, even now, another mystery was involved. "At least he's working to try to get back into society," she noted impulsively. "Hopefully he can put all this behind him."

"That was partly why he wanted to talk to Annabelle. I know that she was pretty traumatized over it all, and why wouldn't she be? It was tough to be a young girl and to have that happen in front of her." Then Mr. Landry asked, "What happened to the family?"

"My understanding is the parents split up and moved."

"Of course they did. Another side effect of a shooting like this, isn't it?"

"It's got to be pretty hard when it's your family. I mean, how do you recover from a loss like that?"

"No, I get it, just more collateral damage. Anyway I'll tell my son. No guarantees." And, with that, he hung up.

She sighed and put down her phone and looked over at her animals. "Horrible stuff like that is just sad, so sad. Nobody had to die that day. Nobody had to get hurt, and yet here it is. Somebody got hurt to the point that there's no return."

Mugs woofed and waddled over to her, his front paws landing on her knees. She bent over and hugged him. And presented with a perfect spot, Thaddeus hopped onto her back and marched from side to side, crowing out, "Thaddeus loves Doreen. Thaddeus loves Doreen."

She chuckled as even Goliath sauntered past just close enough for the tips of her fingers to brush his silky fur. "You minx." He shot her a look, his tail shooting up straight in the air as he circled back around a little closer – but not close enough to cuddle.

The animals were her comfort – her joy. And they did a lot to ease her heartache. This whole mess made her sad. But she could do absolutely nothing about it right now.

# Chapter 12

L ATER THAT AFTERNOON, stymied by the lack of any
progress or direction in which to go on anything,
Doreen looked at the big stack of Solomon files, winced,
then snatched her gardening gloves and called out to the
animals. She would rather work on her garden than sort
through Solomon's research files just yet. "If nothing else,
let's go and get something done outside," she told them.

With them following, she headed out to the garden. She
also needed to get some work done on Millicent's garden.
Doreen worked on hers for a bit, and then, feeling guilty, she
phoned Millicent. "Hey, are you up for my coming over and
doing some gardening?"

"That would be perfect. I'll get the teapot ready."

At that, Doreen smiled because she thought sometimes it
wasn't so much the gardening that needed to be done as
Millicent just needed to be visited. It made Doreen feel so
uncomfortable that she didn't want to charge Mack for
something like that; it felt wrong. Lately it had become more
of a chat period for her and Millicent. Still, somebody
needed to take care of the garden, and that appeared to be
Doreen's job right now.

As she headed over with the animals in tow, she pondered why she didn't want to start digging into Solomon's file on Bob Small, the suspected serial killer. She really did think that it would probably be too big, too mean, too ugly, and she would need an awful lot of help, help that she wasn't certain was even available to her. Sure, she was getting a lot of local help, but she would need Mack in a big way. Which he wasn't up for right now.

Matter of fact he seemed sadder, more tired than she'd ever seen him, and that was a bit of a concern too. Still, she got to Millicent's and, with a wave, started in on the backyard, knowing full well that Millicent would come out and sit on the deck pretty soon. Her animals were content to just sit and roll around on the grass, even Thaddeus strutting about. And, sure enough, when Doreen looked up later, Millicent called out to her enthusiastically.

"Whenever you can stop and join me, dear, the tea's ready."

Doreen smiled at that because most people would reverse it. You came when the tea had steeped enough, so that the tea was ready. She quickly finished off what she was doing, and she and her animals walked over to the porch. Doreen sat down and discussed some of the changes in the garden. "What do you think about doing some of this?" she asked.

At that, Millicent contemplated Doreen's ideas and then nodded. "That's probably a good idea," she agreed. "I was wondering about moving some of those bulbs to the front."

Doreen tried to remember where the bulbs were. "That might be a good idea, but I'm not sure I can find the bulbs now. We have to let them grow a bit."

Millicent gave her a beaming smile and then a laugh.

"No, I hear you. And that's always why we do it right after spring, isn't it?"

"We can do it after they bloom again," Doreen said, then frowned. "Let me ponder this for a little bit and see if I can figure out and remember where they were."

At that, Millicent nodded. "I do have a map somewhere, but we've made a lot of changes lately."

"We have, and we didn't update the map, did we?" Doreen asked, looking over at Millicent. "Or did you?"

Millicent shook her head. "No, I should have. I really should have." And she started to fret.

"It's okay," Doreen replied. "The nice thing about bulbs is they'll come back up next spring, and we'll have another chance."

Millicent smiled and nodded. "Isn't that the truth."

Doreen checked on her brood and was happy to see them all on their best behavior. Then, in an effort to make Millicent feel a little more comfortable, Doreen said, "I'm sure you enjoyed having your sons visit recently. Any sign of Nick coming back?"

"Not soon, but he does have some plans in progress." Then Millicent sighed. "It would be very nice to have him home."

Doreen nodded. "I think every parent says that."

"Absolutely, and every parent wants to have their kids close by," she added, "or at least if you have any relationship with them."

"That's often the trick, isn't it?" Doreen stated. "Not every parent has that kind of relationship with their child."

"I think that's sad," Millicent said. "I had my two boys, and it would have been my greatest honor to keep them both close. ... We knew that Nick needed to go to the coast though, but it was hard. Losing him was hard."

"Yet you didn't lose him, did you?"

She chuckled. "Nope, not at all. So, if he's looking for a change in his life, a little slower pace, I'm really hoping he'll come back here again."

"I did hear some meanderings about it," Doreen shared, "but I don't know that he's ready to make any change like that."

At that, Millicent nodded. "And that's part of the problem. I know he's ready, but it'll take a bit of time, some persuasion. I just would like it to happen more quickly."

Their conversation turned to questions about Nan, a few other cases that Doreen had been working on. Then Millicent added, "I figured you'd be all over this new killing."

*Wasn't that the truth?* "Mack's on that one."

"Sure, but we also know that Nathan's back in town."

Doreen stopped and asked, "Do you know Nathan?"

"We used to know Nathan," she clarified, "but the Nathan I knew wouldn't have gone to jail for shooting somebody. So, once that happened, I'm not sure I really knew him."

Doreen winced at that. "Sometimes the people we know don't end up being the people we thought we knew."

Millicent slowly nodded. "That's very true. I hadn't really considered that. Besides, that boy just got off on the wrong side of the mess."

"How did you know him?"

"He used to mow lawns for us," she replied. "He used to come every Saturday and do it. My husband more or less just hired him to keep the kid out of trouble, and Nathan took the job for pocket change. But apparently that didn't work." She sighed. "He was a good kid."

"And just because he made a mistake doesn't mean he's not a good kid anymore either," Doreen noted. "I'm sure jail was not easy on him."

At that, Millicent winced. "No, I don't imagine it was."

"From what I understand and from what his father told me, Nathan shouldn't have had the gun with him and didn't intend for it to go off. It wasn't an intentional killing or anything. Yet the sad side effect is, he did kill somebody."

"Yes." Millicent nodded. "Broke my husband's heart. He felt like he'd invested his time in the wrong person."

Doreen winced at that. "I don't think that's true, but I can understand how, after years of helping out Nathan, you are entitled to feel that way. What about Mack? Did he know Nathan?" she asked.

"He knew of him. He knew that he was here on Saturdays, doing the lawns and stuff, but it wasn't a case of his knowing Nathan. I know we talked with him a lot at the time because we knew him. Mack, at the time, I guess it's almost eight years ago. ... Yeah, so Mack was on the force. He was pretty young, coming up in the force, and didn't have any power to touch the case either."

"And you wanted to make sure that the kid got a fair shake, right?"

Millicent gave her a smile. "We did—until he confessed, until we realized what he'd done. It was pretty hard to imagine at that time. My husband was really devastated. But you get over things, life happens, and you move on. Nathan went to jail, and then, all of a sudden, he's out. I heard that recently too."

"Has he tried to talk to you at all since?"

Millicent raised her eyebrows in surprise. "Why would he try that?"

"I don't know that he would," Doreen said calmly. "I just wondered."

Millicent shook her head. "Nope, but now that poor Annabelle has been killed, people are going to look at Nathan automatically."

"Well, they might look, but it has to have more than just that in order for Nathan to be in trouble over it."

"You don't think Nathan killed Annabelle?"

Doreen pondered what she knew about this recent murder so far. "I don't know that Nathan had any reason to do it. I mean, Annabelle might very well have been upset to see him, after he was released from prison. Maybe that got ugly, but I don't know." She pondered that and shrugged.

"I don't really know," Doreen admitted. "I was thinking about looking further into Annabelle's case, but I heard the prime suspect's off the hook now. So I guess I don't really have any reason to look into it further. And it would just upset Mack if I get in his way."

At that, Millicent gave her a look. "Get in his way *again*, you mean."

Doreen burst out laughing. "Exactly," she murmured. "So, back to the garden, what would you like me to do?" And they headed back to discussions about a safer topic.

By the time Doreen had finished her tea, she got up and started on the gardening work that Millicent wanted done. It was hard for a gardener to sit here and to know all this stuff needed to be done, but yet Millicent didn't have the energy or the inclination to do it, because of her age and pain level now. So Doreen was quite happy to make it as easy as possible on Millicent.

Done with the gardening work at Millicent's, Doreen and her animals were almost home when her phone rang.

She didn't recognize the number, and, frowning, she turned the corner, wondering if she should answer it or not. Then it stopped ringing abruptly, almost as if the caller had changed his mind. She wondered about it and headed to her kitchen. She'd worked hard at Millicent's and now could use a bite to eat. As she headed in, she looked in her fridge and realized that, once again, she needed to go shopping.

She didn't quite understand how the groceries were always gone. But they were, and shopping never had been something that she considered on a regular cycle. She made a mental note to add it to her list of chores.

She had to make it a habit now, as it was for a lot of people. Giving herself a boot mentally, telling herself to buck up, there were other things to complain about. She fixed herself a quick sandwich, promising to go out and pick up a few more groceries later this afternoon. Just as she finished eating, putting on a pot of coffee, her phone rang again. She looked down at the number, and this time, for whatever reason, decided to answer. "Hello."

"Hello?"

He seemed surprised that she had answered, his greeting hesitant, slow. "Hey, can I help you?"

"I'm looking for ..." And then Doreen heard a rustle of papers, as if somebody were looking for her name. "Doreen."

"I'm Doreen. Who are you?"

"I'm Nathan," he said, his voice scratchy, as if he didn't use it very often.

Her eyebrows shot up. "Nathan Landry?"

First came silence, then he replied, "Yeah."

"Hey, Nathan," she said, her voice soft. "Did your father tell you that I called?"

"Yeah, he did. And I didn't have nothing to do with

Annabelle's death. You know that, right?"

"I know that," she confirmed. "Have the police contacted you?"

"Yeah, I talked to somebody this morning at work," Nathan shared. "I didn't like that either."

"No, they don't have much choice though. They've got a fresh case, so they have to be on it pretty fast."

"Maybe, I don't know." And then Nathan's voice grew stronger. "It would have been nice not to deal with it at work."

"I'm sorry. And thank you for calling me back."

"What did you want to talk to me about?" he asked, hesitant.

"I just wanted to know if, back then, when her brother died, you think anybody in her past might have had something to do with her death now?"

"The cops already asked me this," he said in confusion. "And I ... I didn't have anything to tell them either."

"Well, back then, you had a physical fight with somebody, and apparently Annabelle's father knew you, and you used to mow lawns for Millicent and her husband."

"That's all correct. And a lot of people were really upset at what I did. For that, I spent a lot of years in jail," he noted, his voice getting stronger and stronger, almost agitated.

"Understood," Doreen said. "You've paid your debt to society, and I would very much like to keep you out of jail again."

A shocked gasp could be heard on the other end. "Am I going back to jail?" he cried out almost fearfully.

She winced. "No, not at all. I mean, if you had nothing to do with Annabelle's death, then there's absolutely no reason to even go down that pathway."

But he didn't sound convinced. "I didn't. I swear. I don't have anything to do with this mess."

"Okay, so let's go back a bit. Your dad suggested that you go talk to Annabelle."

He hesitated. "Yeah."

"Did you?"

"Yes, I did."

"And how was she?"

"Shocked, angry, teary, same as me," he admitted. "She wasn't exactly welcoming, but then why would she be?" he asked bitterly. "She didn't have any reason to even be friendly to me."

"Was she friendly?"

"Yes. Annabelle was always a really nice girl."

"Did she say anything to you about it?"

"About what?"

"Like she was worried about anybody, that she was being followed or stalked, or was she angry at seeing you, was she going to call somebody to chase you away? Anything like that."

"No, nothing like that. We basically cried together, and, when I left I, ... I felt better," he declared. "She was perfectly fine and healthy, and I didn't have any reason to do her any harm. I've never harmed anybody wilfully, but ... that one mistake will follow me through my lifetime. I sometimes think it will run me to my grave."

She winced at that because he was right, just no getting out of it. "I'm sorry for that too. Lives were lost."

"Yes, but the biggest loss was of that little boy," Nathan said.

And she heard the catch in his voice over it. "Well, the

good news is, hopefully, if you had nothing to do with this, then the police should check your alibi and let you off the hook."

"I hope so because I didn't have anything to do with it."

And just from the tone of his broken voice, she heard such regret.

"I'm really sorry for whatever happened to her. It's not fair," he muttered. "She was one of the nicest people in the world."

"So I have heard," Doreen agreed gently, "and you're right. It's not fair."

"Life isn't fair," he stated, "I learned that a long time ago. You make a stupid decision, and the results can be so shocking that you don't know how it could have happened."

"Were you alone at the time of her brother's death?" she asked curiously.

"No, I wasn't. I was with another friend, a buddy of mine. He's the one who convinced me to take the gun with us. I realize now that I shouldn't have. It was his gun, but I'd been hanging around with it. I thought I would be a big … tough guy." Nathan groaned. "I was … I was a stupid idiot."

"And this friend of yours, did he have anything to do with this whole scenario?"

"No, not really. I'm the one who had the gun, and it was in my hand when it went off."

"Right. If he was involved at the time, he would have also been charged."

"I think he had information on a different case. I know they talked to him about it, but he never got charged with anything."

"What exactly was your argument about?"

"Does it matter?" he asked, his voice tired.

"Was it your friend who you were arguing with?"

"Yeah, it was," he replied. "Which is another reason why I wasn't too worried about getting him in trouble. I mean, I'm the one who had the gun, even though I had brought it because he told me to."

"So were you going to use it?"

"No, of course not. I didn't want to use it. I just wanted to be a big dude, which I gathered the hard way that I'm not." He sighed. "I'm fairly small, and believe me. The years in prison made me feel even smaller."

"No, I'm sure," she said, wincing at that. "And so what were you and your friend going to do?"

"He wanted to rob somebody. I didn't want to. We were arguing as we walked down the street, where a bunch of kids were playing. He grabbed my shoulder, pushed me hard, and basically said that we would rob somebody, and, if I didn't, he told me to *stop being a pansy* or something like that." Nathan sighed. "All of this is on record."

"Okay. I'll try to get a copy of the police files. That's never easy."

He snorted. "No, I'm sure it isn't. Anyway I pushed back. He pushed back. We got into it. Then he grabbed the gun from my pocket. I took it away from him, and, in the scuffle, … it just went off." His voice was breaking, and, sure enough, she heard him sniffing and clearing his throat. "And that little boy was killed."

"Ouch." She winced at the recounting.

"Yeah, big time," he murmured. "That … That was the end of my life."

"Yet your friend didn't get charged, nothing happened to him?"

"Nope, not at that time. I don't know if he did ever

since. I knew it was all on me. I shouldn't have had the gun with me. It was my fault," Nathan admitted. "Getting my friend in trouble wouldn't make it any better or worse."

"No, but, at the same time, he's the one who wanted to rob somebody?"

"Sure, but that was my story, not his," Nathan clarified in a wry tone. "I don't blame him for making one up to save face, so that he could get out of trouble. I mean, why did we both have to go down?"

She stared at her phone. "So he had his own story, which went against your story, and he got off, and you didn't."

"Yeah, that's it basically," Nathan said. "But the thing is, it was his gun. I had been carrying it around for a few weeks, thinking that I would buy it off him, and I am the one who had the gun with me."

"Yet he's the one who wanted to use the gun to rack up a felony charge."

"Yeah, sure, but we didn't do that."

"No, but that was the intent," she noted. "I'm surprised they let him off the hook."

"I don't know anything about it," Nathan replied. "Believe me. Once I got separated, and we were picked up by the police, that was … that was the end of it. I never had a chance to see him or to talk to him ever since."

"What about since you've been out?"

He groaned. "My dad wants me to stay well and truly away from my buddy, and, since I live with my dad, and I'm trying to go straight, … I won't talk to my buddy."

"Interesting. What's your friend's name?"

"Why?" he asked, with suspicion.

"Because I don't understand some people," she shared. "I just wonder what happened to him in the meantime."

"It won't make any difference," Nathan added. "I don't think he even lives here."

"That would be good, if he didn't," she said. "It'd be easier on you."

"No, you're right there." Nathan nodded. "Anyway, his name's Kurt, Kurt Chandler."

"Thank you for that."

"What does any of this have to do with you?"

"Me? Well, Annabelle's boyfriend was under suspicion for having killed her," she explained. "He came to me and asked me to help him. However, he has an alibi for that night, and now it looks like he's off the hook. So I'm just trying to mentally tie up a few odds and ends."

Silence came on the other end. "You do know that alibis can be broken, right?"

"Yeah, I do, and they can be made to look solid but aren't solid, and people can do all kinds of things, including hiring killers," she suggested. "And you can bet the cops, even if they already spoke with you, will have follow-up questions real soon."

"Ouch. ... I guess, thanks for the heads-up."

"I don't know that they'll thank me for giving you a heads-up on it, but, as long as you talk to them today, I'm not stepping on any toes."

"Oh, yeah, no, they ... they saw me at work today, so not sure they are coming back around soon," Nathan noted, that same bitterness coming back.

"Well, keep your nose clean, and get through this," she suggested. "Hopefully it will be over soon."

"I don't know. It seems like they're only ever fast when it's something you don't want them to be fast about." And, with that, he added, "Anyway I've done my due diligence, and I've talked to the cops, and I've talked to you. I don't know what you've got to do with any of this, and I guess I don't really want to know. But maybe you could just forget I exist after this, please." And, with that, he hung up.

Once she was done with the painful conversation, she sat outside and pondered what Nathan had revealed. With her head so full of bits and pieces, she needed to write this down. She quickly grabbed a notepad and contemplated the whole scenario.

It was just sad. Sad that a little boy had to die. Sad that Nathan had gone to jail and had paid the price, especially when technically two parties were involved, and both must be equally blamed for it. Yet the police probably had no way to charge both of them for manslaughter. Chances were, the cops looked at both versions and believed his friend's story.

And, with one against the other, and Nathan caught with the gun in hand, it looked like self-defense on Kurt's part. Couldn't really blame the police for that either. At the same time, this guy Kurt Chandler got free and clear. Landry did sound like he had done his time and was sad, regretful. And then she thought about Joseph. Did he know about Nathan's visit? Doreen wondered about that. Deciding that it was better to find out than sit here and ponder the possibilities, she quickly phoned Joseph.

When he answered, she asked about Annabelle's last days and a visit by Nathan. Joseph replied right away, "Oh, I didn't realize that you were still looking into this."

A bit of uncertainty filled his voice. "I'm looking into it now from a personal curiosity point of view," she shared calmly. "I mean, as long as you're off the hook, then you don't need to worry about anything that you tell me, right?"

"No, you are correct about that," he said, with relief.

TOES UP IN THE TULIPS

"I just wondered if you had any idea that Annabelle had met Nathan recently."

At that, he got angry. "That sleazebag scum? Yeah, I heard that she'd spoken to him. Now that makes me angry ..."

"Why is that?" she asked curiously.

"That guy killed her brother. Destroyed her family. Did you know that her parents divorced over it? Annabelle ... was a mess afterward."

"Sure, but it was also an accidental shooting," she reminded him.

"Doesn't matter. He was a punk kid with a gun."

She winced at that because so many people would probably think that too. "The gun definitely puts him in the wrong," she murmured.

"Don't defend him," Joseph snapped. "She shouldn't have anything to do with him."

"Maybe she just needed a little closure," Doreen offered. "We all need it. How was she when you talked to her about it?"

"She was teary," he replied. "She was all about sympathy and trying to forgive this guy who'd taken her brother from her. It was disgusting. He should have never approached her, just gave her the chance to deal with stuff and her grief in her own way."

Doreen didn't know what to say to that. "Did she say anything about wanting to see him again?"

"God, like I'd allow that," he sneered. "I was pretty angry about the one visit as it was."

She winced at Joseph's phrase, *like I'd allow that*. Something Mathew told her often during their marriage. "I understand that you'd be upset," she said. "I was just wondering how Annabelle felt about it."

"She wanted to keep in touch with him and to help him get a job and get his life together," he snapped. "But that? That's a load of crock."

Obviously Joseph was one of those guys where, if you make a mistake, it was for life. Whereas for Doreen, she knew perfectly well that everybody should get a do-over, and often people needed a third chance. "When did she see him?"

"I don't know. A week or two maybe before she was killed," he replied, his voice suddenly weary, as if the whole thing was just too much for him. And considering what he'd just lost, it was understandable.

"I'm sorry to have to do this. I don't mean to dredge up bad memories," she murmured.

"Well, you are," he snapped. "Just thinking about that louse makes me even angrier."

She winced at that. "Sorry. If you could tell me *exactly* how far in advance of her death, that would help."

After a pause, Joseph asked, "Are you looking at him for this?" Then his voice deepened. "I wouldn't be at all surprised. That guy's got a one-way ticket to hell. And it would be typical of somebody like that to turn on poor Annabelle."

"You haven't told me exactly when he saw her."

"As far as I know, it was just a few days before she was killed," he noted, his voice gaining in excitement. "You could be right. It could be him."

"And it might not have anything to do with him. Originally you thought one week or two ago. Now you're saying a day or two," she pointed out. "Just like you have an alibi, I'm sure he has one too."

At that, Joseph snorted. "Alibis can be fixed, right?" he

asked, with a snarl. "I wouldn't trust that guy's alibi at all."

She stared down at her cell phone, wondering at that mentality. Same could be said about Joseph's alibi, but he chose to paint himself as trustworthy, while trying to cast suspicion on Nathan. It didn't matter to some people. Everybody else was guilty but not them. And, in this case, Doreen didn't know who was guilty, but she did know that Annabelle needed justice.

"The police have talked to him already," she shared, "so I imagine that they'll be checking it out pretty closely."

"That's good," Joseph muttered, somewhat mollified. "If I find out it was him, I'm likely to kill him myself." And, with that, he hung up.

# Chapter 13

DOREEN SAT OUTSIDE, studying anything she could find on the internet regarding Kurt Chandler. When she heard Mugs bark, she looked up and around to see Mack coming around the house and into her backyard. "Normally you come through the front door," she said.

"You have it shut," he replied, "so I didn't want to ruin a good thing and spoil your record of locking it."

She rolled her eyes at him. "I haven't been out in the front today," she explained, with a smile. "So that's why."

He nodded and asked, "What are you up to?"

"Looking up Kurt Chandler," she stated promptly. He just nodded and headed into the kitchen. She frowned at that and then shrugged.

When he reappeared, she asked, "Do you know him?"

"Yep, I do," Mack told her, "or at least I know of him."

"That brain of your must have an awful lot of criminals floating around in it."

"I try not to let that happen," he teased, with half a smile.

"I talked to both Joseph and Nathan today—and Nathan's father."

Mack winced at that. "I'm sure that was fun."

"Nope, not a whole lot," she admitted, "as I gather it was the same for you."

He shrugged. "We have to do what we have to do. In your case though, you're probably just considered to be a busybody."

She snorted at that. "They were interesting conversations. I didn't realize that Nathan worked and did the lawns for your father."

Mack nodded at that. "I don't remember a whole lot about him from back then, but Dad was really angry when he found out what he'd done."

"Of course. Your father was an upstanding citizen, and Nathan's behavior was something that nobody wants to be associated with—in any way."

He nodded slowly at that. "He also felt betrayed, that whole *I invested in you, and I put my trust in you* point of view, and then *Look what you end up doing.* More than that, I think he was angry at himself for having trusted the kid in the first place."

"Nathan sounds incredibly regretful," she added, "like he's trying to make amends."

"I got the same impression. Doesn't mean that it isn't just all make-believe."

She winced at that. "I keep wanting to believe in people, but I'm not quite so naïve as I used to be."

He gave her a gentle smile. "Life will do this to you."

She nodded. "You're quite right there. On the other hand, Nathan does appear to be working hard and making amends." She looked over at him. "Are you aware he talked to Annabelle?"

He stopped and stared at Doreen, his expression suggesting that he didn't know.

"At least a few days before Annabelle was killed. Now before you ask me or suggest anything, I'm not telling you this to put Nathan on your suspect list."

"I didn't ask him specifically if he had seen her recently," Mack admitted, "but I guess I should have."

"You can always talk to him again."

He groaned, pulled out his notebook, and wrote down a message. He looked over at her. "Anything else that I should know?"

She beamed at him. "Give me a few minutes, and I'll have something for you."

He glared at her and walked back into the kitchen. When he reappeared a few minutes later, he had two cups of coffee.

She sniffed the air and smiled. "Good thing I bought coffee last time I went shopping, *huh*?"

"Good thing you got that reward money," he added, "so at least you had money to buy coffee."

"That's a very good point too," she agreed. "I also spoke to Joseph Moody."

"He's not technically at the top of our suspect list anymore, but remember …"

She cut him off midsentence because she knew what he would say. "I know. I know. It's your case. I did ask him about Nathan Landry."

At that, he stopped and asked, "Did Joseph know Nathan?"

"He knew about Nathan's visit to Annabelle." At that, Mack frowned again but didn't say anything. "Joseph was pretty irate over the whole thing," she added.

"I'm sure he was," Mack noted.

"He wasn't a big fan of her being close to Nathan."

"Maybe not, but that's a whole different story than having anything to do with it."

"I agree with you, and I hope he didn't have anything to do with it because I quite liked Nathan."

"Yeah, I hear you," Mack said, "but you're usually rooting for the underdog anyway. So that's no surprise." She glared at him. He just smiled. "It is the truth, and you know it."

"Maybe I root for the underdog because I feel like the underdog." He stopped at that and frowned. She shrugged. "Ever since I walked away from ... Mathew and that world, my life hasn't been very easy either, trying to rebuild it after supposedly doing something that everybody else considered stupid," she explained. "So rooting for the underdog seems like ... I am rooting for me."

He let out a slow breath on that. "That's an interesting way to look at it."

"And I know, from your perspective, it's probably not the way you'd look at it," she noted, "but I feel like, every time one of these guys gets redemption, then so do I. It makes me hopeful."

"What is it you think you did that was so wrong that you need redemption for?"

"Marrying him in the first place," she declared promptly.

He nodded. "I'm not the person to talk to about that, but I certainly don't think you should hold on to a guilt like that forever."

"I'm still trying to get free, and apparently even trying to get free puts me in the path of being stupid. And then my lawyer, poor Nick, who is even now trying his darndest to get things settled up, he finds that it is not ... easy."

"No, but my brother's on it. And he's good at what he does."

She nodded. "I also worked at your mom's today."

"I have cash on me. How much do I owe you?" When she told him, he frowned. "Unless you can't pay it," she added.

"No, the frown is because it's less than normal."

"I feel like I spend half the time talking to Millicent," Doreen admitted. "I think she is just, … I guess, looking for company."

He handed over the money, placing it on the table. "At least now you can buy more coffee."

At that, she burst out laughing. "I can. More coffee for you apparently."

"Yep," he said. "I also brought a few groceries. I put them away in the kitchen."

She frowned. "Did we make arrangements?" she asked cautiously. "Because, if I forgot, I'm sorry."

He looked at her strangely and then shook his head. "We didn't make arrangements. I just figured I'd stop by anyway."

"You're welcome anytime. You know that. I was just afraid that … I had messed up again."

With that, he reached for her hand and squeezed it softly. "Stop."

"Stop what?" she asked, looking at him in confusion.

"You didn't mess up anything, not now, not then. Let yourself off the hook for making a decision that you came later to regret," he told her. "If we all didn't have things that we later regretted, we wouldn't be human. We make decisions by looking at the circumstances, and you live with the consequences until you change them. It took you a little longer to change it, and that's fine. So, no, you didn't mess up. And even if you had forgotten? ... It would be totally fine by me." She stared at him for a long moment. He raised an eyebrow. "What?" he asked. "You're looking at me like I'm from Mars."

She grinned. "I think women are supposed to be from Venus and you guys are supposed to be from Mars, so maybe you are."

He rolled his eyes at that. "What psychobabble stuff is that anyway?" he asked. "We're all from Earth, and we're all just on this journey to find our happy endings. All of us, in this world, ... we are together."

She stopped and considered that. "Oh, I like that."

"What?" he asked, looking at her confused. He picked up his coffee and took a sip.

"Just a life journey to head toward a happy ending," she repeated. "I think the world would be a much better place if we were all just happy."

"And yet it seems to be the challenge, just to be happy," he noted, with a smile.

"You're right there too." She tossed down her pen. "That's enough of those notes anyway."

"What notes?" he asked.

"Just about your case." At that, he glared at her. She shrugged. "Joseph's case then," she clarified. "I mean, he asked me to look into it, right?"

"What about now?"

"No, now that he's more or less off the hook, I'm kind of hooked on it, which is not good because it's your case."

"Thank you," he replied, with exaggerated politeness.

She gave him a misty smile. "I did try to stay out of it. You know that, right?"

He sighed heavily. "Well, you might *try* ..."

"I fail a lot, yes. I know." She chuckled. "Yet I don't always fail, and sometimes I'm even a big help."

"Sometimes you are," he agreed, "and that's one of the reasons why I try to be patient when you get in my way. Sometimes I really can't have you close because you'll mess up a case that we can't prosecute much less convict because of civilian interference. I am sure you don't want to let a criminal off the hook on a minor technicality."

She nodded. "I'm slowly understanding that. In this case, I don't get it."

"What do you mean, *you don't get it?*"

"I don't understand why anybody would kill her." Then she turned and asked, "Did ballistics get back to you yet?"

"Why would they?"

She shrugged. "I just wondered if it would be the same gun used in the shooting of her brother."

He froze, turned to face her. "That wouldn't be good."

"No, of course not, because I presume the gun was recovered from him back then."

"Yes."

"And he wouldn't get it back, so how did somebody get it?"

"It should be in lockup—although a lot of those things are destroyed over time. I don't know what happened to that one."

"You mean, evidence goes missing?" she asked, with a wry look in his direction.

"Sometimes it's sold, but I have not heard from ballistics yet."

"You may want to have them run it against that case." He glared at her, and she raised both hands. "I know. I know. I know. You are fully aware of how to do your own business. … I get it. I really do. However, at the same time, it would be an interesting twist."

"It would be an ugly twist."

"Meaning that he's out of jail and now he'd be really stupid to use the same gun?" She glanced at him sideways. "Even *any* gun. I mean, anything that implicates him this time, it would be planned."

"And is there any connection—outside of the fact that her brother died at the hands of Nathan and that Annabelle gave witness testimony against Nathan?" Mack asked.

"Of course she was a witness." She nodded at her own answer. "The thing is, I believe Nathan, and I think he's trying to get his life back on track."

"Then you think he was set up?"

"I don't …" She froze and added, "I only spoke to him on the phone, so I have to be careful what I say about him." Mack raised his eyebrows at her, and his lips twitched. "I am learning," she said apologetically. "I'm slow, but I am learning."

"Stop knocking yourself down," he retorted. "You've done a phenomenal job and made all of us look like idiots a time or two."

She shrugged. "Wasn't hard." He glared at her. Then she burst out laughing. "Anyway, it would be something if Nathan were to get blamed for this. He's only been out for so long, so he's a pretty easy patsy."

"You didn't think we would look at that?" he asked in astonishment.

"I'm not saying you wouldn't. I'm just saying that it looks very suspicious and that you'd still have to find an answer, one way or the other."

"What you're saying is, it's easy for Nathan to get blamed for this, but I'm telling you that we wouldn't go by something easy. We want to get to the truth."

"No, you wouldn't want easy," she agreed earnestly. "What ..." She stopped, shrugged, and said, "I'm not trying to upset you."

He shook his head, and she almost heard him mentally say, *Good, because you are upsetting me.* Without even trying to glean it out of him.

She sighed, her shoulders slumping. "The thing is, just because Nathan makes an easy target to blame doesn't mean that he had anything to do with Annabelle's death or that this was even somebody trying to pin it on Nathan. It could just be happenstance for the killer. And that still doesn't give us anybody to look at."

"Us?" he asked, his tone suspiciously neutral.

She glared at him. "I get it." She raised her hands in surrender. "Not so much *us*. You."

He nodded. "Thank you for that."

She snorted. "When you get so polite like that, it's almost funny."

"I'm not trying to be entertaining."

"Nope, I know you're not." She gave him a big grin. "Yet you are in many ways. This will be an interesting case. And I want to get out, and I want to do something on it. I want to search for answers, but I don't have anything to search for."

"And that is what our job comes down to," Mack noted. "We want to jump out and do something too, but, if there's no angle, no direction to go, we don't have a choice. We are forced to sit here, twiddling our thumbs and looking like idiots."

She nodded. "You do that so well." Then she snickered. "And, yes, I'm joking."

"Sometimes—believe me—it doesn't matter if you're joking or not. That's how we feel too."

"And that's not fair," she stated. "As I'm starting to understand, answers don't just show up because we want them to. Everything happens in its own time."

He gave her an eye roll. "I'm glad you're finally getting to that point."

"Oh, it's not easy," she admitted. "I get it, and here I'm sitting, trying to figure out where to go, what to look at. I mean, Annabelle was shot before Joseph got home from his shift, so early evening. He called the cops, but why didn't somebody hear the gunfire? Somebody ought to have called the cops, but nobody was seen, and there is ..." She looked over at him, with a side look. "No forensics on that either, right?"

He shook his head. "Let's just say too little."

"So no forensics," she stated, "and you haven't got ballistics back or a tox report, I presume."

"What makes you think a tox report is coming?" he asked, looking at her curiously.

"It's a murder," she declared. "You have got to check everything."

His lips twitched. "You're right. It is a murder, and, yes, we do have to check everything."

She took a slow breath. "Now the real question is, do we know it's a murder?" she asked, her voice low. "Why not a suicide?"

"There was no note, there was nothing, as far as we can see, in her life that would point in that direction. The way she fell, she would have dropped the gun and then fallen beside it."

"But that's not impossible. I just don't know if there's any GSR on her hand, things like that," she explained. "And that's back to the forensics again."

He stared at her. "You're really getting into all this stuff, aren't you?"

She nodded. "I'm starting to learn, put it that way, and it's not the easiest stuff to learn. However, over time, I'm getting there. And I have a much better idea of just how hard all this is."

"Good, because it really is a challenge sometimes."

"And people go out of their way to make it even more difficult on us," she added, staring at him. "Of course I get that they don't want to get caught, but, at the same time, it's ... it's really not fair."

At that, he turned to see if she was serious and burst out laughing.

She grinned. "See? Now I made you laugh. You really do look tired."

He groaned. "Yes, I am tired. I haven't been sleeping well."

"What am I supposed to tell Nan, when she starts worrying about you?"

He stared at her. "You can come up with something, I'm sure. Definitely don't get her on my case."

She smirked. "So let me just get this straight. You're scared of Nan?"

He glared at her. "I'm not scared of Nan."

"No, no, it sounds to me like you're scared of Nan," Doreen declared, with a head nod.

He sighed. "So shall we change the subject again?"

"I don't know." She stared at him. "Is there anything to

change it to?"

He sighed. "We don't have any reason to consider this as suicide."

"But then how did somebody get in the building? And how did somebody get into her apartment? Without being seen by anyone?"

"We are still figuring out all that," he replied.

"You sure there's nothing wrong with you? Health-wise, right?" she asked.

He realized she was serious, and his face softened. He shook his head. "No, I'm fine. Just a little tired."

"A little tired is to be expected," she said. "You work so hard."

"Well, thank you," he replied in an exaggeration tone and then grinned at her.

She grimaced. "It doesn't seem to matter what anybody says, but, as soon as you get defensive about your health, it means something else is going on."

"Nothing else is going on," he stated firmly.

"Okay then. Back to the case. So it's not a suicide, which means it's a murder, which means somebody got into the building somehow, got into her apartment somehow," she recapped, with an eye roll.

"She wasn't known to lock her doors," Mack offered.

Doreen stopped. "Oh."

"Exactly, and Joseph often didn't take his keys, so she left it unlocked so he could get in."

"I suppose she went to sleep that way too."

He nodded. "Remember. Kelowna is still in many ways a small town, and a lot of people don't consider locking their doors a necessity here." She frowned at him. He shrugged and added, "How many times have you gone to bed without locking up?"

She winced. "A couple times, but I don't try to make a habit of it."

"Maybe not," he admitted, "but it is possible that somebody would have done that here, particularly in this town."

"Right. So somebody gets in and shoots her, takes nothing, doesn't mess up anything, isn't looking for anything, so why?" she asked.

He studied her intently. "I was going to ask you that." She stared at him in surprise. He shrugged. "We might be on the outs a lot of the time over *my* cases," he noted, with an emphasis on the *my*. "However, I do appreciate that you come at things from a very different point of view, and sometimes your viewpoint opens up all kinds of other avenues."

"Right," she agreed. "And sometimes people just talk to me."

He smiled and nodded. "You already got more out of our convict than I was expecting."

"It's not even that I got anything out of him. I spoke to his father first, and his father's pretty sad and upset about his son's actions, but I really do believe that his son is trying."

"It wasn't something that he tried to do. It wasn't a deliberate shooting," Mack acknowledged. "So I won't argue with you. I think you're probably right. And, yes, it's sad that this happened in the first place."

"And Nathan has served his time."

Mack shrugged. "Yet a lot of people think, over something like this murder of a small child, that there is no time served."

She frowned at that. "Meaning?"

"Meaning that, sometimes there's just no forgiveness

ever. So, even though Nathan did his time, for a lot of people, it is still fresh. You have to remember that, with people in small towns, we have long memories, and it won't matter to them one bit that Nathan served his time."

"Okay," she began, "so let's take a step back a bit. Who else, apart from Nathan Landry, was affected—outside of Kurt Chandler, who walked away from it. Well, pleading self-defense on his part," she added, "was an understandable move, but the fact remains that the two guys got into a fight, and the gun went off, and the little boy was killed."

"Remember. Nathan's the one who came to the party with the gun, and he's the one who was holding the gun," Mack corrected. "He and Kurt weren't in the act of wilfully committing a crime, so there was absolutely no reason to go after the other kid. He didn't commit the crime is what's different here."

She pondered that. "Even though Kurt was the one who told Nathan to bring the gun, and Kurt was the one who was planning to go rob someone to get some money?"

Mack stared at her. "Where did you get that from?"

"Nathan," she replied. "He doesn't hold any grudge against Kurt because Nathan understood that it would be normal for everybody to try and save their own skin. Kurt bought the gun, but Nathan carried it because Kurt told Nathan to. Nathan had been hanging on to it, looking at maybe buying it from his buddy. Nathan said it made him feel like a big man, and he didn't learn—until it was too late—that it just made him a fool."

At that, Mack's eyebrows popped up.

She nodded. "So unless Nathan was just saying the right words—and I'd be the first to say that a lot of people out there do that—I believe he was sincere, and he doesn't blame his buddy for having gotten away scot-free."

Mack sat back and pondered that. "At the time—and, yes, I've gone over the case since because I had to talk to Nathan today—I was invested in that old case also because of my dad. Still Nathan didn't say anything to me about that intent to rob."

"Well, Nathan believes," she added, "that because it was already his buddy's version against his, Nathan knew nobody would believe him, and he felt terribly guilty because he did kill that little boy. If he hadn't brought the gun with him, it wouldn't have happened, and that's quite true."

"I can see that as well," Mack admitted. "Yet I did not get any of this from Nathan."

"But you probably didn't ask those questions," she noted.

"No, I didn't, which is something I'll have to rectify now," he confirmed, swearing under his breath.

She wanted to tell him off for cursing, but, considering the look on his face as he stood, she asked, "You'll do that now?"

"Yeah, I'll do that now," he snapped, kicking himself. He looked over at her. "Thanks for the coffee."

And, with that, he left.

# Chapter 14

DOREEN SURELY DIDN'T expect Mack to leave so suddenly, obviously listening to what she had to say. So when her phone rang an hour later, somehow she knew that it would be Nathan.

"Did you talk to him?" he cried out.

"I did," she confirmed. "I told him that I thought you didn't have anything to do with Annabelle's murder and that you were sincere in your belief that somebody else was involved. I am sure you would agree that you are working hard on getting your life back together."

There was silence on the other end. "Oh," he finally replied, confused.

"You might be confused. I get it. I mean, Mack is pretty big, and he's pretty domineering, and he's very official and all business. Yet he's also a good guy. He's the one trying to solve Annabelle's murder. So regardless of what he puts you through and your fears and your reservations, whatever that brings up," she explained, "realize that Mack's just trying to get to the bottom of the truth."

"Yeah, but it's me he's rattling," Nathan told her.

"But you didn't do anything," she stated. "And he'll

know that as soon as he checks out everything. Your name will be cleared."

"I hope so," he muttered. "So do you, like, help people for real?"

"Yeah, I do. I mean, as much as I can try to," she noted, with a laugh. "Why?"

"I just wondered if I could hire you to help solve this case."

She stared down at her phone. "Oh."

She loved the word *hire* but also knew that she didn't have any official capacity to do that. "It's not something that people hire me for. I'm just somebody who keeps digging for the truth."

"So what'll it take to have you keep digging for the truth?" he asked glumly. "I really don't want to go back to jail."

"Did you do anything wrong?"

"No, I told you that already," he declared crossly.

"And people will continuously ask you the same question over and over again, especially when you say things like that."

"Why?" he asked. "The police don't always get it right."

"Did they get it right in your case?"

"Sure," he agreed. "The gun was in my hand."

"But you didn't tell him about your buddy, did you?"

He hesitated and then replied, "I did at the beginning, and then I didn't bother trying to reinforce that because my buddy had already basically said that I was the guilty party. I knew it, so what would I do about that obvious truth?"

She nodded. "I get that. I really do. It's not helpful, but I get it, and now what you have for a problem is trying to come up with answers as to what you'll do about it now."

"I want to get clear of this," he stated. "When I talked to Annabelle, although she wasn't terribly happy, we were both in an okay space when I left."

"When you say *an okay space*, what does that mean?"

"She was teary. I was teary," he shared. "I went home and had a long talk with my dad, and there's, … there's … I can't change anything. Talking doesn't change anything, so it's not as if I could make it right. And that's hard because, if I could have brought back that little boy, I would have. But I didn't have that option. I didn't have any of those options available to me, so it feels very much like it was all for naught."

"And did Annabelle feel better at the end of it?"

After a moment of silence, he said, "I don't know. I would like to think so, but I don't have any way to know that."

"Right," she agreed. "It's hard, isn't it?"

"It sure is," he said. "So I don't know what it'll take to have you turn your attention to this case …"

"What makes you think I'm not already doing it?" she asked, a smile in her voice. "I did already contact you, and I would love to get a hold of your friend and talk to him."

"He's dangerous," Nathan warned her. "You should stay away from him."

Surprised at the warning, she asked, "Oh? In what way?" When Nathan hesitated, Doreen continued. "Kurt's not being charged with a crime, but, if you've got a warning for me, it would help a lot to know exactly why."

He sighed. "I got in trouble from being around him, but he's the one who had already been busy doing other things."

"Other things like what?"

"He'd already done a few robberies, and some of them

were much less than nice."

"Did he kill anybody?"

"No, I don't think he killed anybody, … but then I don't know that for sure."

"And that gun, the cops have it, right?"

"Yeah, the cops have it."

"Okay. Would Kurt have had any trouble getting any other guns?"

"No, not at all," Nathan replied. "He arranged for that one in the first place."

"Right, so if he wanted to get a gun again, … he wouldn't have been upset at you for the loss of that one."

"No, they're easy to get. You just got to know the right people."

She winced at that because that's true. Everybody just needed to know the right people. That was always the problem. "Okay, so, if that's the case, what would be the issue with him?"

"He's just dangerous," Nathan repeated. "You're one of those nice people, and he eats those kinds of people alive."

"Is that how you got sucked in with him?"

"Yeah, and it's not fun. I'm doing my best to avoid people like that from now on. I'm hoping that, after being in jail and meeting a ton of them, I have a better radar as to who is like that."

"I don't know," she muttered. "I think snakes have a really good way of shedding their skins."

He gave a quiet sigh. "No, you're right. Still I'm not as young and stupid as I used to be." And, with that, he hung up.

And it surprised her in a way because she had just said something similar to Mack. She had been young and stupid about the things that she had allowed her husband to do, just that whole mind-control power trip was something that really bothered her. And now to hear this guy—trying hard to better himself, yet getting stuck and feeling like he was nothing but a loser—hurt. It wasn't in her to ignore his plea.

# Chapter 15

NOT IGNORING SOMEBODY'S plea was a whole different story than trying to get somewhere on a case that wasn't providing any clues. In frustration, Doreen dropped the phone book on her kitchen table yet again. She was looking for this Kurt Chandler, and, as Nathan had warned her, that was probably a lost cause and also a dangerous one. She would enlist Mack's help to try and get Kurt as well, but so far she had not reached Mack. Finally she wondered—knowing it was possibly the wrong thing to do, but feeling that she didn't have any other options—she phoned Nathan's father. When he answered, she explained who she was again.

"What do you want?" he asked suspiciously. "My son's not here."

"I already spoke to your son," she shared. "He did ask me to look into the case, to help to keep him clear of all this regarding Annabelle's murder." After that, Mr. Landry was a little more amiable to talking.

"I don't know what you can do though," he replied, "especially as the cops are on it."

"They are, indeed," she confirmed. "This friend of Nathan's who got him into trouble years ago ..."

"Yeah, what about him?" Mr. Landry asked, his voice suspicious again. "That one's bad news. I told Nathan at the time to get away, but he didn't listen."

"Young men have a habit of not listening, don't they?"

"Yeah, unfortunately in this case, it got Nathan into major trouble," he muttered.

"Have you seen or heard from Kurt since?"

He hesitated and finally replied, "I've seen him around every once in a while, but I haven't talked to him. I won't either."

"No, and your son has told me to stay away from him because he's dangerous."

"Then you should listen," Mr. Landry said. "Guys like that, they're survivors. And they just take everybody else down, without having to work for it."

She'd met more than a few like that too. And they usually hung around with her husband. "I get that. I'm just wondering if Kurt would have any reason to kill Annabelle."

"I don't know why he would," Mr. Landry replied slowly.

"No, but that's not an answer where I can just mark it off. I mean, is there any way that she would have seen something back then that might have been triggered now?"

He hesitated. "I don't know what that trigger would have been."

"One trigger would have been your son getting out of jail," she noted. "I mean, I'm not saying that is what happened, but I have to mark that off as a possibility and make sure that we know even if it's a part of this equation."

"Well, Kurt's the one who got Nathan the gun. So, outside of purchasing a gun, that's small fry for this guy."

"And I get that too," she agreed. "So the question is, is there any reason for Kurt to have contacted Annabelle?"

"I don't think so," Mr. Landry answered slowly. "But the trouble is, guys like that, they're kind of sick. ... Sometimes they like to contact their victims, maybe in order to twist the knife a little bit. And maybe Kurt contacted her and warned her that my son was due to be released from jail soon. I can see Kurt doing that," Mr Landry stated. "It would have been a sorry thing to do, and it would have hurt her a lot more, and she didn't need to suffer like that, and it is something somebody like Kurt might do."

"Right, so the question is whether he was seen around the murder site. You don't happen to have a picture of him, right?"

"No, I sure don't," he muttered in disgust. "Even ... even if I did, I wouldn't give it to you. My son's right. This guy's dangerous. You need to stay away."

"Right," she mumbled. "Do you have any particulars about him at least? How could I recognize him to stay away?"

"Well, Kurt's the same age as my son. He had really jet-black hair, and he had a bit of a scar on his cheek," Mr. Landry shared. "Always added a more dangerous look to him."

"And he probably loved it," she guessed, "added to his big bad wolf persona."

"Which he is," he declared sharply. "Please, stay away from him." And, with that, he hung up the phone.

She put down her phone and looked over the animals. "So where would a guy like that hang out?" she asked. "I feel like the pawnshops, pubs, things like that, but to find somebody in town? That'll be a whole different story."

She had his name but didn't know anything about him. At that, she started to dig through the internet, and, on a quick note, she picked up the phone and called her grandmother. "Hey, Nan. Kurt Chandler."

"Yeah, what about him?"

"Do you know that name at all?"

"Nope, I don't."

"Could you see if anybody else around there knows it?"

"Why?" she asked.

"Because I think he was also involved in that mess from years ago." And she quickly explained the story.

"And why would he have anything to do with Annabelle now?"

"I don't know that he did. I'm just wondering about this Kurt guy. ... Nathan's father thought that he'd be the kind of person to let Annabelle know that Nathan was back in town. To salt the wounds."

"Oh, that's interesting," Nan replied. "So, in other words, make it seem like either she was in danger or to rev up all those hard feelings again."

"Exactly. Mr. Landry told me that Kurt's that kind of a person who likes to rub it in and to make life difficult for everyone around him."

"Oh, *nice*," Nan muttered. "Why can't you have some nice clean-cut murderers right now? That one sounds nasty."

"I think they're all nasty," Doreen noted, with a laugh. "And there's absolutely nothing nice about any of these guys."

"So why do you want to have anything to do with them?" Nan asked.

"It's not that I want to, but this is where it's led me. So I'm following through on this, until I can get to something else."

"Well, let's hope it comes to something else pretty fast," Nan noted. "So, yeah, I'll ask around."

After the phone call Doreen got up and worked in her garden for a little bit, trying to keep her mind busy. And just as she was about to give up on that and maybe head to the library, Nan called back.

"Nobody knows anything specific," she said. "Sounds like he's a two-bit loser."

"Yeah, he's a two-bit loser all right," Doreen agreed, "but the kind who likes to torment people."

"Well, we don't like that," she snapped.

"Nope, I hear you." And, with that, she said goodbye to her grandmother and phoned Joseph. "Hey, did Annabelle have any other visitors in the couple days leading up to her death?"

"Man, I wish this was over," he grumbled. "Every time I see your phone number come up, it scares me."

"Why should it scare you?" she asked. "Now, if the cops were calling you, that's a different story."

"Why would the cops call me?" he asked, his voice wobbling in panic.

She shrugged. "Mostly just because they'd have more questions."

"Right." He sighed. "I've never been the kind to get into trouble, so every time you even say things like that, … it just makes my heart pound."

"Yeah, I'm the same," she agreed, "so back to that question."

"She had a couple customers come by. I don't really know too much about it though."

"So you didn't really have anything to do with her business?"

"Not like that," he said. "I mean, obviously I was interested and tried to stay partly involved, but it was *her thing.*" And his tone was so dismissive about it being *her thing.*

"Would she ever make a successful business out of it?" she asked.

"I don't think she could have. There wasn't enough demand for this. She really needed to get a real job."

At that, Doreen winced because that whole *real job* comment was a touchy subject for her too. "So you said that to me, but did you also say that to her?"

"Well, we had a few discussions about it," he replied. "I mean, I was working at the pub, and she was doing this flower stuff, but we were barely covering all the bills."

"Ah, yeah, the bills are one of those ongoing issues, aren't they?"

"Particularly when this wasn't really a business," he stated. "And, yeah, she'd get really angry at me if I even said something along that line."

"Of course she would. You were knocking down a dream of hers."

"Maybe. … I don't know."

"Maybe, maybe not," she hedged. "So you don't really know if she had any other visitors."

"No, I don't. Some days I was there, and some days I wasn't."

"Because you only work evenings, don't you?"

"Yeah, I work six p.m. till eleven p.m. usually."

"So you only work five hours a day."

For some reason that made his back bristle. "Yeah, I do, but I made more in those few hours than she did in her forty-hour workweeks. And sometimes she did a lot more than that too."

"Hey, hey," Doreen said, "I'm not trying to upset you. So you weren't there during the daytime, when she worked, and then you left for the evening to do your job. You two didn't get much time together, I gather." At his groan, she reminded him, "I'm trying to get to the bottom of Annabelle's murder."

"Well, I'm sorry I ever brought it up," he declared. "Can you just, like, get past this?"

"Wouldn't that be nice," she said in a harder tone. "I'm trying to solve Annabelle's murder."

"But you're not even the police or anything, so I don't know how you'll solve anything," he noted.

"Maybe I won't, but I won't give up until I have at least followed every lead I could. So back to visitors."

"A couple guys came one day, another woman one day," he replied unwillingly, "but I don't know who they were. They were just people. They were people talking to her about some of her stuff. One of the guys wanted a bouquet done for his girlfriend. I don't know anything else."

She stared down at her phone in disgust. She was beginning to understand why everyone liked Annabelle and was weary of Joseph Moody. "I'm sorry that you weren't interested enough in her business to even answer a few questions. Did she have a binder or something?"

"Yeah, sure, she had documents, but the cops took the laptop."

"Of course they did." She rotated her neck in frustration.

"I mean, a bunch of her receipts were there though."

"Good, you want to take some photographs of them and send them to me?" He hesitated. "You did get back into your

149

place, didn't you?"

"Well, yes, but I'm not staying there," he said. "I mean, how would that feel ... to be in the same room but not having her there," he explained, his voice choking up.

She winced at that. "No, you're right. Are you allowed back in?"

"Yes, I just told you that, didn't I?"

"Good. Why don't you meet me there, and I'll take a bunch of photos and have a look around. I wanted to see the crime scene anyway." He hesitated again. She added, "It would be a good thing to do for Annabelle."

"Fine," he relented in exasperation. "But after this, we're done."

She stared at the phone. "Done?"

"Yes, done. I need to put this behind me."

"Well, good luck with that," she replied, "because, until there are answers, there's no *putting this behind us* for anybody."

# Chapter 16

WITH THE ANIMALS in tow, Doreen got everybody into the vehicle and then headed over to Annabelle's apartment. The boyfriend had been less than pleased about meeting her there but had finally given in, wanting to go right now, so that he could be done with this. She pondered somebody who thought he would get past all this so fast. He was a character after all. If it were her, no way. If something happened to Nan, it would take Doreen a long time to get past it, and Nan was older and had had a good run.

Somebody like Annabelle—who was young and full of life, who had already suffered so much tragedy—how was that even remotely something that people got over so quickly? Doreen didn't understand that mentality, and no doubt Joseph was grieving. Yet she certainly didn't feel that that was the main issue, just his need to compartmentalize this and to move on—which she could understand, but she didn't think she could do that.

Particularly where you lived with that person, and supposedly he was in love with her. Although they'd obviously had a lot of problems, from what everybody had said, Annabelle had been an absolutely lovely lady. Therefore, the grief and the shock of her death would be that much harder for everybody to deal with.

Doreen could already imagine that by the number of people saying, *such a waste, such a loss, died too young.* And all those statements were true, but then it went for anybody who was taken before their time by another's hand. That's the part that Doreen was aggravated about. Disease was bad enough. Accidents happened too, but to think that people were dealing with a loss because of a murder—and the second one in that family—Doreen couldn't even imagine how the poor parents were getting along.

It's almost as if they had left to get away and apparently had split up over the son's death, but now having lost their daughter as well, she wondered if there was any hope of the parents finding a way past this. ... It would have been unfathomable, but people somehow deal with this, day by day, coping in ways that she had never seen. She walked up the stairs to the right door. She saw Joseph, restlessly shifting from foot to foot.

He saw her, and a look of relief washed over his face. "Finally," he cried out.

She stated, "I'm early."

He glared at her, stiffening. "I don't want to be here."

She nodded. "And if there was a way to get in without asking you, I would have done it already."

He sighed, nodded, and pointed. "Let's just get this done." With that, he opened the door and let her go in first. With both Mugs and Goliath on leashes, she walked into the apartment and stopped almost at the entranceway. He came in behind her and slammed the door. She looked back at him and frowned.

He shrugged. "It's not a place I want to be."

b

"Are you moving out?"

"I was just going to take my stuff and run," he muttered. "I don't have the rent money anyway, and the police are still keeping us on a short leash over this," he said, with a wave of his hand. "Not being able to pay the rent just means that I'll take my stuff and go."

"You haven't taken anything yet?"

"No, I have to get my clothes and stuff out," he said, with a sigh. "And I'm staying at a friend's but on their couch, and couch surfing is not my preferred state either."

"No, I don't imagine it is," she agreed, raising her eyebrow at the concept. "But at least you have friends you can go to."

He shrugged. "Sure, for a little while, but I mean it's not an ideal long-term solution."

Privately she thought that there was a shortage of long-term solutions when it came to something like this, but what did she know? "I need to wander around, if that's okay with you."

"Yeah, you go do you," he said. "I'll grab a few things while I'm here."

As she followed him to the bedroom, he opened up the closet, grabbed a bag on the floor and started tossing in his clothes. And she realized that he really was likely to just take his stuff and run. "How much of this is all yours?" she asked curiously.

He shrugged. "We've lived together for quite a few years, so I don't know what's mine versus hers, but most of it's just old and won't be of any value."

"So you're not worried about the furniture?"

He shook his head. "No, God no."

And, with that, he returned his attention to the dresser,

and he quickly emptied his drawer, then went back to the closet. She went to the dresser beside his and went through everything there. When silence filled the room, she turned to see him staring at her.

"Why are you going through her things?"

"Because you never know what you'll come up with," she replied. And ignoring him, she went to the closet and took a careful look at everything that was Annabelle's. Then she went to the bed and asked, "Which side did she sleep on?"

He pointed to the far side, close to the closet.

She walked over and checked out the contents of the night table. It was pretty usual, pretty normal. A couple books, a pack of Kleenex, a few personal items, like pictures. Doreen picked them up, looked at a few of them, and asked Joseph who they were.

He shrugged. "Friends of hers from school."

"Okay. Do you mind if I keep them?"

He shrugged. "I don't care what you do with them. I'm taking my stuff and leaving the rest."

It wasn't the way she would want to be treated, if she were a landlord, but not much she could say about it to this guy. If he couldn't pay his rent, then chances were the landlord would need everything here to sell just to recoup what he had lost. She didn't know how the tenant laws worked, having never been in that position.

She quickly went through the rest of the bedroom, but, with just a few pictures in her hands, she tucked them into her purse, and then asked, "Where's her paperwork for the office?"

"Out here," he said.

And he led the way to a crowded dining room table that

she had obviously been using as an office. Her flowers were still tossed on the floor, which Doreen studiously ignored, yet it was a little hard when they were everywhere. "Did she normally keep these neat and orderly?"

"Sure, but when she was being creative, nothing was neat and orderly about it." He shook his head. "It was one of the ongoing arguments between us," he noted awkwardly. "I just wanted her to leave the dining room as it was."

"Where else would she do her work?" she asked, looking at him.

He just shrugged.

"In other words, you wouldn't have minded if she didn't do this at all."

"No, I wouldn't have." He glared at her. "Is that so wrong? I wanted her to get a regular job that would have a regular paycheck."

"Got it," Doreen replied. The last thing Doreen had was a regular job with a regular paycheck, so her sympathies were entirely with the victim.

She sat down at the nearest chair and studied the layout and how the woman worked. She wasn't sure what it would tell her, if anything, because everything was such a mess.

Joseph even said as much. "You can't tell anything from this place right now. Between the attack, the cops, the searches and all that, this place doesn't look like it used to."

"Okay. Did you check to see if anything was stolen?"

"I did," he said. "The TV's here. Her laptop the cops took, so it was still here. I didn't notice anything gone."

"Where's the paperwork?"

"Right there." Joseph pointed to a stack off to the side.

She picked up the entire stack, quite a bit to it. "Do you mind if I take this?"

"Take it all. The sooner, the better. I want to get out of here."

At that, she took a step back because something was just so noticeably jittery about him, as he kept looking around the apartment, almost shuddering at the room. Doreen wasn't sure whether it was just a nervous thing or he maybe had a bad premonition.

She went through the rest of stuff slowly, deliberately taking her time, not trying to make him any more upset but obviously not wanting to give in to the same feelings that he had.

None of her animals seemed to pick up anything, and that was enough for her. If anything, there was a certain solemness to their actions, as if they knew what had already happened to the poor woman. By the time Doreen was done here, she went to the kitchen.

He asked, "Can we just get this over with?"

She turned to him. "You can leave if you want. Do you care if I'm here?"

Startled, he shook his head. "I'm out then." And he grabbed the bag that he had with him, and he bolted for the door.

Surprised, she expected him to put up a bigger argument, but then why would he? Something was seriously bothering him.

She listened as he raced down the hallway and went back to her search. When a knock came on the door, and then the door opened abruptly, she turned to see the building manager. When he saw her and her animals, he was shooting daggers.

"Hey," she greeted him. "Joseph let me in to take a look at the crime scene. I'm not trying to interfere, but I am here to see how she lived and if anything here might lead us to whoever murdered Annabelle."

"Yeah, whoever did this is probably the jerk who just left." He looked at the room in disgust. "He's not coming back, is he?"

She winced. "Joseph was really jittery, and it's one of the reasons why I told him that he might as well just leave."

"Yeah, thanks for that." He continued glaring at her. "How will I get my rent money now?"

"I don't know what to say, other than to tell you that he didn't have it."

"He never had it," he declared bitterly, looking at her. "It was always her."

"So then you already know that he won't pay. I don't know how much damage the rest of this place sustained," she noted, looking at the floor and wincing at the dried blood.

Even Mugs was staying away from it, for which she was grateful.

"Yeah, I know." The manager raised both hands. "Not only is it a loss of a month's rent but I have to get this cleaned up and this stuff disposed of." He was disgusted as he looked around. "It's a sad end for that beautiful girl." And, with that, he left and slammed the door behind him.

Doreen finished looking the place over and then went back to the bedroom to where Joseph had been pulling out his stuff. She hoped he'd only taken his stuff, and she had tried to watch him, but it was hard to know. With the cops being all over him, she wouldn't be at all surprised if he didn't just bugger off somewhere, take a bus to nowhere.

It seemed like something important was here that she just couldn't put her finger on. She went through the room again slowly. She had the stack of business papers in her hand, and she took several photos of the rest of the apartment, just to ensure she had something as a reference. And then slowly, with the animals, she moved outside. As soon as she closed the apartment door behind her, the neighbor's door popped open.

"You."

"Yep, me," Doreen responded. The nosy neighbor looked suspiciously at the door to Annabelle's apartment, so Doreen had to clarify before that woman called the cops on her, "Joseph let me in. Then he left, and the manager came in."

The woman nodded slowly. "I suppose Joseph came back to get his stuff and run," she declared in disgust.

"That seems to be the general consensus, yes," she murmured.

The woman nodded. "That's his kind of style. If he can get out of taking responsibility, he's out the door the first chance he gets."

It was an interesting unanimous assessment of the guy. And yet she didn't have anything to offset it. She just nodded and added, "He seemed jittery, really spooked by being here."

The woman frowned. "I would be too. No way you'd catch me still in the same room where my partner died. I don't know that anybody would ever come back here, and the police certainly didn't seem to think that the killer would return here and shoot anybody else," she shared. "But believe me. I've been keeping a close eye on the place ever since."

At that, Doreen nodded. "Have you seen anything else? Anyone come by?"

She shook her head. "No, not even sure what it would be that I could have seen," she noted. "It's just so wrong and heartbreaking."

"I got it," Doreen replied. "Did you have much to do with Annabelle when she was alive?"

"Nope, not at all, but she was good people. She was always friendly, always happy, always willing to help out. Him on the other hand …"

Doreen smiled. "Yep, I already met him."

The woman gave a cackle. "And having met him, you probably don't need anybody else to tell you what he's like."

Doreen just smiled and didn't say anything. The guy was obviously traumatized, and maybe he wasn't the most upstanding citizen, but she hardly had any reason to crucify him. "There certainly isn't anything in their apartment to lead us to whoever has done this though," she shared.

"No?" The woman studied Doreen with an eagle eye. The nosy neighbor stared at the papers in her hand.

"This is her customer information," she explained. "I'll call a few of them just to see if anybody was hassling her, if she made mention of anybody in her world causing her trouble, if anything was just off."

"Her boyfriend couldn't help?" she asked, with a raised eyebrow.

"No, he sure couldn't," Doreen replied. The two women exchanged knowing glances, and Doreen smiled and added, "Anyway, that's it for me for then. I guess I will see you around."

And, with a wave, she tugged her animals back toward her car. Mugs wanted to visit the older lady, but Doreen wasn't sure what kind of reception he would get, so she kept pulling him toward the main door.

# Chapter 17

WHEN THEY FINALLY got farther away, Doreen looked down at Mugs. "What's the matter with you?"

He woofed at her and went out the door willingly, now heading for a big patch of grass. There he relieved himself, while she waited. She studied the area around her. It was open, friendly. She had already seen people come and go without too much trouble, which just meant that it would cause her and the cops much more problems to find out what the heck was going on here. And that was troubling too.

She took several deep breaths, wondering at the horrible tightness within. Whether it was just being in that poor woman's home or the meeting with the boyfriend or if it was literally just a reaction from talking with the older lady, Doreen didn't know.

Her hands were trembling slightly. She wanted to swear, but that would make her sound much more like Mack, and that she wouldn't do. There was never a reason to swear, at least there hadn't been in her world up till now. She would hate to think that this is what it took for her to start. Still, it was sad to even carry on doing what she was doing, and, on that note, she headed to her car.

As she pulled away and glanced up at the windows of the apartment building, sure enough, there was the old lady, staring down at her. Doreen gave a wave, and the lady, instead of waving back, just closed her curtains. As if by pulling them closed, she could put some closure on what had happened across the hall from where she lived. That had to be one of the hardest things too. How did you reconcile a murder so close to your home and stay?

So close that you had to wonder whether it was targeted or an accident.

Doreen frowned at that, wondering if the police had considered that maybe this killer had the wrong apartment. Knowing that it was probably foolish, but deciding that she needed to at least see if Mack had considered it, she pulled off to the side of the road and sent a quick text. She was only a few minutes from home, but then she was only a few minutes from home no matter where in town she went. That was one of the nice things about living in Kelowna. Everything was so close and handy.

After sending the text, she pulled her vehicle back into traffic and drove home. As soon as she got to the house, she let the animals off their leashes, and they raced up to the front door. Mugs waited impatiently for her. "I don't know what your problem is today, but it seems to me that everything's off for everybody."

She wasn't sure what that was all about. Maybe they were picking up on her own odd mood. Which was most likely, and she was pretty sure anybody who dealt with animals would tell her to smarten up because it was affecting everybody.

With a groan she went inside, dropped all the paperwork

onto the countertop in her kitchen, and put on a small pot of coffee. She deserved a cup after that visit to Annabelle's apartment. It's not that Doreen was trying to slow down or to cut back on her caffeine intake, but she was very aware when she had too much. However, now definitely a second pot was needed.

And, with it done dripping, she headed down to the river, where she sat quietly for the longest time—she didn't want to say meditating, but, yeah, sure, meditating. Just communing with nature, with the good things in life, which she needed to calm her nerves.

When Mugs barked after a while, she didn't even have to turn around to know that Mack had arrived. He came and sat down beside her, wrapped his arm around her shoulders, and just tucked her a little closer to him.

She leaned into his embrace. "Hey, it's good to see you."

"In that case, you might want to look up at me," he noted in exasperation.

She looked up and smiled. "Just an off day."

"You've had a lot of them lately."

"I have?" she asked. "What about you?"

He smiled. "So we're both having a couple of *off* days."

"Maybe," she muttered. "I got to thinking that maybe Annabelle wasn't the intended victim."

Mack frowned.

"I don't know why, but it's just a thought," she noted. "It doesn't look like a terribly wealthy area, but what if somebody else on that block was the intended victim?"

He pondered that for a moment. "I was actually wondering whether the boyfriend was the intended victim."

She frowned and then nodded. "That almost makes it too easy though, doesn't it?"

"In what way?" he asked curiously.

"Nobody likes him," she stated bluntly.

He smiled and nodded. "You've got a point there. He does not have a very big fan club, does he?"

"Not at all," she declared. "I'm not sure anybody's got anything good to say about him."

"That's too bad."

"And yet, for all intents and purposes, Annabelle seemed happy. So, if that's the case, then I'm happy to let everything else slide because, if he made her happy, then that's all that matters."

Mack sat silently at her side, a cup of coffee in his hand.

She looked at it and shook her head. "Why did I make a small pot?" she muttered, groaning inwardly. "I should have realized, after I texted you, that you'd be here soon."

"No, I was heading home anyway."

"Really?" she asked.

"Yeah, I am, and I stopped off at Mum's earlier to check on her. So, when I got your text, I needed to see if you were doing okay."

She smiled up at him. "See? You stop to make sure I'm okay, even when I don't text you. And, when I do text, you make sure that you come?"

"That's what I just said." He frowned again. "What's wrong with that?"

She smiled. "Nothing. It just shows that you care."

"Of course I care," he replied, his tone turning slightly raspy.

She nodded. "And you show it so well, all the time," she teased. "I guess that's what I'm still adjusting to."

He gave a heavy sigh. "That husband of yours ... de-serves to have somebody take him out in the back alley and give him a good beating."

She raised one eyebrow and replied, "As long as it's not you."

"And why is that?" he asked, glaring at her. "You mean I don't have a right to be pissed off at him?"

"Oh, absolutely you do," she agreed. "Believe me. I'd like to take him out in the back alley and give him a good beating myself. But chances are, between us, we'd do too good a job, and we'd be spending too much of our lives in jail."

He chuckled. "Then we'd have to make sure we don't do that."

Almost as if Mathew had heard their conversation, her phone rang and her Caller ID confirmed it was her ex. "Speak of the devil."

Mack looked at her screen and frowned. "How often does he call you?"

"Not very often," she said, "so I'm not sure what I should do about this one."

"Well, maybe answer it," he suggested. "Let's see what he's up to."

"Nick would tell me to hang up on him or to not even answer."

Mack contemplated that, while the phone rang incessantly. "Well, I'm here with you. So let's just see what he wants to say."

And with that decided, she answered the phone, putting it on Speaker.

"About time you answered," Mathew said crossly. "I haven't got all day."

"Wow. How nice to hear from you too," she muttered. "You think I don't have something else to do?"

"Yeah, what?" he asked. "Go out and interfere in other people's lives some more?" At that, he snickered.

She stiffened and glared at her phone. But Mack reached out a calming hand.

"Did you have a reason for calling?" she muttered. "I should probably remind you that you're supposed to be talking to my lawyer."

"But I don't like talking to your lawyer," he said in that silky manipulative voice. "I'd much rather talk with you."

"Not anything that you need to say to me though," she stated, glancing over at Mack. "I certainly don't have time to sit here and listen to you."

"Well, you'll make time. I want your lawyer to back off."

She frowned at her phone, glanced at Mack. "What's he done that's pissed you off?" she asked curiously.

"What do you mean?"

"It's a simple enough question. So what's he done?"

"I wouldn't sign this last round. I changed my mind," Mathew declared. "And now he's applied for a court date for irreconcilable differences."

"What's the problem then? You can't come to an agreement, right?"

"Right."

"So that makes sense. He is entitled to take any course of action that he is due." She looked over at Mack to see a big grin on his face. It made sense to her, but obviously Mack thought it was pretty funny.

At that, her husband gave one of his exaggerated sighs. "You see? That's the stuff you just don't understand, which is why I always handled the business."

She stiffened again and glared at the phone. "Well, guess what? That's exactly why I hired a lawyer," she barked, fuming. "So I don't have to deal with your talking down to me all the time."

"Oh, is that what this is all about?" Mathew asked. "Well, if you had any brains, you wouldn't have got yourself into this situation."

"Okay, if this will just be a mud-slinging match, I'm not taking part. You can talk to my lawyer."

As she went to hang up, Mathew cried out, "No, wait, wait."

"What?" she snapped. "You think I need to sit here and listen to you insult me like that?"

"Look. I'm sorry," he replied, though his tone was not apologetic. "There is just something every time I talk to you."

"Yeah, believe me. I've noticed."

He groaned. "Okay, look. I just need you to back off, to get your lawyer to back off. I'm sure you and I can come to some sort of an agreement."

"You just told me that I didn't have any business sense and that's why you did the business in our relationship. Why would I trust you to do that with my interests right now?" she asked, with a snort. "From where I stand, I think Nick definitely understands what he is doing. That's the reason I have him. So, if you want to talk, you know where to reach him. I would certainly appreciate it if you would man up and quit complaining to me about it."

"Nope, nope, nope, nope, nope, nope, we're not going there," he growled.

"Not going where?" she asked.

"We're not going back to the lawyer. I need you to deal with this on your own, and let's just get it over with."

"Get what over with?"

"Oh, stop being dense," he stated crossly. "We just need to sign the agreement, so we can both move on with our lives."

"Yeah? I'd like to see that happen too. Remember? That's why I hired the lawyer."

"Yes, but your lawyer is not being very cooperative."

At that, she smirked. "Pretty sure he would say the same—that you're not being very cooperative." She almost felt the glare reach through the phone and snag her in the throat. "Look. Enough is enough. Stop calling me. Call him. The sooner you get this dealt with, the faster it'll be over. And, if the judge is the way to go, then the judge is the way to go. I don't see a problem either way."

"What do you mean, you don't see a problem?" And then he stopped. "Good God, you don't even know."

"Don't even know what?" she growled. "You better watch it. I'm getting a little sick of your attitude." She looked over at Mack to see him staring at her. She shrugged at him, asking Mathew, "So what?"

"They'll hit me a lot harder if we go to court."

Frowning, she asked, "So why are you not settling now then? Why do you want to go to court?"

"I don't want to go to court," he snapped. "Obviously I don't want to go to court."

"Well then, come up with an arrangement that my attorney is okay with. How hard is that to understand for somebody who's dealt with business all his life," she taunted, unable to keep the sting out of her voice, followed by an eye roll.

"Why do you want so much money?" he asked. "You won't even be able to look after it."

At that, she glared into the phone again. "So this conversation is over," she ordered in a very calm tone. "As I told you, don't bother calling me again. I won't answer. You can talk to him." And this time she disconnected the call with a furious tap. She glared at Mack. "Your brother will still get angry with me."

He smiled at her. "He might, but it was actually good for me to hear that conversation."

"Why?" she asked.

"Because you were standing up for yourself. I'm really proud of you for that." She stared at him in surprise. He looped an arm around her shoulders in a quick hug. "Sometimes we're afraid that people will revert back to where they were—in a very unhappy and unhealthy relationship," he explained. "People tend to give in, and I didn't want to think of you going back to your ex because of something he said."

She shook her head. "He wouldn't tolerate me now anyway," she noted, with a smile. "I'm a very different person than when I was married to him." She looked down at her phone. "Do you really think they'll throw the book at him?"

"Not only will they throw the book at him but he will quite possibly go up on legal charges, depending on how the judge sees his sexual involvement with your divorce lawyer."

She stared at him in shock. "That'll make it even harder for him to get out of this."

"Sure it will," Mack agreed, "but all he has to do is make a proper agreement, and then he won't have to go to court."

"Will I have to go?" she asked, staring at him in sudden worry.

He shrugged. "Maybe, but you won't be alone. You'll have Nick on your side, and he is all you need. If need be," Mack added, "I'll take time off, and I'll come for emotional support too."

She smiled up at him. "You would do that, wouldn't you?"

"Yep. Not to mention the fact that I'd like to have a little personal talk with this guy."

She stared at him in alarm, but he gave her a wolfish grin. "I promise. I won't hurt him." She was about to relax when he added, "Not too badly."

She sighed. "He'd have your butt in jail pretty fast, if you were to do anything like that. He lives for lawsuits."

"Now he's got one that he really needs to deal with," Mack noted, with a sly smile.

"And, yeah, next time he calls, I won't even answer my phone."

"He's obviously got a bee in his bonnet, so let's get Nick to deal with it from now on." Mack pulled out his phone and called his brother, putting it on Speakerphone. When he filled him in on the details, Nick was laughing.

"Yeah, he's pretty upset about the whole thing," Nick confirmed. "He's got a couple months, but the closer we get to the court date, he is losing more of his stuff. I mean, if he settles now, it would be good, but, if he lets it drag on, the harder it'll be. And, if we end up in court, he knows he'll be in a lot of trouble."

"What kind of trouble though?" she asked.

"That's up to the judge to decide."

"But, if he finds out who the judge is, Mathew could possibly get to the judge. You know that, right?"

A moment of silence passed. "Our assigned judge happens to be somebody who is very highly respected for *not* being the type of guy who takes bribes, and he does not like anybody who does," Nick explained, "so we couldn't have gotten a better shot at winning this thing."

"That's good," she noted, "because Mathew will try it."

"Then rest easy because this judge will throw the book at him," Nick stated cheerfully.

"Yeah, but if he goes to jail, I won't get any money, will I?"

"You will. That will happen regardless of whether he goes to jail or not," Nick added. "It'll still take a bit of time, but we're getting there."

"I'm glad one of us is enjoying this," she muttered.

He laughed, and it came bright and cheerful through the phone. "I am. There are very few cases where I'm as happy to go after the husband as I am in this case."

And, with that, he and Mack talked for a few more moments, and then he signed off. Mack picked up his coffee, finished it in one gulp, and asked, "Have you eaten?"

She shook her head. "No, I haven't. And I should tell you that I picked up a bunch of paperwork from Annabelle's place today."

"What kind of paperwork?" he asked.

She filled him in on what she'd found.

"What good do you think that'll do you?"

"Probably nothing," she admitted. "I just wanted to check on her mental state to see if there was any threat that anybody else detected."

He nodded. "We have already talked to quite a few of her clients."

"Good," she said. "If nothing else, people should be reassured that we're doing everything we can."

He repeated, "*We?*"

She shrugged. "Yeah, *we.*"

# Chapter 18

MACK LEFT SOON after they had dinner. It was a simple meat-and-veggie meal, and then he got a call and had to leave. She hated to see him go because another work-related call just meant he wouldn't get the rest he needed. Keyed up and still uncertain as to what direction she should go, she started phoning Annabelle's past clients. Several phone numbers were more business-oriented, and she could only leave messages. Others were private personal phone numbers, and she did manage to speak to a few people.

When she explained who she was, most people had no clue, which was a good thing, and they just asked what she was doing looking into it. She explained that she was doing it for a friend of the family. By the time she'd had a chance to talk to as many as she could, nobody could say anything was wrong with Annabelle. She always seemed happy and bubbly. She was excited about running her own business, and that was very important to her.

When asked about her partner, nobody seemed to know anything about him. Joseph was never there when they had spoken to her. When Doreen reached the last name on the list, she identified herself again and went through the whole spiel.

"Oh that poor girl," the woman replied, sounding teary. "I've used her services several times for different events. She's always come through for me."

"Everybody has such good things to say about her," Doreen confirmed.

"Yes, and to think that somebody so young should be taken from us and so senselessly too is a shame. It's a crime that it hasn't been solved yet either."

"The police are working on it," Doreen murmured. "I'm trying to find if anything may have been amiss in any way. For example, somebody in her acquaintance that she may have had a problem with, or a past client who may have had a problem with her—something, anything."

"Oh, dear, it's that bad, is it?" the woman cried out. "You would like to think that it would be easy."

"No cameras were at her apartment, and nobody saw the shooter or heard the shooting. She wasn't expecting any-body—or rather it wasn't in her calendar. The police don't think she was targeted, but we can't rule out the possibility that she was shot when someone else was expected to be there. Maybe when they found Annabelle was alone, they shot her and just took off."

"All of that's possible too." The client dropped her voice a little bit and added, "Her boyfriend wasn't terribly nice."

"Did you talk to him?"

"I did. I was there one day, and he was, … well, upset because dinner was being pushed back, and he had to go to work."

"Ah, of course," Doreen replied. "I'm not surprised at that."

"No, he looks like the kind who requires a lot of her attention, at least when he wants it." The client chuckled, and then she sighed. "But still, everything in his world's flipped now too, so I shouldn't make fun of him."

Doreen winced at that. "You're right, and it is a crying shame that it happened at all."

"Oh, it's just so terrible."

"But you didn't see her with anybody else, did you?"

"No, I certainly …" And then she stopped. "Oh, wait a minute. Another man was there one day I met her," she shared. "He looked a little bit familiar. It was a couple days before she died. I stopped by to bring her back some vases that she had left at one of my events. I was supposed to bring them back a few weeks earlier, but I got really busy," she explained apologetically. "Anyway, another was man there, and they were both teary-eyed."

"Ah." Doreen gave a quick description of Nathan Landry.

"Yes, that would be him," the client confirmed excitedly. "I wasn't sure what was going on, but Annabelle just told me that everything was fine, and it was just a trip down memory lane."

"Yes, I do know who that was."

"Well, that's all I have to give you then. Sorry, dear," the client said. "You might want to check with the neighbor though. She often keeps tabs on everybody around there. She seemed to listen in on all the conversations."

"Did you see her there?"

"I did. She had her head poked out a couple times. I know Annabelle would just smile at her, and then, when we got inside her apartment, she'd roll her eyes and say, *She's just one of those nosy women.*"

"Yeah, I got that impression too," Doreen agreed. "And she thinks she heard the shooting but didn't see anybody."

At that, the other woman gasped. "Seriously? Because even the slightest sound from Annabelle's, and the woman was at the door, knocking."

"I'm wondering if a gunshot might have scared the neighbor enough to keep her inside."

"I suppose," the client replied slowly. "That would be shocking, but I'm not sure I would know what a gunshot sounded like."

Long after she hung up, Doreen had to think about that. It was a good point. Had a silencer been used? Did anybody even know what a gunshot sounds like with a silencer? Even without one? Knowing Mack had been called back to work, she didn't want to bother him. Yet, at the same time, how would she find out about a silencer? And, if it was a silencer, it would have meant that it was a much more professional hit. But they said it was Joseph's gun, so that completely blew that theory out of the water.

And that also bothered her because she didn't see Annabelle getting caught up in anything like that. Doreen pondered that for a long moment and then went back to her research on Nathan's buddy, Kurt. And it wasn't long after that where she caught sight of his father in a newspaper article on the internet. And, from the father, she tracked down the son in the article, but it still didn't say anything about what he did and where he lived.

She frowned at that because that still, to her, was one of the better leads of all this. So, if they could at least find Kurt or see if he was around here, that would help her get a better understanding. She considered that for a long moment and then called Nan. When Nan answered, she sounded more tired than Doreen expected.

"It's just been a very long day, dear," she said. "Are you getting anywhere?"

"It doesn't seem like it, no," Doreen replied in frustration. "I was trying to find Nathan's buddy from way back when, Kurt Chandler, and it is pretty hard."

"And I don't know anybody who knows Kurt or otherwise knows anything about that one."

"Right. So tell me what you know about getting a gun in town?"

Silence came on the other end of the phone, and then Nan went off in peals of laughter. "I think those are questions you should be asking Mack."

"I would, but he got called out to another case," she stated. "I just wondered if any of your cronies there had any idea how easy or how hard it is to buy a gun in town."

"I think it's no different than any other town," Nan suggested. "It's all about who you know."

Doreen mulled over that afterward as well because it really was all about who you knew. But the question was, how did anybody in that corner know Annabelle? Why a connection to her? Doreen was still thinking about it when her phone rang. Her Caller ID revealed Private Call. She hesitated and then finally decided to answer it.

A man on the other end said, "Stop asking questions or else."

She didn't know what to say to that, and, by the time she had formulated a response, the line was already dead. As soon as she took a deep breath and hit Redial, it didn't go through. Apparently she had no way to get a redial for a Private Call. She snorted at that. "I should get one of those for myself," she muttered.

Mack phoned her a few minutes later. "What's the matter?" he asked.

She stared at her phone in surprise. "How do you know something's the matter?"

"I don't," he admitted. "I'm just assuming it is."

She chuckled. "Well in a way there is." She told him about the warning phone call.

"Crap. Did you recognize the voice?"

"Nope and it happened so fast I didn't have time to respond." She waited a beat. "I'm not always in trouble you know. Although from your own tone, it sounds like something is off. What's up?"

"Richie phoned Darren to ask how hard it would be to get a gun in town."

She gasped. "Oh, dang. I called and asked Nan that."

"And she asked Richie, who then called his grandson." He groaned. "It's like a never ending bad comedy."

"Well, it'll be a little hard to get a gun, if people keep going to the cops," she replied, with a note of humor.

"I figured it was you right away. Are you asking about how to get a gun?"

"I was asking how hard it would be to get a gun," she clarified. "And really the point here, which I was trying to find out, is how hard is it to get a silencer for a gun?"

After a second or two, Mack asked softly, "Why?"

"Because how was it that the nosy neighbor across from Annabelle's place, who apparently hears everything and sticks her head out at every sound—to the point that sometimes she even comes across to Annabelle's, when she has clients there—because she can hear things, and she wants to know what's up. Yet, on the night that Annabelle's shot, she doesn't recognize a gunshot and doesn't open the door and doesn't call the cops? I'm not buying that."

# Chapter 19

*Sunday Morning...*

THE NEXT MORNING Mack came by Doreen's house bright and early, and he looked pretty worn out. He glared at her.

She raised both her hands, exclaiming, "It's not my fault."

"Yes, it is," he groused. He walked over to the coffeepot and poured himself a cup. "It's easy to find a gun in town. It's easy to buy a silencer for a gun in town. However, I haven't yet figured out how to explain away the shot fired and the nosy neighbor."

"I was thinking of one thing that could explain it," Doreen noted. He turned to stare at her. "Maybe she wears a hearing aid and takes it out at bedtime."

His eyebrows shot up. "I should have thought of that." He glared down in his coffee. "I did think of all kinds of things, but nothing that really made any sense."

"That's the one thing that I kept coming back to is, if she heard a gunshot, why didn't she phone 9-1-1? And, if she said that she heard it, maybe she really didn't. Maybe because her reputation is so important to her—of knowing all that's going on—so maybe she made it up."

"But that would throw the timeline completely off," Mack grumbled, looking at her in astonishment.

"And yet," she pointed out gently, "we don't know for sure from anybody else that that *is* the timeline. And if that *isn't* the timeline …"

"Then Annabelle's boyfriend's alibi is no good." He threw back the last of his coffee and said, "I'll be back." And, with that, he stormed out of Doreen's house.

She winced as she headed outside to sit on her deck, wondering just what kind of chaos was coming around, because it sounded like Mack was pretty upset over this thing. And with good reason because, if the nosy neighbor had done so much to throw off the timeline that made Joseph the main suspect now, that would be a huge headache for everybody. On the other hand, it's better to find out now and to get back on track.

She waited all morning, working outside, working inside, until finally she couldn't stand it anymore, and she sent a text message. **Well?**

Mack's reply came back almost immediately. **I'll stop by in a little bit.**

She frowned at that, not sure that she believed him, and maybe he was just trying to distract her.

It was possible. Still, not a whole lot she could do. She went back over her notes, pondering everything that she'd heard, wondering just what else she was missing here because it felt like something was missing—something simple, something easy. And she couldn't quite figure out what it was.

Then she realized she didn't have that old lady's name. Realizing her mistake, she was angry with herself because that was something she did want. She quickly asked Mack if he would give her the name of the old lady across from Annabelle's apartment.

He came back with **Why?**

She frowned, not sure what she should say here. And then she just sent back a simple one-liner. **I need to know.**

Finally he sent her a name. **Hannah Hartley.**

She stared at that, wondering if she'd heard it before. However, even as she went through her notes, she couldn't find a match. Frowning, she turned to the internet, and even that wasn't giving her anything.

With a look down at her animals, she hopped up and promised, "I'll be back in a little bit." And she bolted to the library.

She walked in to see what had been the difficult librarian but who now was one who appeared to have made peace with Doreen's curious hobby.

And she looked up, saw the determined look in Doreen's eye, she nodded and said, "You're on Annabelle's case, aren't you?"

"How did you know? I usually work the cold cases."

The librarian shrugged. "Not too many murder cases around right now, and that one's pretty fresh."

"It is. It also means that I'm not really allowed to be on it." Doreen winced. "Because it is a fresh case, then Mack's on it."

"Of course he is," she noted, "but that doesn't mean he doesn't need help."

Doreen laughed at that. "He would say he doesn't need any help."

"Of course he does," the librarian replied. "So what is it you're looking for?"

"Information on a Hannah Hartley," she said.

"*Hannah.*" She frowned. "I don't think I know that name."

"She's an older lady who lives in the same apartment building as Annabelle did."

At that, the librarian's eyebrows shot up. "Interesting. What's she done?"

"Maybe nothing, but I need to see if I can find any history on her." And she headed back to the archives. There she poured over newspapers until her phone rang, jarring her out of her silent concentration. She looked down to find Mack on her Caller ID. She answered the call, catching several other people's disapproving looks because the library was supposed to be dead zone, and here she was with a phone ringing off the hook. She quickly got up, realizing that she was mostly done on the microfiche anyway, and walked out of the library.

Outside, she said, "Okay, I'm on the front entrance to the library, and now I can talk."

He gave a snort. "You mean, they kicked you out of there."

"No, they didn't," she argued, "but I really don't want to lose one of my best resources."

He sighed. "Anyway, I went and talked to her. The neighbor."

"Okay, and?"

"It took quite a bit to get it out of her, but she was sound asleep, and it's not that she has a hearing aid but that she sleeps with earplugs."

"Seriously?"

"Yes. Apparently her hearing is so acute that she can't sleep in the night without getting woken up by various noises, so she sleeps with earplugs."

"How does she know then when Annabelle was shot?"

"And that's where we come to the problem. It was a guess on her part, as the boyfriend found Annabelle after his shift, and the neighbor didn't hear anything at the time."

"Oh, good Lord," Doreen muttered.

"Yeah," Mack agreed, his tone grim. "So I've gone back to the coroner to confirm the time frame and to get something a little tighter that we can look at."

"Well, *looking at* is one thing," Doreen noted, "but pinning it on somebody is a whole different story."

"I know that," Mack stated, adding a word of warning. "I don't want you contacting any of the people involved in this case right now."

"Fine," she grumbled, flinging up her free hand. "Hopefully with this correction, it'll bring enough to the case that you can pop it wide open."

"I don't think that happens in real life," he replied. "That sounds more like a movie plot."

"Hey, it sounds good to me though," she teased.

"I'll talk to you later then." And he quickly hung up.

She stood here for a long moment, realizing just how much more of a problem that was for him. It could mean all kinds of people who had been crossed off the list now had to be brought right back in again—and one in particular. Joseph Moody.

Sure enough, when he called a couple hours later, he was almost panicked.

She was sitting outside on the lawn, had just finished weeding, the animals all around her on the grass. When she realized who was calling, she sat up. "What's the matter?"

"What's the matter?" he roared. "I'm back on the stupid

suspect list," he snapped. "It's that stupid neighbor's fault."

"I don't know what you're talking about," she lied. Of course she did, but he was too irate to even deal with.

"She apparently didn't have a locked-in time frame for when … Annabelle was shot, and apparently it could have been earlier and/or later. So now I am potentially back on the suspect list."

"I'm sorry. I guess that means that your alibi's no longer holding then, *huh*?"

"I was at work, and I didn't have anything to do with it."

"If you didn't have anything to do with it," she noted calmly, "then give the police everything they want, stay calm, and let them do their job."

"Well, if they'd done their job in the first place," he growled, "I wouldn't be in this position."

"What position is that?" she asked curiously, not sure exactly why he was so irate. Obviously nobody wanted to be back on a suspect list, but, considering his reaction and how irate he was, that didn't scream "innocent" either.

"What it's like to have them poking and prying through your life?" he snapped in an ugly tone. "I don't want anything to do with this. I just want to leave town and start over."

"Are you moving on?" she asked.

"I was hoping to. Why? Why wouldn't I?"

She stopped and shrugged. "We all process grief in different ways, so it's not for me to say how you're supposed to act in a situation like this, but I guess maybe, to the police, it would seem suspicious."

"How can it be suspicious?" he cried out, almost in tears as he was so upset. "I lost the one person in my life that I could count on. She was always there for me. That was the reason I came home every night," he admitted. "And now? Now it's like I've gone back to all my old habits. And believe me. They're not pretty." And, with that, he slammed the phone down hard.

She stared at her phone, trying to figure out just what bad habits he might have had and what trouble he was in and whether it had anything to do with Annabelle's case. The problem was, if he wouldn't talk to her, not a whole lot that Doreen could find out on her own.

# Chapter 20

DETERMINED TO GET something solved, Doreen decided to go talk to the nosy neighbor again too. Doreen had some information on Hannah that Doreen needed to go through first. She sat down with her laptop, downloaded the documents that she had sent to herself from the library's archives, and sat here with a cup of tea to read through them. It wasn't long before she had a few notes to sort out herself. She wondered how involved this woman could even be with the earlier murder.

With her list of questions, she looked down at her animals. "Let's go back. We'll drive partway, and then we'll walk."

With that, Mugs rolled onto his back, his feet in the air, almost like he was playing dead.

Surprised, she asked him, "Don't you want to go for a walk?"

Then Mugs hopped to his feet and wagged his tail. Goliath joined him. She looked over to find Thaddeus sound asleep on his roost. She contemplated leaving him behind, but the thought of him waking up to find himself alone was enough for her to walk over and gently stroke his feathers and ask if he wanted to go for a trip. He opened his eyes, seemingly smiled at her, and bobbed his head up and down. "Thaddeus is here. Thaddeus is here."

But his voice was sleepy, as if it was all he could do to stay awake long enough to answer her. She chuckled softly and let him walk up her arm to curl up in the curve of her neck. There he snuggled in close. She smiled and whispered, "It's all right, buddy. We'll be fine."

And she walked out with the animals, quickly set the alarm, and headed down to Hannah Hartley's place. As she got there, Hannah was out in the hallway. She turned and saw Doreen and frowned.

"Why are you back again?" Her tone was cross.

"I came to see you," Doreen replied, with a smile. But instead of the reception she was expecting, Hannah just frowned at her. Doreen waited, her head tilted, trying to figure out what was going on. "You seem to be quite upset."

"Of course I'm upset," she spat. "The police think I lied."

"Ah," Doreen replied, a wealth of meaning in her voice.

"What does that mean?" she asked crossly. "How am I supposed to keep track of everything? That's for them to do."

"Meaning that the time of death wasn't exactly when you thought it was?"

The woman stared at her. "It's as close as I thought it would be."

"But in a court of law," Doreen pointed out, "and in a case like this, it's not based on what you think. We must know for sure."

"Well, it's not for you to know either," she snapped. "You're just a wannabe detective."

"That's quite true," Doreen agreed, "although I am officially looking into this for somebody else."

Hannah stared at her for a moment. "Oh."

"But that's all right," Doreen said gently. "How was it that you got the time wrong?"

"It's not so much that I got it wrong, but I guessed. I didn't check. When I first woke up, I might have dozed off a little bit," she explained. "So when I thought that the shooting happened, it might have, I think, occurred earlier," she muttered. "But now I'm very confused, and I don't know when it happened."

"I'm sure that the coroner will come up with some idea to go on."

"Well, they should have," she declared. "I'm not the one here with all the answers."

"Of course not," Doreen agreed.

And it was obvious Hannah was quite perturbed at having been wrong. And being wrong was hard on a lot of people. In this case Hannah's self-worth or sense of belonging or being needed or whatever drove her seemed to be very much aligned with what she knew.

"You've spent a lot of time keeping an eye on the place, haven't you?"

The older woman nodded slowly. "And, for some people, that just makes me a nosy busybody. But, when you're lonely, that drags you down." Hannah looked quite distraught.

"I'm sorry," Doreen said. "Obviously it's shaken you."

At that, Hannah turned and glared at her. "Most people don't question me," she stated stiffly. "It's a position I'm not used to being in."

"And that makes you uncomfortable."

"Of course it does," she replied crossly, "but I don't deliberately try to send the police in a different direction."

"Oh." Doreen asked, "Is that what they suggested?"

Hannah shrugged. "I don't know what they were trying to suggest, but it certainly set me off anyway." She glared at her. "What do you want?"

"I wondered what the sound was like."

She stared at her. "What difference does it make?" she cried out.

"I wondered if he used a silencer."

She stared at her. "Now what difference would that make?"

"Besides the intent," Doreen began, "it would also be a case of somebody with a lot more experience in this."

Hannah shook her head. "And it doesn't matter. Annabelle's dead."

"Annabelle is dead," Doreen confirmed. "But what we don't know is, if it's connected to her brother's death."

The other woman paled. "That would not be fair. That poor woman has been through enough already."

"Oh, I agree," Doreen said. "And what we don't want is to have anything that leads back to her brother's death. And you do know something about that, don't you?" It wasn't so much a wild guess as her instincts were prodding her to say that.

Hannah glared at Doreen and said in a harsh voice, "I'm not talking to you anymore." Hannah walked into her apartment and slammed the door hard in Doreen's face.

Chances were that she'd react this way. Doreen had just hoped that somebody who liked to talk and to gossip would have been a little more open. Doreen looked down at Mugs. "Not even you seem to have had any magic uplift with her."

Mugs was lying on the carpet and staring at Hannah's front door.

It opened almost immediately, and the woman started yelling, "Get those animals out of here, before I call the super."

"Right." Doreen frowned. "Like that's been a problem up till now, hasn't it?"

"Well, now it is," Hannah snapped. "You need to get out of here. We'll start posting No Trespassing signs around here." She was almost yelling.

"Hardly trespassing," Doreen declared cheerfully. "I came here for a visit."

"Well, you're not welcome anymore." At that, Hannah stepped back inside and slammed the door again.

Slowly Doreen walked back outside with her animals. Even Thaddeus clung deeper into her neck. "I'm sorry, guys. That visit wasn't very much fun, was it?"

As she stepped outside, she looked up at the woman's window to find her staring at her. The curtain was quickly twitched back into place but not before Doreen saw Hannah. Doreen waved in a friendly motion and turned to the parking lot. Several other people were coming in at the same time.

One guy in particular, an older man, brought up the rear. He stopped and asked, "Did you need something, my dear?"

She smiled at him. "I came to talk to Hannah Hartley, but she's not in a mood to talk."

"Ah, the police were up there this morning. I'm sure she's just more upset about that poor dear girl's murder," he replied, shaking his head. "I don't know what this world's come to."

"I know," she murmured. "It's pretty upsetting for everybody."

"It absolutely is," he agreed. "I've been here for a long time, and that girl's been no trouble to anybody."

"I don't suppose you were home on the night of the murder, were you?"

"I was. I came in and got to bed pretty early," he shared, "so I didn't hear anything. Afterward I heard all the commotion from the police coming and going. The gossip is pretty rampant at that point in time."

She nodded and smiled. "I guess. Annabelle's boyfriend asked me to help look into what happened because the police are coming onto him pretty heavily."

"Of course, of course," the older man agreed, giving a wave of his hand. Then he stopped and said, "I know who you are."

She winced. "I'm not sure when people say that whether it's a good thing or not."

He burst out laughing. "You're that amateur sleuth in town, aren't you?"

"Not really what I would like to be called," she murmured. "However, I'm somebody who's had a hand in solving some cases, yes."

He nodded enthusiastically. "I've seen you around. I just didn't recognize all the animals." He paused. "Don't you have a bird?" At that Thaddeus poked his head through the curtain of her hair, and the man burst out laughing. "Oh, I am charmed. Thank you, thank you, thank you. You've just made my day." She raised her eyebrows, and he shrugged. "I go to work. I come home, and it's pretty boring. When my wife was alive, a lot more was going on in my life. However, now? Now it's almost like you just sit here and wait for death to take you." He sighed. "It's pretty sad."

It sounded terribly sad to her. "Are you happy here?" she asked. "What about a retirement home?"

"Oh, those things are terrible," he replied, with a shudder.

"Even Rosemoor? My nan lives there." Then Doreen added, "She's really happy."

He grimaced. "I've never heard of anybody being happy in a home."

She chuckled. "Well, maybe you should pop over there one time and take a closer look. They have a lot of fun. I mean, if lawn bowling isn't your thing, and poker isn't your thing, and the pool table isn't your thing, then maybe it isn't someplace you would like to be. However, I can attest to the food. It's pretty great." She added, "I'm forever over there, getting snacks and tea and coffee, sitting out in the gardens and whatnot."

He looked mildly interested. "My wife was pretty young when she went, and I was thinking I'd end up in a home, down the road, but it's not really where I want to be."

"But if you're all alone here," Doreen noted, "wouldn't it be better to have friends over there?"

"I don't know," he hedged. "I'd have to think about it. Rosemoor, you say?"

She nodded. "Yes, exactly. Did you have anything to do with Annabelle and her boyfriend?"

He shook his head. "Nope, I don't even really know them. They were just one of many couples that I passed all the time, coming and going."

"What about Hannah?"

He rolled his eyes at that name. "I live directly below Hannah. So unfortunately I do have to deal with her on regular occasions."

"Is she a problem?"

"If my music's too loud, I get her banging on my ceiling, her floor," he replied, by way of explanation. "If I have anybody over, and we're talking too loud, she pounds on the door."

"She does apparently have supersensitive hearing," Doreen shared. "And then sleeps with earplugs in."

"Ah, that's why she rarely complains after eleven p.m.," he noted. "It seems to me that she always calmed down at that point in time."

"I suspect that's when she puts in her earplugs," she murmured. "And the night that Annabelle was shot, I guess you didn't see or hear anybody in relation to who might have been here causing trouble."

He shook his head again. "Nope, I really don't have very much to do with anybody in the building. It was different when my wife was alive. She was a little more social than I am," he said. "I just got into that rut. I go to work, come home, just have my own little world."

"Even if you're working, you should have at least some outlet for social activities."

"And that's one of the reasons I do keep working," he admitted. "I don't really need the money, but otherwise I would sit at home and do nothing all day."

"So then you need to contact Rosemoor and see if it would be a place where you might be happy," she urged. "I can tell you that my grandmother—and she's older, in her eighties—is really happy there."

"I'll think about it. Sometimes, every once in a while, you think that you're good to go, and then you realize you've gotten a little bit more limited in what you do and a little bit more housebound than is really good for you," he stated, with a shrug. "If I didn't work, I can't imagine where I'd end up."

He gave her a wave, and she stepped out of the way and said, "Thanks very much for talking to me."

He chuckled. "Anytime I don't stop and talk with a beautiful young woman, something is wrong, and I need to fix it." And, with that, he gave another wave and headed inside.

She smiled, liking a lot about him. He probably would do just fine at Rosemoor. Not only that, he would probably find lots of friends and potential girlfriends for him, if he did move. That was still a concept Doreen struggled to get her mind wrapped around when it came to Nan, but, as long as Doreen didn't spend too much time focusing on it, it was easier.

Nan was happy, and that was all Doreen cared about. She headed over to her vehicle, intent on going to the beach and spending a few hours there, when she looked up to see Hannah staring out the window at her. She smiled and waved again. But this time, Hannah, in a surprising motion, stuck up her middle finger in that age-old salute to tell her off. Surprised at that behavior, Doreen stared at her window for a long moment and then slowly turned and headed to her vehicle. What on earth would have caused Hannah to be so angry? The last thing Doreen had said to Hannah was something about linking the two murders, Annabelle's brother's death to Annabelle's.

So was Annabelle's murder all caught up with the old murder of her little brother?

And that thought just wouldn't let Doreen's brain go. It was a pretty extreme reaction on Hannah's part, and that meant something was there. And, if something was there, Doreen would find it. And then she'd figure out if and when it had anything to do with this mess. Because sure as heck she didn't have a whole lot to go on. Except that somebody had walked into Annabelle's apartment—apparently let in or got in so fast that no fight ensued about their presence inside—and then had shot Annabelle dead.

And a lot earlier than eleven p.m. At least as far as the murder window probably would be per the autopsy, something like nine p.m. to midnight. And, yeah, that would bring Annabelle's boyfriend back into question, but still it wouldn't have been easy. He was at work. If he'd stepped out during his shift, that would easily be found out.

It's not as if he could have walked home, shot her, and then left again, without anybody at the bar knowing that he'd left. At that thought, she stopped and winced because surely he had a break during his shift. And if he did have a break, how long a break? She headed to the beach with her animals. Her mind buzzed with everything that she had learned but yet not learned.

As she sat here in the sand, just off from the area where the animals could sit and enjoy, the place was pretty empty. She stayed here for about an hour, until she got a text from Mack, asking where she was. She texted the name of the beach and added that she'd be heading home in a few minutes.

**I'm picking up steaks**, he announced.

She smiled. **Enough for two of us?**

Instead of texting back, he phoned. "Since when do I not bring enough for the two of us?" he asked curiously.

"Hey, it was just a question," she replied, as she hopped up, bringing the animals with her as she headed back to her car.

"What are you doing at the beach?"

"I came to talk to Hannah and didn't get the reception I was really expecting," she murmured. "We'll talk when I get home." And she quickly hung up, raced to the car, and said, "Come on, guys. Mack's meeting us at the house."

At that, Mugs, for the first time in a while, picked up his ears and woofed in excitement.

She laughed. "Well at least he makes you happy," she noted. And, with them all loaded up in the car, she headed home.

# Chapter 21

DOREEN PULLED INTO her driveway, around Mack's truck, as he'd gotten there ahead of her. She hopped out from the car in her garage, quickly closed the door, and stepped out in the front yard to say hi to him.

He looked down at her. "You look to be in a better mood."

"It was just a weird scenario. Mugs was so happy when I told him we were coming home to meet you." She chuckled, as she got her animals out of her vehicle. "He's been off all morning too. Actually for a couple days now."

"Yeah, a lot of that going around." He smiled, looked down at Mugs, and gave him a big greeting. "But this guy, he's special."

"He's very special," she agreed. "And I'm very suscepti-ble to their moods, especially when they are not quite the same as what I expect." She walked everybody to the front door, unlocked it, and they all trooped into the kitchen. Doreen fed her animals and checked their water bowls, while Mack put the groceries in the refrigerator for now.

"How did they greet Hannah?" he asked, as he took a seat at her kitchen table.

"They were not their usual selves from our first visit. Hannah doesn't like animals and had yelled at me about how no animals were allowed. She was even more unpleasant this time. She was probably pretty shook up after your visit this morning, I think," she added, fixing a pot of coffee for them.

He nodded. "She was by the time we finally finished grilling her. She didn't want to talk to us, wanted to kick us out of the place. I told her that she'd have to come to the station for questioning or she could talk to us now. By the time she finally confessed to not knowing exactly what time the shooting happened, she was in tears, and I suspect that, for a while, she'll be very hesitant about what she says to anybody."

"You're right there, and, in this case, she should be quiet because she didn't know what she was talking about, and that wasted a lot of our time." She shrugged. "All it did was let the boyfriend off the hook, and now Joseph's back on the hook."

Mack laughed. "I suppose you've talked to him too."

"Didn't have much choice," she told him cheerfully. "Joseph called me in a panic."

He nodded.

"He wants to leave town," she shared.

At that, Mack turned slowly.

She shrugged. "I told him that leaving town was probably not a smart idea."

"Not only not smart but that'll get him picked up for questioning pretty darn fast."

"But you've already questioned him, haven't you?" She poured two cups of coffee and joined him at the table.

"We have. I just don't have any motive."

"And yet it's often the partner."

"It is often the partner," he confirmed. "However, we can't just decide it's the partner without proof."

"No, of course not," she agreed. "Still it does make you wonder."

"It does, indeed."

He had said that in such a distracted tone that she asked Mack, "Do you really think he would have done it? Why? By the way, was a silencer used?"

He frowned. "No. Why would you ask that?"

"It just goes back to the fact that Hannah Hartley didn't hear anything."

"We addressed that though."

"We did," she noted, "but it was a residual question."

"No, a silencer was not used," he confirmed.

"So it would have been a loud *pop*. What about the rest of the neighbors?" she asked.

"We've questioned everybody in the building on floors on either side," he shared, "and nothing. Nobody heard anything. But then sometimes even a vehicle outside can backfire, and people think it's a gunshot. Or it's a gunshot, and people think it's just a backfire."

"I know," she said. "I've heard things like that too."

"Exactly. So, even though we think we might have heard something, we aren't really sure. Plus, when there is only one gunshot, then people tend to just dismiss it."

"Until Joseph got home from work."

"Exactly. And that's when he found her, and that's when he called the cops."

She sighed. "Hannah did get very angry, when I brought up the old murder."

He asked, "What do you mean, she got angry?"

Doreen quickly explained what had happened. He sat

back, nonplussed. She nodded. "See what I mean? That's not normal."

"No, it's not normal, but we can't really say that it's much worse than *normal* when it comes to Hannah."

"Maybe not," Doreen agreed, "but it's definitely something that's got my neck itching like crazy. I need to figure out why she feels that way."

"Do you think she had something to do with that prior case?"

"My research just confirmed that she has lived here for many, many years. Other than that, I don't know," she muttered. "It makes no sense."

"Well, it will."

"I know. I know. I know," she said, holding up her hand. "It will when we get all the information, but you also know that sometimes we don't get all the information."

He frowned at her gently. "Too often that's the truth, yes."

"And that gets very frustrating too," she lamented.

"How do you think we feel?" he muttered. "We only get so many days to keep a case in front of us, and then things go cold, and other cases pile on top."

She nodded. "And I get that. Believe me. I certainly don't judge you guys for the job you do. It's not easy, and the more I do this, ... the more I realize that."

"Good," he replied. "Makes us feel not quite so bad. Yet we do the best we can. It's just that sometimes even our best isn't good enough."

She winced. "I didn't plan to make you all depressed again. So let's cook dinner and forget about this." She hopped up and asked, "Did you pick up anything to go with the steaks?"

"No, last time I was here, you had carrots and lettuce—although I probably should have checked again, just in case."

"I still have the carrots." She pulled them out and set them on the counter. "Can you put them on the barbecue?"

He nodded. "We can, or we can make a carrot salad."

She looked at the carrots and frowned. "You can make a salad out of carrots?"

He burst out laughing, wrapped an arm around her, and gave her a quick hug. "Don't change. You're way too much fun to be around.'

"Ha. I'm fun until all this becomes not fun, and then everybody just wants me to smarten up."

"Nope," he disagreed. "That's not true. Everybody just wants you to be you."

# Chapter 22

*Monday Morning...*

THE NEXT MORNING, Doreen woke and decided that she would start in right away on this Annabelle case. And as soon as she had her first cup of coffee, she phoned Nathan. He was just getting ready for his construction job.

"Is there a reason why you're calling me?" he asked hesitantly.

"Did you know a Hannah Hartley from way back when?"

"Sure. I used to do her lawns too."

"Ah, I never even thought of that."

"Well, I did know a lot of people because I did those kinds of jobs, ... a lot actually," he replied. "She was pretty upset that I had gotten involved in this mess. Like a lot of people."

"Did she have any connection to Kurt, the friend of yours who was involved in this?"

"I don't think so," he replied, but then he paused. "Honestly I don't remember. That was a long time ago."

"That's fine. Think about it, and, if you come up with something, just let me know."

"I still don't understand why you're going back over all this old ground again," he said.

"Have you seen your friend Kurt since you've been out of jail?"

He hesitated, then reluctantly replied, "Once."

"Ouch, that wouldn't have been good."

"No, it wasn't. Basically he warned me to not cause him any trouble." Nathan sighed. "As if I went to jail and did eight years just to cause him trouble now."

"Nope, that sounds sensible on your part," she stated gently.

"I don't know. I just ... I just want to stay on the straight and narrow and do my dad proud now. He's got enough health issues. I don't want to be getting into trouble and stressing him more."

"No, and I'm not trying to get you into any trouble at all," she said. "I am trying to solve Annabelle's murder."

He sighed at that. "I wish I had some answers for you. I really do, but I've got to go to work right now. I can't afford to lose my job."

She let him off the hook quickly and sat here sipping her coffee, as she thought about this more. And then she picked up the phone and phoned Millicent. As soon as Mack's mother answered the phone, Doreen asked, "Did you know Hannah Hartley?"

"Oh my, that's a name from the past."

"Well, the woman is still alive, so I'm not sure how much in the past it is."

"It's a past because that's how we prefer to keep it," Millicent responded. "That woman is one of the nosiest people in town, a gossip, a terrible, ... terrible gossip. And if she didn't have something to say and didn't know something, she'd make it up."

Doreen winced at that because that's essentially what Hannah had done when giving the cops the wrong time frame for the shooting of Annabelle.

"Hannah may have learned her lesson now," she said gently to Millicent.

"Oh, I don't know. We haven't had anything to do with her for years. Why would you even bring up that name?" she asked.

"I just met her the other day," Doreen replied. "And wondered, when I mentioned something about the old murder with Nathan Landry, why she got so really angry about it."

"Well, she used to hire Nathan, the same as we did, and I know that she was pretty fond of the kid at the time. So I'm not surprised by her reaction to your questions," Millicent stated. "But then another boy was close to Nathan as well, and I think he was close to her too. So I'm not sure how that worked out. I don't know the details on that, but I do know that Hannah is somebody you should stay away from," she declared in a severe tone. "Mark my words, that old gal's up to no good."

"Well, that's a good warning," Doreen noted carefully. "I mean, obviously I don't have any reason to have anything to do with her."

"Good," Millicent said, her voice pretty strident. "I don't have much bad to say about anybody in this world, but I do want to warn you about Hannah. ... That woman is trouble."

"Just because she lies and gossips?"

"Yes, and something was always *off* about her. Part of the reason that we stopped having anything to do with her was she was pretty protective of some of the kids around here, *too protective*, as if they were hers, and they sure as heck weren't hers," Millicent shared. "And I'm sure Mack doesn't remember her, but, even years back, we had to warn her to stay away from him and Nick."

"Seriously?"

"Yep, she just wanted them to come over and to spend time with her, but it was *off*. Like she should have had her own children. If she did, I never heard about it, and she certainly never shared any information as to whether she had children, at least I don't think so. Or maybe she had them and lost them. I don't know. Something was dodgy about the whole thing."

"Interesting," Doreen murmured.

"Again, I don't know about *interesting*," Millicent disagreed, getting visibly upset.

"Sorry. I'm not trying to upset you. I just wondered if you knew Hannah."

"Well, I do, and she is bad news."

"Okay, good enough," Doreen noted. "In that case, I'll try to minimize my contact. I don't think she'll want anything to do with me anyway right now. She was pretty angry at me the last time I saw her."

"Good," Millicent declared. "Angry is better than friendly."

"No, not necessarily," Doreen clarified. "Sometimes angry people do all kinds of stupid stuff."

"They do," Millicent agreed. "You're right there. Just stay away from her, please, please."

As she sounded even more and more worried, Doreen assured her, "Honest, I'll try to. I was just looking for anybody connected to Nathan's case back then, that's all."

"You need to find that other boy," Millicent suggested. "That's the one who's got all the answers to this mess," she stated. "Now I'll go have a cup of tea and try to forget that woman's name." With that, Millicent hung up too.

Doreen was definitely surprised at Millicent's strident view of Hannah. Yet, having seen Hannah's change of personality while Doreen was there yesterday, she could also confirm Millicent's view. With a sigh, Doreen made herself breakfast, fed her animals, checked their water bowls, and sat outside again.

When Nathan called her a little bit later, he said, "The answer is yes. I did see him. *Kurt.* Just briefly and again, yes, he did warn me, but he didn't threaten me or anything."

"Did you two know Hannah Hartley?"

"Yes, but, like I said, not very well."

"Did Kurt know her better than you did?"

"I don't know. However, because we hung out all the time together, then he would see Hannah sometimes when I mowed her yard."

"Right. Would Kurt have had anything to do with killing Annabelle?"

"No. Why would he?"

"I don't know. You went and talked to her. Is there anything that you would have mentioned to her that would have upset Kurt, if he had seen you there at Annabelle's apartment?"

"How could he have seen me?"

"Hannah Hartley lives across the hallway from her."

At that revelation, he stopped a moment. "I would have stopped in and said hi, if I knew."

"Well, you still can. I can't because she's quite irate with me at the moment."

"She does have a temper," he noted apologetically. "You also don't come off as someone easy to be around, with all your questions and stuff."

"Right," she murmured. "Anyway she is living in the apartment literally across from Annabelle."

"I wonder if that was on purpose," he muttered.

"Why?"

"Well, because Hannah always kept close to the family after the shooting. I know that Annabelle's parents had some problems right afterward, and Annabelle used to go over to Hannah's all the time, just more as a way to be in a safe zone. Like where people were around you."

"How do you know that?"

"Because she told me. Annabelle and I kept in touch while I was in jail."

"Seriously?"

"Yes, that's one of the reasons my father told me that I should contact her afterward, after I got out."

"I didn't know that," Doreen muttered.

"Well, it doesn't change anything though, does it?"

"No, I don't think so," she replied cautiously. "I mean, it shows that you and Annabelle at least had a reasonably civil relationship prior to that face-to-face meeting."

"Yes, but we didn't have a *relationship*," he corrected, with quiet emphasis. "Yet I did count her as my friend. At the same time, I know I was somebody that her family wouldn't have liked her to be hanging out with. They never liked me, and she didn't tell them about me being pen pals with her while I was in prison. At least I don't think so. And when I saw her that night, we were both crying."

"Of course you were," Doreen noted, with quiet empathy. "It was a hard time in both your lives."

"Yeah, and yet then, just a few days later, she's dead," he muttered bitterly. "She was a good person. She didn't deserve that."

"No, none of that family deserved anything that happened to them," she reminded him. "And that just adds to the family's pain now."

"I can't imagine," Nathan replied. "I just can't imagine what they're going through."

"No, I can't either," she admitted. "And obviously it's a trying time for them now. I don't know if they're coming into town for her funeral or what they're doing about Annabelle's body, but I know that the boyfriend just left the apartment with everything as it is."

"Of course he did," Nathan said in disgust. "I did ask her if she was happy, and she hesitated. I told her, if she wasn't, she should get out and find someone better because life was too short. Even when you thought you had all the time in the world, … sometimes things happen, and you end up in a really ugly place in life. Then, before you know it, your freedom is taken away from you."

She was silent for a long moment.

He added, "And I shouldn't complain about it because I am alive. Lots of people in jail didn't even get that far. … It wasn't an easy life there, but I kept hanging on to the fact that I would do my time and that I would get out and that I would never get into trouble again."

"And, as soon as you get out, look what happens," she muttered.

"Right? And just after I saw her."

"Which is why I had to seriously wonder if somebody was setting you up to take the fall."

He gave a startled exclamation. "It's possible," he replied

cautiously, "but I don't know who that could be. The case was pretty simple."

"I was thinking of this friend of yours. What benefit would there be for Kurt to send you back to prison is the real question."

"I don't know. No reason as far as I can see."

"Did you do any robberies with Kurt ahead of time? Is there any money that he thinks that you might be after, now you're out, that he doesn't want to give you?"

"I don't know," he said. "I certainly didn't rob anyone. Besides, it was so long ago that I, … I basically wrote it all off."

"Maybe, and maybe there's another reason," she murmured. "We need to figure out what it is before somebody else gets killed, just to make you look guilty. You look after your dad," she added, "just in case."

"Don't even say things like that," Nathan cried out. "I mean, if my dad were to die, I don't know what I'd do. But again, why would anybody want to kill him? I don't even wanna go there." His tone was utterly bewildered.

"Did that friend of yours ever stay at your house?"

"Yes."

"And did Kurt know Annabelle ahead of time?"

"Sure, we all did. She was just a kid, our age, and her brother was just a little boy," he related.

"So you didn't have any relationship with her?"

"No, no. I mean, my friend kept making comments about her all the time because she was pretty special, but that's all it was."

"He didn't get to be obnoxious? He didn't do anything to hurt her or anything like that?"

"No, no, not at all," Nathan said. "You're way off base

there."

"Okay, I'm just trying to figure out why Kurt would want to take you out or to make it look like you had killed somebody else again because you would go back to jail, and why would Kurt want that? What is it that you know that he doesn't want you to tell me, or what is it that he has that he doesn't want you to have?"

"What I don't have is freedom. Even now. ... Everybody's looking at me sideways. They are waiting for me to mess up again."

"I know. I get that. I guess Annabelle's boyfriend wouldn't have had anything to do with your friend Kurt, would he?"

"I don't know why or how. They don't exactly move in the same circles."

"Does your friend ever go to pubs?"

"What do I know?" he replied. "I haven't seen Kurt in years, except for that one time, and at that point he was more or less telling me to get out of town and to stop being a pain in his backside."

"See? I think he got the impression that, when you were released, you'd go anywhere else but here."

"Why? I mean, I did my time. I'm allowed to be here. I have less of a life here, but my family is here."

"Sure," she agreed, trying to feel her way through all this. "So it comes back to the possibilities that Kurt either thought you weren't going to return here, or that you would not contact Annabelle.

"But again how would he know?" Nathan asked Doreen.

"Because of Hannah. I know she saw you there, visiting Annabelle. And, if she has any contact with Kurt, she could easily have told him."

"But why would Kurt care?" Nathan cried out. "We didn't have anything to do with each other since the accident, so it makes no sense at all."

"Okay. Let me just work my way through this, and then we'll figure it out," Doreen explained. "So stay calm, don't do anything rash. You stay in town, go to work, look after your dad—and whatever you do, don't go out to pubs, don't go out anywhere for the next few weeks, okay?"

He hesitated.

"I mean it," she declared. "You need to keep your nose clean, to have an alibi for every moment to ensure the cops don't have any reason to look at you sideways. At least for the next few days, okay?"

"No, that's fine," he replied. "You just spooked me when you mentioned my dad."

"I don't want anything to happen to you or your dad, and I sure as heck don't want anything to happen because of something from a long time ago."

"No, I don't either," Nathan agreed, "but now? Now you got me worried."

"So go to work and then go home and stay home," she repeated. "I mean it. If I come up with anything that makes any sense, I'll contact you."

"Fine," Nathan said, "but it needs to happen fast, I can't handle too much more of this. I'm already getting completely stressed and overwhelmed."

"I get that," she noted, "but some of this could take time."

"Why, why does it take time?" he cried out in frustration. "You'd think people would want to help," he muttered bitterly. "Annabelle didn't deserve any of this."

"No, she didn't. She was a sweetheart, and she loved

everybody. But not everybody loved her, if she was shot point-blank."

"No," he agreed. "And I hope that jerk rots in a cell."

"I do too," she said gently. "But hoping won't get us answers. What we need is to find out who would have been there that night of Annabelle's death, who could have seen him. But the biggest thing is motive. Why Annabelle? And if it's connected to the shooting of her brother, then it's connected to you. And we have to make sure Kurt doesn't take you down again."

"I deserved it the last time," he admitted, "and I'll spend the rest of my life paying for it, but I didn't have anything to do with Annabelle's death."

"And you also know that," she began, "although the police will try to be fair, if the case looks good, they'll take you to town and hope that they can pin it on you regardless."

"I know," he said, his voice heavy. "So you've got a few days, but that's about it."

"And then what?" she asked, her voice rising in alarm. "You need to stay out of this because anything that goes wrong, it'll come back to bite you."

He gave a bitter laugh. "It looks to me like it's already biting," he snapped. "I just want to make sure that I won't get charged with something I didn't do. I'm the first one to admit, I screwed up last time. I screwed up in a big way. And my buddy got off because I didn't want to do anything except pay my price and walk forward again. But I won't do that a second time, not if it's not necessary. I didn't do anything here. I won't go down for this. And, if my buddy's involved, you can bet that I want to make sure he pays this time around. Not me."

"The only person who'll pay," Doreen stated, "is whoever did this. That's all we care about, making sure the truth comes out and Annabelle's death is not left unpunished. And I don't know whether it's connected to your deal, to one of her customers or to one of her boyfriend's customers. We have to make sure that, whatever the deal, it's something the police can convict for. We do not need a mess. And, as Mack mentioned, I swear I cannot have this guy get off the hook on technicalities."

"Got it," Nathan agreed. Then he reminded her, "Remember, you got a few days."

"But you can't do anything stupid now or later," she warned. "I do want to find that friend of yours though."

"Good luck with that. That won't be easy."

"Maybe not, but now that I have a name, it'll give us something."

"Maybe, maybe not. This guy's a chameleon. We were young and stupid back then, but he's had eight years to perfect his skills," Nathan noted. "So I wouldn't count on it. He could look like anybody that you see on a regular basis, and nobody'll know the difference."

"So then really," she added, "if he's in town, and if he's using a disguise, it all comes back around to Annabelle and what she might have said or seen that makes this guy so scared that he killed her. That's what I want to know."

# Chapter 23

K URT CHANDLER WAS just the name on her mind, but one that wouldn't let go. She couldn't understand what possible reason he could have had for contacting Annabelle or for wanting Annabelle dead. The only connection Doreen could even begin to see was her brother's murder. Nathan had already been convicted and had done time for it. He should have been safe now, able to walk away.

And yet Nathan had seen his friend Kurt once, and Nathan was trying to stay away from him, and Nathan had spoken to Annabelle too. Yet apparently they had corresponded over the years while he was in jail and afterward too. At that, she picked up the phone, determined to see what Joseph Moody had to say about that.

When he answered, he said, "I sure hope you have something to get the cops off my back."

"Oh, so now I'm supposed to look into your case again?" she asked in a dry tone.

He groaned. "This is hardly the time to joke."

"Maybe not," she agreed, "but again, if you haven't done anything wrong, just give them a chance to sort through this."

"Have you seen how well they're doing at that?" he asked in disgust. "I'm on the suspect list. I'm off. I'm on. I'm off."

"Well, until it's solved, just expect yourself to be on the list," she told Joseph.

At that, he freaked. "I can't be on it. I need to leave. I need to get out of here."

"I wouldn't suggest you running off because the cops will look at that in a very dim way," she muttered.

"It's not running off," he snapped. "But how do they expect anybody to survive this?"

"The same way anybody else does," she said. "You persevere. One day at a time."

He snorted through the phone, and, if he had been here in person, she imagined he would have had an awful lot more to say to her face. But, as it was, the phone gave him a little bit less personal interference.

"I don't even know what to say anymore," he replied, calming slightly.

"Well, only say whatever answers the questions that people need."

"Sure, but why these kinds of questions?" he asked in bewilderment. "I don't know anything."

"Maybe that says something too," she pointed out. "I mean, it sounds like you didn't know Annabelle all that well."

After a moment's hesitation, he said, "I'm starting to realize that too. Not so much from the relationship but because I can't answer a lot of these questions everybody keeps bugging me about."

"Who has been asking you questions?"

"The cops, *you*," he snapped.

TOES UP IN THE TULIPS

"Anybody else?" she asked.

"No, no, no, and no." Then he added, "Well, yes, a couple of my friends. They're all asking me what's going on and how come the case hasn't been solved yet. What am I supposed to say to that? I don't have any answers for them."

"You might not have answers, but the police are working on it."

"Well, you have more faith in the police than I do," he snapped.

She winced at that because she was always about keeping things positive and knew that Mack was doing the best job he could. Even now she had a much better understanding of just how hard it was on anybody to do that job, especially when people lied and cheated all the time. "That's true. I do have a lot of faith in them. You need to keep the faith as well."

"Why?" he snapped. "It's not as if they're doing me any favors."

"They're solving your partner's death," she reminded him. "A little compassion and understanding would go a long way."

"That's bullshit," he growled into the phone. "I had nothing to do with it."

"And now I have a few other questions I need to ask. Whether you can answer them is a different story."

"The answer is probably a no right off the bat," he declared.

"Hopefully you can shed some light on it."

"What?" he snapped.

"Did you know that Annabelle had kept in touch with her brother's shooter while he was in jail?"

There was a moment of silence. "She what?"

Doreen sighed at that. "I gather you didn't know that she kept in touch with the guy who was charged and convicted and in jail for the killing of her brother."

"Why would she do that?" Joseph asked in astonishment.

"So all this time you didn't hear her mention emails or letters back and forth or visits?"

"Visits too? I'm not sure she would do something like that," he muttered. "She never said anything to me about it."

"Are you sure?"

"What do you mean, am I sure?" he asked. "Of course I'm sure. I don't remember her talking about him at all."

"She didn't say she wanted to keep in touch? You didn't have a fight about it?"

An odd silence followed.

She pressed her point. "Are you sure? It's very important."

"Do you think that jerk killed her?" he asked, his voice dark, threatening.

"No, I don't," she said.

"Then why are you asking?" he cried out.

"Because it's a connection that I need to follow up with somebody else," she replied, "but I need to know what she knew, what she was doing, and what she might have had to say about him."

"I called him a loser," he snapped. "And we obviously argued on that point."

She winced at that. "What was the outcome then?"

"The outcome was, we didn't talk about it again."

"How long ago did you have this argument?"

"I only found out a little while ago," he admitted. "Even then I was pretty pissed off about it."

"Why?" she asked.

"What do you mean, why? I mean, she's keeping up conversations with a criminal. Who does that?"

"Lots of women," Doreen replied.

"Yeah, I know about those supposed jailhouse romances," he said. "I just never thought that she would be the kind to do it."

"Activists are also involved in the wrongfully accused and jailed. But you don't know all that much about why she was doing it, correct?"

"No, she said she felt bad about it. She knew it was an accident and didn't agree with his going to jail."

"What about the other guy? Did she say anything about that?"

"What other guy?" Joseph asked.

"Two men were involved in the altercation when the gun went off."

"I don't know anything about that," he said. "She had a soft spot for this guy, and I certainly didn't agree with it."

"Right, because, once you make a mistake, it's always a mistake, is that it?"

"Exactly. The guy shot a kid, for crying out loud. Who does that?"

It seemed to be his favorite comment at the moment. Doreen thought about it and asked, "So Annabelle doesn't have any correspondence from him?"

"I'm sure she does in her emails, but I don't have the laptop."

"You might not have her laptop, but I'm sure you know what her log-in is."

"Yeah, sure." And he rattled off a series of numbers and letters.

Doreen just managed to capture it on paper. "What's her email address?" she asked. He gave it to her. "And yours?"

"Why?" he snapped.

"In case there's any information that I need to send you," she replied smoothly.

He groaned and gave it to her. "Now would you leave me alone? Unless you've got something to give to the cops that'll get me out of this, I don't want to talk to you again. I just want to leave town. Besides," he added, "even if there was some mention of this other guy, who cares? The guy's probably still in jail."

"I'm not sure whether he is or not," she said. "I just want to make sure that there wasn't any odd connection there that I need to know about."

"Well, Annabelle certainly had an odd connection with people. But I can't tell you whether it was this guy or someone else," he snapped. "She was a good person, so you can't judge her for that."

"I have no intention of judging her at all," Doreen stated. "I mean, if she felt bad because he ended up serving time, I can understand that."

"How? How can you understand that?" he cried out again. "This guy killed somebody. And he deserves to pay for it."

"But he did," she replied. "When does he ever *not* pay for it?"

"As far as I'm concerned, never. And, if he did it once, … I guess he'll do it again. As far as I'm concerned, he's the one who killed her."

"And yet you saw them."

"I did. Well, at least I knew when she'd talked to him face-to-face," he amended. "I still think it's ridiculous. I was pretty angry, and we had a hell of a fight over it."

"You keep mentioning that you had a hell of a fight over it," she mentioned. "And why would I then not wonder if that fight had brought out a little bit more anger on your part than you were expecting."

He snorted at that. "Oh no, you don't. I'm allowed to be angry when she talks to an ex-con all the time," he snapped. "That's BS to try and pin this on me just because of that."

"I need more information then," she stated calmly. "As in everything you can remember about the conversation and didn't mention. Did they talk at all about this other guy?"

"She didn't mention it."

"Nowhere along the last few years did she mention this other criminal."

"No, not as far as I know. Just that he was more to blame than this Nathan character."

Even hearing Nathan's name brought up made her eyebrows shoot up. "Interesting," she murmured.

"Why?" Joseph asked.

"Just interesting that Nathan's name had come up enough that you would remember it."

"It's hard not to remember it." Joseph shrugged. "I was around town when the shooting happened way long ago, you know."

"Right. That's an interesting point too."

"Why? So that makes me guilty in his murder now?" he asked in disgust. "You're just trying to find something to pin this on me. You're supposed to be finding something to get the cops off me." And, with that, he hung up.

She pondered that for a long moment. He was right. In theory she was supposed to be helping the cops to prove that Joseph had nothing to do with Annabelle's murder. But, at the same time, something was there. He had not mentioned before that he knew Annabelle back when her brother had been murdered. Doreen hadn't expected that. Yet he was in her life early on, so maybe that was part of the connection that Annabelle had with him now. Maybe that was why she stayed with Joseph because he was part of that whole mess with her brother. Maybe because it kept her connected in some twisted way to her brother.

Doreen was sure the shrinks would have a heyday with that theory, but it made a sad kind of sense. Some people, like Joseph Moody, seemed to want to run away and to start fresh, and others clung to the sense of familiarity. Doreen wondered whether a scenario like that actually helped them move away from the trauma or caused them to keep all that trauma with them?

In Doreen's case, it had all just come with her. She'd ended up taking a long time before she could start to deal with it. That thought alone had urged her to consider seeing a therapist. But not right now. She had things on her mind, things to do, places to go, and people to talk to—somebody else, like Millicent.

And almost as if Millicent were listening in, Doreen's phone rang, and she looked down to see who was calling. "Hey, Millicent," she greeted Mack's Mom. "Everything okay?" There was a moment's hesitation, at which Doreen frowned. "Are you okay?"

"I'm ... I'm fine," she replied. "I'm just getting a bit forgetful."

"I think at your age you're entitled to that," she murmured. "Did you need something? Is there something in the garden bothering you?"

"No, the garden's fine," she said. "I just thought maybe

TOES UP IN THE TULIPS

you were coming soon."

"I'm not due to come for a few more days yet," she noted, making a generalization. "Would you like some company?"

"Oh my, yes. Would you mind coming for a cup of tea?"

"Not at all," Doreen replied. "I was looking to call you anyway. I have a couple questions I wanted to ask."

"Oh, perfect," Millicent replied in joy. "Then I don't feel bad."

Doreen chuckled. "You don't have to feel bad anyway. I'll walk over with the animals."

"Oh, that would be lovely." And, with that, she hung up.

Doreen looked down at her animals and asked them, "Instead of Nan's, how about we go over to Millicent's?"

Mugs woofed, and Thaddeus just cocked his head, staring at her, as if he didn't make a connection.

She smiled at him. "We'll go over and see Mack's mom and do some gardening."

The gardening she would do just if something really bothered Millicent. Doreen had to keep in mind that Mack was paying for all the work that she did, so she couldn't exactly go overboard on that just to get a few extra bucks. She was fine with money at the moment too, and that was something else she had to remember.

With the animals in tow and a bottle of water, Thaddeus walking this time because he didn't want to ride—at least for the first bit—she slowly started her menagerie in the direction of Millicent's place. The walk was a bit longer, but that was okay. She would make it there eventually.

By the time they arrived, Millicent was peering around the backyard, looking for them. When she saw them, her

225

face lit up.

And Doreen realized just how lonely Millicent was. It wouldn't be a hardship to visit a little more often, but some of the time Doreen was just busy, and it was hard to remember. She'd have to mention it to Mack and see if he could make more visits. Plus Doreen needed to talk to Nick to ask if he was planning to move back.

With those thoughts, she pulled out her phone, and, even as she walked toward Millicent, she texted Nick. **Your mom's lonely. Can't you move closer?** And then she put away her phone and walked up and greeted her.

"Oh, there you are, dear," Millicent said. "Sometimes it just seems like the days are endless, and nothing ever changes."

Doreen didn't have the same boring routine in her world, but she could understand from Millicent's perspective. "I'm here now," she said gently. "So let's have a visit, and, if anything's bothering you in the garden, I can take care of it."

"Oh, thank you, dear. I think the garden's just fine." Yet she was looking around, as if something were off-kilter.

"Not that I'm looking for the work though," Doreen reminded her. "I am fine now. At least for a little while."

"And thank heavens for that," Millicent cried out. "I mean, you've done so well, and at least somebody is helping you."

"Well, the reward money is always nice," she admitted. "And to know that I'm doing a job to help other people, well, that's nice too."

At that, Millicent pointed to a large coffee urn. "I thought maybe you'd like coffee this time."

"I always like coffee," Doreen said, with a bright smile.

She walked up to the small deck and sat down beside Millicent.

At that, Thaddeus, who had long ago given up walking, poked his head out from under her hair and cried out, "Thaddeus is here. Thaddeus is here."

Millicent laughed and laughed. "Oh my. It's such a joy to have them here."

"They certainly bring a lot of joy to my life," Doreen murmured, "especially Thaddeus, with all his craziness."

"Yes, but it's a good craziness," Millicent noted gently. "We all could use a bit more of that too."

Doreen smiled and watched, as the older woman poured coffee for her. Doreen really was happy to have another cup of coffee.

And when their cups were filled and Millicent sat back down again, Doreen began, "I wanted to ask you about Annabelle and Joseph."

She frowned at Doreen, shook her head, and clarified, "I didn't know them. I just knew Nathan."

"Okay, and what about Nathan's friend, Kurt Chandler?"

She paused at that and frowned. "That's a name from a long time ago."

"Yes, exactly," Doreen murmured. "He was involved in the altercation that killed Annabelle's brother."

"Oh dear, that was such a sad story," Millicent replied. "I mean, such a horrible thing to happen. And that young girl, she was so close to her brother too."

"So I understand," Doreen added. "And apparently she also kept in touch with Nathan, while he was in jail." Millicent seemed surprised to hear this. Doreen nodded. "I guess Annabelle felt like her brother's death had been an accident and that Nathan shouldn't have gone to jail for so long."

"That was very sweet of her," Millicent noted, looking at Doreen, "but somebody does have to pay the price for these kinds of things."

"And sometimes people, and not always the right people, pay a bigger price than others," Doreen murmured.

At that, Millicent raised an eyebrow.

"Apparently this other person, Kurt Chandler, was at the scene, and he and Nathan were fighting, and that's when the gun went off."

"Yes, yes, I remember that now." Millicent gave a sage nod. "But Nathan fired the gun. And the other guy was defending himself."

"Exactly." Then Doreen stopped and asked, "But what if it was the other way around?"

Millicent frowned in confusion. "What do you mean?"

"What if the other guy was attacking Nathan, and the gun went off."

"But it doesn't change anything, does it though?" Millicent asked. "It was Nathan's gun. He brought it to the fight. It was in his hand supposedly." She looked at Doreen, still frowning.

Doreen shrugged. "I'm not exactly sure on the details on that case, but I presume so."

"So, even if they were in a fight, I mean, it still doesn't change anything."

"No, except for the fact that one person didn't have to pay a price."

"Maybe," Millicent agreed, "but I don't think anybody'll convict him on something that was buried eight years ago, especially where somebody else already served time."

"You see? That's the part I don't really understand." Doreen smiled at Millicent. "I'll have to talk to your sons about it."

"You certainly know how to contact them." Millicent laughed. And then she got serious and stared at Doreen. "I really would like to see Mack settled."

Doreen froze. "Oh?" she asked carefully. "You don't think he's settled?"

At that, she steadily shook her head. "He's never married, and I had him very late in life, and I'm definitely feeling the pressure of age."

"So you want to put a little pressure on me, *huh*?" she asked, with a laugh.

Millicent almost looked relieved to hear Doreen's response. "You are such a good person. I'm really hoping that you and Mack can make this work."

"I'll tell you what I tell everybody else about this right now," Doreen began. "And believe me. You're not the first person to bring it up, but I am still legally married. So, until all that is settled, I am not prepared to move forward in any way."

Millicent nodded. "Oh, I didn't realize you were still married."

Doreen gave a one-arm shrug. "And it's not something that I like to talk about because that was a very difficult time in my life. However, it was the impetus that sent me here. Your other son, Nick, is the one who's helping me finalize my divorce."

"Oh, well, in that case, I'm pretty sure I can leave it in his capable hands."

Doreen went off in a peal of laughter. "Please do. Now I don't know why or how he decided to take on my case, but believe me. I am grateful. My husband is not a nice person, and I wasn't looking forward to a fight."

"Right, right, right. It was your other lawyer who died too, wasn't it?" Millicent asked in fascinated curiosity.

"Yes. Yes, it was." Doreen made a funny face. "You know what they say about lawyers."

At that, Millicent chuckled. "I do. I've heard so many attorney jokes in my life. And I used to tell them too, until my son became one." She grinned. "And then you have to wonder because Nick is a good guy."

"He is, indeed," Doreen agreed.

"But it's Mack you're stuck on, isn't it?" Millicent asked, probing.

Doreen sighed. "Yes, I do like Nick, but it's Mack I'm stuck on."

"Well, I'm grateful," she said. "I think Mack really likes you. I think it would break his heart if you weren't as stuck on him as he is on you."

Even just the phraseology made her uncomfortable. And yet *stuck* seemed to be not a bad definition of what was going on in their world. "We will sort it out in our own time. Mack knows perfectly well how I feel about still being married."

"Yes, yes, yes. That's absolutely fair," Millicent said, "and I have to applaud you for your morals in that regard."

Doreen wasn't sure that it was something to be applauded because a lot of people thought Doreen was just being plain stupid about it. However, that's how she felt, and, if that's how she felt, then that's how she would live her life. She took a sip of the coffee. "So back to these two men in question, Nathan and Kurt," she said. "Do you know anybody else who was connected to the case back then?"

"Just that Annabelle had to give witness testimony."

Doreen nodded at that. "Maybe I need to see that testimony."

"Well, if you could, that might clear up any confusion in your mind," Millicent noted gently.

"That's worth a lot too," Doreen murmured.

"Absolutely it is," Millicent confirmed. "I mean, nothing is worse than thinking that something is going on but not having any way to prove it or even to have any means to check out whether something is there or not."

And, with that, the two of them returned to a different conversation.

As Doreen was readying to leave, Millicent added, "Don't keep him waiting too long, will you, dear?"

She looked down at the older woman and nodded, seeing the worry of a mother's despair in the back of her eyes. "I wasn't planning on it, but these things must happen in their own time."

Millicent nodded. "I'm glad Nick's helping you."

"I am too. He's a good guy. You've done very well with both of them."

Millicent brightened. "Thank you. I don't think we get very much credit in this world for being a mother. It's one of the most thankless jobs, and yet, at the same time, one of the most rewarding."

Doreen chuckled. "And that I have no doubt, yet I have no experience at all in any way with kids," she admitted. "So I really don't know what I could even say to that."

"You'll find out, just give it time." And, with that, Millicent slowly stood. "I'll go lie down now."

"You do that," Doreen replied, watching the older woman walk inside, and a little bit of worry gnawed at how slow her movements were. But still, it had been a slightly uncomfortable and yet probably necessary talk in order to make Millicent feel a little bit better.

As for Doreen, an awful lot of people were curious about her relationship with Mack, and she just didn't know what to say to anybody anymore. She could hardly tell people to back off and to get out of her life when what did she spend her time doing? Poking her nose into everybody else's business.

So it seemed fair that other people were poking their noses into hers.

# Chapter 24

DOREEN WAS ALMOST back home again when her phone buzzed. She looked down to see it was Nick. She answered the call, "Hey. Problems?"

"No, not problems. What was that about Mum?"

"Oh, yeah. I just came back from there. She invited me for coffee."

"Coffee or gardening?"

"In this case, coffee. I think she was just really lonely. Of course then she had a chance to dig into the, you know, the *parent special*."

He gave a bark of laughter. "I'm not sure I want to know, but what is the *parent special*?"

She chuckled. "What are my intentions with Mack."

After a moment of dead silence, he laughed and laughed. She was grinning herself, when he finally calmed down. "Oh my, I cannot imagine."

"Well, that's good. Believe me. My imagination was more than enough for both of us."

He gasped into chuckles again. "So, as a brother, do I get to ask what your intentions are as well?"

"No, you don't," she snapped. "I'll tell you what I told

your mother. Until I am divorced, there is absolutely no forward progress. Mack and I are great friends, but I'm not prepared to do more than that or to go in any other direction, not while I am still legally married."

"Got it," Nick confirmed, but still laughter filled his voice. "I guess I'd better get that divorce done fast, *huh*?"

"Yeah, I guess it depends on who you're talking to at any given day. Your mother wants grandkids, so she wants you to hurry up with that paperwork," Doreen shared. "Yet some days ... I think your brother wishes he had never met me."

"I'm sure everybody has those days, but I'm also sure that he's overjoyed to have you in his life."

"Well, that's a lovely thing to say," she murmured. "It still doesn't change anything."

"Are you sure?" he asked in a teasing voice. "You could become my sister-in-law."

"Oh my God," she said. "I am so far away from even thinking about something along that line. Don't even mention that to Mack."

He burst out laughing.

She closed her eyes and stood still, even though she was at the creek. "Have you guys already discussed this?" she demanded to know.

"Of course not," Nick said. "I would never interfere."

She snorted at that. "You would in a heartbeat."

And again he burst out laughing.

When he finally calmed down, she muttered, "I'm glad you're having such fun at my expense."

"Oh, it's not at your expense," he clarified, "but I can't imagine how Mack will respond to finding out Mum was grilling you."

"She's a darling," Doreen responded, "and, as I said,

she's lonely."

"Ah, so you managed to get that back around onto me again, didn't you?" he asked.

She almost heard him shaking his head.

"Are you sure you don't want to be a lawyer?"

"Nope, I definitely don't want to be a lawyer," she replied crossly. "Look at my experience with lawyers."

"Yeah," he agreed. "But what about me?"

She stopped, winced, and admitted, "Okay, fine. You? You're the exception. Robin is the only other exposure I have to lawyers," she noted. "Hardly awe-inspiring."

"Sometimes I think lawyers get a bad rap."

"Yeah, and sometimes they deserve it." She reminded Nick once again about Robin's participation in making her life miserable.

"No, you're right there too," he agreed. "Still, I am in the process of getting things in order, so I can move closer to home."

"That would be good for you and your mom," she noted. "I know your brother would like it too."

"Do you think so?" he asked in a contemplative voice. "We were close growing up, but we went our own ways, and that's been much harder to connect now."

"I think he's just happy to have you around when you can be here," she replied. "There's really no easy time once you're adults and you're off living your own lives. I think it's just sad that it takes a long time for people to reconnect, and they don't realize until they do just how much they missed each other."

"If I get back up there, you'll see a lot more of me," he declared.

She laughed. "You're warning me? Maybe I should be

warning you because I do get Mack into trouble a lot."

Nick groaned. "Maybe you could try *not* getting him into trouble."

"Well, that would go along with *me* not getting into trouble," she noted, "and apparently I don't do that well."

At that, Nick sighed. "It will be a change of pace for both of us."

"And a good one," she murmured. "Just remember that Mack's very special."

"I'm glad you think so," he said in a teasing voice.

She sighed. "Why does everybody want to be a match-maker?" she muttered.

"Only if it'll make you guys happy," Nick stated. "The last thing I want is for Mack or you to be unhappy."

"Right. And who would ever think that I could make him happy?" she asked, groaning. "I think most of the time he's just very frustrated with me."

"Most likely, with good reason. Well, let's table this. I have got to go." And he quickly rang off.

# Chapter 25

I T WAS HARD for Doreen to understand how everybody was worried about her and Mack right now. There was time for both of them to sort it out. At least she kept telling herself there was time. She didn't want that to be something that she had to worry about between them. Back home again, and hours later, everybody's conversations were still rolling around in her head.

What she was really looking forward to was a way to find this Kurt Chandler's address. When she found another name in the phonebook, she called and asked if this was Kurt Chandler's family.

A crotchety voice came from the other end. "No, he spells it differently, for heaven's sake," the woman muttered. "You should get him if you spell it another way."

"Sure," she agreed, "but it's not in the phonebook that way."

"Well, I don't know where he is," she snapped.

"Do you know of him?"

"Yes, I do. Why?"

"I was just wondering what he's up to these days."

"No good, like he always has been," she replied in a

shrill nasally voice. "You want to stay away from that one."

"So I've heard," Doreen noted. "I still need to ask him some questions."

"Well, he ain't the kind to answer any questions. He's bad news all the way." And, with that, the other woman hung up.

Just as Doreen stared at her phone, it rang again. This time it was Nathan Landry. "Nathan, what's the matter?" she asked.

"He called me ... to meet me," he said, his voice nervous.

"*Uh-oh*, you're talking about Kurt?"

"Yeah, I am. He says he just wants to talk, a visit for old time's sake."

"But do you want to meet him for old time's sake?"

"Hell no. Not at all. I mean, I don't hold any grudges against him, but I know he may not be too sure about me."

"Well, if you didn't cheat him out of something back then, why would you now?"

"I don't know," he cried out, almost in tears.

"Have you told your father?"

"Yeah, and he told me to not even, ... like, don't even think about it. He is keen on me to lose Kurt's number and to not go near him."

"That's probably a good idea," she noted.

"But I can't," Nathan said. "He won't leave me alone. What if he did have something he wants to tell me?"

"I'm sure he does, but it's more like he wants to know what you have to tell him."

There was silence on the other end. "In what way?" he asked cautiously.

"I don't know, but there's no reason, not a good one, for

him to want to get together again."

"Sure there is," Nathan argued. "We were buds before."

She questioned that, but then gave him full points for that. "Maybe, but I think this is a bad deal. What we don't want now is to have you get into any trouble that you could be put on the spot for."

"So what am I supposed to do? I need to see him, or he'll hound me forever."

She wanted to go see him too. "Well, why don't we go together?"

He gasped in shock. "Oh no," he snapped. "I mean it. He's not the guy who would take any interference in stride, and you? … *You* are not easy to be around."

She frowned, then asked, "What if instead you make a recording or wear a wire?"

"No, no, no, no," he argued. "I'll be way too nervous, and he'll know."

And that she didn't in any way doubt.

"Besides, the cops won't believe me," he added. "My dad doesn't want me to go at all."

"Of course he doesn't," she said gently. "He's afraid something bad will happen to you."

"But he's a friend of mine," Nathan argued. "Or he was."

"So then why are you nervous?" she asked him.

"I don't know," he whispered, his voice failing. "I don't know. I think it's you. I think you just made me really nervous about this whole thing."

Her eyebrows shot up at that. "Or it's your gut instinct. Maybe inside you a problem is here, and you'll have to deal with it. But let's not have anything happen that has your father losing his son again."

"No, no, I don't want to, but I don't know what to do."

"Where are you going to meet him?"

"Up at the pool hall in Rutland, beside the stripper bar."

She thought about the stripper bar and Cassandra who she'd met there last time. "Right, and it's not in an area that has any lights, where it'd be nice and bright, is it?"

"No, of course not," Nathan said, "but it's the place we always hung out before."

"Why? Because it was cool?"

"Yeah, exactly." But a note of self-condemnation filled his voice.

"Okay, maybe you should go."

"I plan to go," he said.

She stopped, hesitated, and asked, "So why are you calling me?"

"I don't know," he said, his voice breaking.

"Are you hoping that I'll talk you out of it?"

"You can't talk me out of it," he stated.

She wasn't at all sure what to make of this, but it sounded like a plea for help of some kind. "Okay, so I'm a little confused. You don't think I can talk you out of it, and you plan to go, but you still called me. So obviously you're worried. I'm not sure what it is you want me to do."

After a long moment of silence, he said, "I guess there's nothing anybody can do."

"Whoa, whoa, whoa, whoa," she cried out. But it was too late, he'd already hung up.

She stared down at the phone and now her stomach was knotting. But she didn't know what she was supposed to do here. Nathan didn't seem to want to listen to anybody, and yet maybe that's because his focus was just so paranoid. She frowned, and, not sure what Mack was up to, she called him anyway.

"Hey. What's the matter?"

"How do you always know when something's the matter?" she replied crossly.

"We'll go into that later. Tell me what happened."

And she quickly filled him in on the details. When she finally calmed down, she added, "Nathan's really panicked about meeting up with Kurt."

"Yet he's still going?" Mack asked, puzzled.

"Yeah, he is. I'm not sure what to make of it." And more silence passed, and she added, "I know. I know. This really isn't your problem, but, at the same time, I think this will end badly."

"Why do you think it'll end badly?"

She told him about Annabelle having contact with Nathan during jail and then how the nosy neighbor had seen him at Annabelle's.

"You think that that's connected?" Mack asked.

"I do. I really do. I think that not only is Nathan connected to Annabelle but this Kurt Chandler is also connected to the nosy old lady across the hallway, Hannah Hartley."

"And?"

"I think she told Kurt that Nathan had been at Annabelle's."

"Now what difference would that make?"

She hesitated. "I think it goes back to the little boy's accidental death."

"You mean, the shooting that Nathan did time for?"

"Yeah," she agreed. "But I can't get into the emails from Annabelle, at least I haven't managed to crack her password yet," she said, looking down at her laptop that she had walked away from in frustration.

"What will that show you?"

"I'm not sure," she admitted. "But I feel like there's a connection between that killing and this one."

"Any killing is a connection in and of itself," he noted, "but I'm not sure that we have anything to go on with this one."

"Would it be so hard to go and make sure that Nathan will be okay?"

"No," he said slowly. "Is that what you're asking me to do?"

"I don't know what I'm asking," she cried out. "I'm really worried right now. And the feeling's getting worse."

"Was he leaving now?"

"Yeah, pretty soon," she said, "and they'll meet up at the pool hall, not exactly an environment that I'm terribly comfortable in."

"Whoa, whoa, whoa, you're not going." And Mack's tone was flat but an order was behind it.

She sagged in place. "And neither can I sit back and watch this young man suffer yet again."

"I don't understand why you're defending him," Mack admitted, a curiosity in his voice that she wasn't accustomed to.

"I don't know, but it all goes back to whether he was ..." She stopped, trying to marshal her thoughts. "According to what Joseph said, Annabelle thought that Nathan shouldn't have done all that time and that the other guy was equally guilty."

"And yet nobody'll reopen a case in which this guy already did the time. He confessed, remember?"

"I know," she replied. "But what if Kurt doesn't know that? What if he thinks that maybe something he heard from

Annabelle or maybe just his own fears has him afraid that Annabelle or Nathan will try to reopen the old murder case, so that Kurt takes the fall as well."

"Why would that be?"

"According to ..." She stopped, trying to gather her thoughts again. "God, this is getting confusing."

"Your cases tend to be confusing," he muttered.

"Anyway—according to Annabelle, I believe, and what Joseph was telling me—she had told him about corresponding with Nathan in jail, and they had a couple big fights about that. And Annabelle and Nathan had discussed this other guy, Kurt Chandler. The gun had gone off when he'd attacked Nathan. But, according to you guys' police reports—which I haven't seen, nor the case files or the interviews—Nathan apparently said that he was holding the gun, and Kurt is the one that said it was self-defense—that Nathan had jumped Kurt and tried to kill him. According to Nathan, Kurt took the gun from Nathan and was avidly planning an armed robbery. He jumped Nathan, but Nathan already felt terribly guilty for having killed the kid and took the fall."

There was silence on the other end. "And you think this Kurt Chandler has something to do with Annabelle's murder?"

"It's about the only thing that's coming around as being possible."

"Which isn't the same thing as being guilty," he said in a dry tone.

"I know. I know. I know," she wailed, "but what am I supposed to say?"

"What is it you think will happen during this meetup?"

"I think that this Kurt Chandler is trying to figure out

what the conversation was with Annabelle and what Nathan will do about it."

"So you think he's in danger?"

"Yes, I do."

"Well, I don't really have any proof positive that Nathan's in danger, but I can go pay a visit and maybe play some pool while I am at it."

She stopped and looked down at her phone. "Would you check on Nathan?" she asked.

"I've been asked to do an awful lot crazier things in my life. So, if you think that this Nathan guy is in trouble, and potentially we've got some connection to our current case," he said, "then, yes. I'll go take a look."

"Can I come?" she asked.

"No."

She groaned.

"You'll look conspicuous. There's no way."

"And you won't?" she asked.

"Yeah, and I've got a couple other cops here who have done undercover work. We can go shoot a game of pool and just see if these guys are around and how it goes."

"Fine," she muttered.

"You're not to come, do you hear me?" And such a stern note filled his voice that she groaned.

"Fine, but you're really a party pooper."

His tone turned superquiet. "A party pooper." And then he started to laugh.

"Oh, stop," she said.

"You're really worried, aren't you?" he asked, as his laughter stopped midgurgle.

"Yes, I really am. Nathan did time, and I'm not sure he should have. And now I think the person who should have done time—and maybe for a second murder too—will try and take out Nathan to keep Kurt safe forever." And, with that, she hung up on Mack.

# Chapter 26

HOURS LATER, LONG and hard hours of pacing, hours of wondering what the heck was going on, Doreen finally gave up trying to figure out why Mack hadn't gotten back to her. So Doreen then spent hours trying to get into Annabelle's emails. Doreen had Annabelle's email address but did not have her password. Joseph had given her some logins though. But nope. She tried all kinds of other things. And then, as she sat here, staring at her laptop, she gave a startled laugh. She quickly called Millicent, asked her what was Annabelle's brother's name.

*Charlie.*

She quickly typed it into the password box, and, sure enough, that was it. Annabelle's emails loaded, and Doreen crowed in delight. Annabelle's inbox wasn't stuffed, but it had a decent amount to wade through. She had a lot of orders, a lot of contacts, a lot of suppliers, a lot of queries, and then Doreen found a folder named Nathan. As she went through it, she realized this was correspondence back and forth between the two of them, and it was pretty extensive.

Doreen quickly scanned through it, looking to see if anything, one way or another, would help in this murder investigation. But it was mostly Annabelle trying to keep Nathan positive, as he made his way through jail. She believed in him and didn't think he deserved what he'd gotten.

He'd tried to refute it at times. *I killed your brother. There is no forgiveness for me.*

And her response had been *There is forgiveness for everyone,* which revealed a lot about the person Annabelle was.

Doreen sat back, tears in her eyes. Annabelle had been a beautiful woman who had had her life cut way too short. Even as Annabelle dealt with her own pain, she was trying to help somebody else deal with his. The sadness of what had happened to her just kept compounding.

Finally, a little bit farther down in these emails, Annabelle had written *You're almost out. I'd like us to meet.*

Nathan had sent her back a happy face. *I'd like that, but I don't want to upset your partner.*

Her response had been equally casual. *He won't know about it. I won't tell him. He gets pretty upset about this anyway.*

*And so he should. I'm now a con.*

*Stop it,* she'd responded. *Just stop it. What happened to my brother was an accident, a horrible accident, yes. And it was tough for all of us, but it doesn't have to define who you are now.*

The more Doreen read Annabelle's emails, the more Doreen loved Annabelle. Her spirit was soft and gentle. And she'd been full of forgiveness for a man who had been full of guilt.

*You know yourself that your fight wasn't the way he said it was. You shouldn't have done time. It should have been him in jail.*

His response was more of the same. *It doesn't matter. It's old news. I killed your brother.*

*No, you didn't. It was him. He killed my brother,* she had snapped back.

*Don't say that. There's absolutely no path forward on that.*

*I get it. I get it.*

All of this and more was in their emails. As far as Annabelle was concerned, Nathan had been attacked by Kurt. And the gun hadn't gone off accidentally. Kurt had tried to shoot Nathan. So Nathan had dodged that attempt, his hand still on the gun, and it had fired, hitting Annabelle's brother.

But because of his guilt, Nathan had taken the fall and continued to believe Charlie's death was his fault. Whereas the truth of the matter was, Kurt Chandler had killed Charlie Hopkins. It should have been Kurt behind bars, or, at the very least, it should have been both of them. Instead, Kurt got off scot-free.

Doreen still didn't think anybody would open a case if the wrong person had been convicted and had already done time, especially when Nathan had confessed, and so this case seemed pretty much open-and-shut. She didn't know what Annabelle had testified to at the time of trial. Doreen still didn't have any copies of the court transcripts, and that would help. However, since Nathan had confessed and testified that the murder was all his fault, the cops had pretty well just closed the case on it.

Doreen pondered that for a long moment and then picked up the phone and contacted Nathan's father. "What do you want?" he asked, his tone tired, upset, almost depressed.

"I want to keep your son out of jail," she replied.

"Good luck with that," he said bitterly. "That boy is just

going to end up in more ugly trouble, and, no matter what you and I do, it's like ... he's got this death wish."

"Maybe when he first went to jail," she admitted. "I don't have a copy of the court transcript, but I understand he confessed."

"Yeah, he sure did," Mr. Landry grumbled. "Confessed and didn't even tell me the truth of it, not until he got out of jail quite recently."

"You mean, the fact that he was attacked by Kurt, who tried to kill him?"

"Yeah, exactly." Then he stopped. "Wait. Did he tell you that too?"

"No, it's in Annabelle's emails," she stated.

"Jesus," he muttered. "That girl was gold. You know that, right? He told me about all their correspondence, and how sometimes he got really depressed, and she always made him feel better, tried to get him off the hook, saying it wasn't his fault."

"Yet he was so racked with guilt at the time that apparently he confessed."

"Yes, and no one could talk him out of it either," his dad complained. "Nathan firmly believed that he was responsible and that, if he hadn't taken the gun that day, Charlie's murder wouldn't have happened."

"And for that," she replied, "I agree with him. If he hadn't, it probably wouldn't have. But that's not a reason to have to die right now."

After a silent moment, Mr. Landry asked, "Do you think he'll die?"

And such fear and yet a sense of knowing filled his voice that she sighed. "You know where he is right now, don't you?"

"I told him not to go," he said. "I tried to get him to not go."

"I know that," she confirmed. "I tried to get him to not go too. So I don't know that it will do any good, but I called the cops on him."

Mr. Malone hesitated. "You called the cops on my son?"

"Well, not in that sense," she corrected. "I called one of my cop friends to have him go to the pool hall, to be there at the same time as this meetup was going on, to get a lay of the land and to see how it is. I just wanted Nathan to have someone there to watch his back."

His father didn't seem to know what to say.

"Now I can't guarantee it will help," she added, "but I am also very concerned that it's quite possible that Kurt Chandler killed Annabelle."

"Why would he do that?" Mr. Landry cried out. Then he stopped. "Yes, Kurt would do that."

"Do you know that for sure?"

"He's the kind who likes to clip any loose threads," he told her bitterly. "He likes everything neat and tidy, and, if he thought that my son would screw up Kurt's life right now, ... you can bet Kurt would take out Nathan *in a heartbeat.*"

"That's an interesting comment," she noted wryly, "because, as far as I'm concerned, he's our most likely candidate. However, without any proof, the police don't have anything."

"He's slippery," Nathan's father confirmed. "I just ... Please keep my son alive."

"I'm working on it." Then, letting some of her exasperation show, she said, "Nathan's not being very cooperative."

Mr. Landry gave a bitter laugh. "No, and he's still racked

with guilt, and now I'm afraid he's feeling guilty over Annabelle."

"I'm sure he is. He was in town when she was killed, and he couldn't stop it. And now it's as if her whole world has been for naught, and she had been very supportive of Nathan," Doreen explained. "So I'm sure, from Nathan's perspective, this is just a bad news event that never quits."

"You're right there," Mr. Landry agreed. "But the cops are up there now, right?"

"Yes. Is your son home yet?"

"No." His voice was filled with worry. "Not yet."

"And yet that's not all that unexpected, is it?" she asked. "He could be out for hours."

"Yeah, but only with this guy," he grumbled, "only with this one. Talk about bad news. I keep trying to keep Nathan safe, but it seems like he didn't learn anything in jail."

"Yeah, he did learn something," she said. "I think he learned who his friends were. What I don't know is what he'll do while he's out there. Is it likely that he'll try to avenge Annabelle's death, if he finds out that this Kurt guy had something to do with it?"

"Absolutely," Mr. Landry replied.

"And that's what we don't want to happen then," she said. "Absolutely no way do we want him involved."

"As much as I agree with you," he added, his voice despondent, "I don't think there's anything we can do about it now."

She heard the sobs in his voice.

"I really wish he was home." And, with that, he hung up.

She got up and paced around her small living room. She still had no response from Mack. Just nothing. And her nerves were getting harder and harder to control, almost to the point of snapping. It was pitch-black outside, and she knew, if she even showed her face anywhere close to that pool hall, no way she would walk back into Mack's good graces easily.

He'd given her a direct order. Since she had brought him into this meetup in the first place, she could hardly change that now. Yet, at the same time, something was wrong. She knew it. Not knowing what else to do, she phoned the captain. When he answered, his tone was jovial, as if he had been having a nice dinner with his family. "Captain, I'm worried about Mack."

"Why is that?" he asked in a surprised tone.

She quickly explained about her worries up at the pool hall and Mack volunteering to go up there with somebody else.

"I did hear about that," the captain noted, "so thank you for telling me the truth." A note of humor filled his voice. "And you know that pool hall stays open till two in the morning, right?"

"Oh. No, I did not know that."

"It does, and Mack is supposed to check in with me pretty soon anyway," the captain shared. "So let's just give Mack the benefit of the doubt and see where this goes."

"Fine," she muttered.

"And we do like to hear that you're worried about Mack." He chuckled. "It makes us feel better. Besides, I got twenty bucks on you." And, with that and a big laugh, he hung up, leaving her staring at her phone.

"Twenty bucks?" she repeated, looking over at Thaddeus. "The captain has twenty bucks on me," she cried out in horror. "Is the captain gambling on my love life?"

And then she realized *no*. The captain was gambling on

his own men's love lives. She just happened to be one of the partners involved.

She groaned, closed her eyes, and muttered, "I guess we have a few more hours to wait."

And, with that, she headed up to have a shower and to get to bed, hopefully ready for when Mack decided to check in.

# Chapter 27

*Tuesday Morning ...*

DOREEN WOKE THE next morning, her brain fuzzy, her body exhausted, everything ringing in her ears. It took a moment to realize her phone was ringing in her ears. She quickly answered it to hear Mack on the other end. "Good God, what time is it?"

"It is seven a.m.," he replied, his voice sober.

"What's wrong?" she asked.

"Definitely somebody is dead," he noted. "And you were right. Lots of that action was coming from the pool hall, but you're wrong about one thing."

"What's that?"

"It's not Nathan who's in trouble. Although maybe he's in trouble because Kurt Chandler is dead."

She sat up and stared down at the phone in her hand. "What?"

"Yeah," Mack said. "Who figured?"

"How did he die?"

"He was shot. But no ballistics back yet."

"Oh, no, no, no. Did you guys pick up Nathan?"

"We did. And we'll hold him, until we figure out what's

going on."

She closed her eyes and pinched the bridge of her nose. "I was really hoping that sending you up there would avoid all this."

"That would be nice. It's a long story, but let's just say that Nathan and Kurt ended up in the back alley," he explained. "It's been a very long night, and the captain just contacted me and let me know that you called him last night." There was a rebuke in his voice.

She got defensive. "And, if you had contacted me, I wouldn't have had to contact him. Besides, I knew something was wrong. I just didn't know what."

He sighed. "It is what I do. You know that, right?"

"And worry is apparently what I do," she said. "Can I visit Nathan in jail?"

"Why?"

"Because I got into Annabelle's emails."

"And?"

"It was obvious that she was trying hard to save him. I don't think there's any way Nathan killed her."

"And so you're ... you're back to thinking Nathan killed Kurt because Nathan thinks Kurt killed Annabelle?"

"That makes the most sense. How were they in the pool hall?"

"Talking, joking back and forth. It got a little heated a couple times, and, at one point in time, it got quite heated, and they ended up going outside. By the time I walked toward the back of the pub, my buddy went around outside the front, and I went out the back door. Then we heard the shots fired. When we both got there, Kurt was already dead."

"Nathan?"

"He was sitting beside him, crying out for help."

"Okay. Was anybody else there?"

"I don't think so."

"Okay, that'll be one of the hardest things for Nathan to explain, right?"

"It is," Mack confirmed.

"And the gun?"

"That's the thing. The gun was on the ground beside them."

"What does Nathan say?"

"He just stared at me with a very resigned look and then stood and didn't say anything."

"Did you ask him what happened?"

"Of course I did. Then he gave me this story about some other guy shooting Kurt."

"Nobody saw a third party, I suppose."

"No, you can bet nobody did."

"Fine. I still want to talk to him."

"I'm not sure that's a good idea."

"Maybe not, but I still want to talk to him."

"I'll see when I get back to the office. I'll crash for a few hours, then I'll call you in a bit." With that, he hung up.

She walked through the kitchen, put on coffee, propped open the kitchen door, and stepped outside. Two men came immediately to mind as being the possible shooter. The trouble was, Kurt didn't live an easy lifestyle, and it could have been any number of guys wanting to take him out. But she thought two in particular might have had something to do with this.

The question was how to find out and how to do it in such a way that he would get caught. She pondered that for a long moment, and then Nan called.

"Did you hear about the shooting?" she cried out.

"Yeah, I just got off the phone with Mack," she said sadly. "Kurt, the man I had pegged as Annabelle's killer, was killed last night."

"That's just insane," Nan murmured. "This is such a nice and quiet little town."

She didn't even put it in past tense. Doreen shrugged. "That's what you told me before I moved here. I'm not so sure that I believe you anymore."

Nan chuckled. "I guess maybe it seems I lied to you, considering all the stuff that you've found out in this last while," she noted, "but honestly I don't think so. I think the goodness is still here."

"Maybe," Doreen murmured. "I'm not so sure right now."

"Do they know who killed this Kurt guy?"

"Not yet," she told her. "To add to the frustration, the cops weren't far away at the time. Yet somebody supposedly came out of the blue and killed Kurt."

"Supposedly?" Nan asked delicately.

"Yeah, but you can't say anything, Nan," she warned.

"No, I'm sure. Why don't you come down for a nice cup of tea? You sound rattled."

"I am rattled," she muttered. "I'm just not sure if I'm rattled for the right reason."

"*Can* you be rattled for the right reason?" Nan asked.

Doreen groaned. "Maybe not."

"You need to come have a cup of tea," she repeated.

"Okay, fine. I just put on coffee though." She looked at the coffeemaker and frowned. She had yet to push the button. "Change that. Apparently I didn't even push the button to start the pot dripping."

"You definitely need to come here," Nan said. "I'll see if

I can roust you up some coffee from the kitchen." And, with that, she ended the call.

Doreen sat here, looking at the coffeemaker, wondering just how rattled she really was.

Something was going on in the back of her brain, and she was struggling to bring it forward. She slowly made her way with the animals to Rosemoor. As soon as she stepped onto her grandmother's patio, Nan bustled forward, Richie at her side.

Richie took one look at Doreen and murmured, "Oh dear. You've had a tough time, haven't you?"

She smiled at him. "I'm fine."

"You look awful." Richie was nothing but a blunt instrument. "Still I found coffee for you." And he produced a big thick mug of steaming brew.

She cried out in delight. "Now this will go a long way to make me feel better."

"I hope so, dear." He patted Nan on the shoulder and disappeared back to his side of the hallway.

Doreen watched him leave and asked, "Did you tell him?"

"No, I didn't. Just that you were worried about a case."

"That's one way to say it," she replied.

"Do you have any idea who did the shooting?"

"I have a good idea," she admitted. "The trouble is, I'm torn between two suspects."

Nan looked at her in surprise and then in delight. "That's marvelous."

"No, not really," she muttered. "I have to find out which one it was, and that'll be a problem."

"Why?" Nan asked.

"Because I don't want the wrong man to go to jail, not

again."

"Again?" Nan asked.

"Yeah, I'm pretty sure that Kurt was the one who fired at Annabelle's brother years ago. And now? Now I just don't know what to think."

"Oh, dear. Drink your coffee," Nan ordered. "That'll make your brain work better."

Doreen chuckled and sipped her coffee. It was such a thick, heavy brew that she wondered if she'd even get it down. Nan got up and returned with several cookies and a little pot of cream.

Doreen smiled at the cream and laced a heavy ring into her coffee. "It's a bit rich, the coffee, isn't it?"

"With the cream, it will be fine."

And they turned their discussion to something more pleasant. By the time Doreen had finished her coffee and had eaten a couple cookies, she felt a little bit more like herself. When she got up to leave, Nan seemed worried. Doreen leaned over, kissed her grandmother on the cheek, and said, "I'm fine. I just need to get a few things sorted in my brain."

"You have a magnificent brain," Nan declared. "I'm sure you'll get it sorted in no time."

Doreen chuckled at that. "I hope so, ... but I am not at all sure about it."

"You'll be fine," Nan said. "Do what you always do. Take the animals, go for a walk, and let it just rattle around in your head."

She nodded and then, with a wave, said her goodbye and led all the animals to the river. As soon as they got to the water, Mugs wanted to play and splash around. She let him have his fun for a while, even as she slowly meandered toward home. As they made their way back along the river, she stopped several times to just spend a few moments enjoying the view. It was important that she get her head wrapped around some of this, but how was she supposed to know which suspect was the right one?

When Mugs's barks turned to shrieks she turned to see Goliath riding his back in the water.

"Goliath, stop," she hollered at him racing back to the two of them. She kicked off her shoes and stepped into the stream gasping at the cold. "Come here, right now," she ordered.

His ears went back, then didn't he sit back on his haunches, and looked from Mugs, who was standing still beneath him, to her, back and forth.

In a movement that took her off guard, he launched himself into the air and into her arms.

And down she went. She sat half on and half off the rocks, water washing over her legs, as Goliath meowed loudly in her ear and continued his river hop skip and jump to the safety of the pathway. Of course using her shoulder as a launching pad.

She groaned as she tried to stand up and make her way over the slippery rocks only to find him and Mugs on the pathway lying side by side – waiting for her.

And then she heard it…

"Hehehe."

Thaddeus, who'd somehow managed not only to stay safe, but also, of course – dry.

Glaring at the three of them, she quickly raced back home, her feet squelching with every step.

Mugs caught up with her as she turned onto her path and whined. She leaned down and gave him a good scratch. "Hey, buddy. You're doing just fine." Then added. "And despite how I look, I'm fine too."

And the antics of the past few minutes still did nothing to help her solve the problem of determining the right suspects.

She could not phone them. As soon as she did that, they would know what she had found out. And chances were, neither of them had an alibi. Pondering that even more, when she got home and inside, she phoned the police station, asking if she'd be allowed to talk to Nathan. Instead she was rerouted to the captain.

The captain was friendly, but his harried tone could not be ignored. "Doreen, you can't see him right now. He's confessed to the murder."

"Oh, good God." She closed her eyes. "He didn't do it."

After a moment of shock seemed to pass on the other end, the captain asked, "He didn't?"

"No, he didn't," she stated. "I was afraid he'd do this. Please, let me come talk to him."

"What good would that do?"

"Maybe I can get him to tell us the truth this time," she said.

He hesitated. "What do you mean, *this* time?"

"Please, Captain. Nathan already did time for one murder he didn't commit."

"What are you talking about?" he asked.

She quickly gave him the gist of it.

"But that just reinforces his motivation for taking Kurt out," he noted. "You're not helping his case."

She considered that, then asked, "Well, if I'm not helping, then I can't hurt it either, can I?"

He groaned at that.

"Please."

"Fine, you can come talk to him, but I want Mack in there with you."

"Sure, but then you're waking him up, not me."

At that, he sighed and then chuckled. "Good point. Still, that's the condition."

"Fine, fine," she muttered.

She got dressed into more worklike attire, leaving the animals at home, even though she hated to. Then realized that they were more therapy animals for her, so she walked back up to the front door and let them all out again. She loaded them all up into her car and headed to the police station and pulled into the parking lot. By the time she got everybody out and walked toward the front door, Mack stood there, huge, imposing, his arms crossed, and a frown on his face.

"Don't frown," she said, as she walked up the steps. "I'm hardly in trouble."

He just stared.

"Okay, fine, maybe I am in trouble," she said, raising both hands. "But I'm telling you that Nathan didn't do it."

"You weren't there," he replied. "You don't know that."

"No, I don't, so let me go talk to him."

"I don't know how you convinced the captain to let you do this," Mack admitted, with a headshake, "but you know that you shouldn't get involved."

"I know. I'm not involved in your current case, honest. It was the old case."

"Sure, but Kurt's dead now, so there's nobody to deal with on the old case."

She smiled. "No, but I think in this case ... Nathan's taking the fall for somebody else. But he's wrong there too."

Mack shook his head. "You'll have to explain this to

me."

"No point in explaining anything until I talk to Nathan and see if I'm right." He glared at her. She shrugged. "Sit in with me."

"Oh, I will." He nodded. "I absolutely will."

She sighed. As they walked deeper inside the station, Mack led her to another room. It was empty. As she sat here, she looked around. Two of her animals were at her feet, Thaddeus on her shoulder, all quiet and circumspect, as if knowing this was a momentous occasion. She just didn't know what an occasion it really was.

A few minutes later, Mack walked in with a cup of coffee and placed it in front of her. He said, "Nathan will be here in a few minutes."

She nodded. Mack left. When the door opened next, and Nathan came in with Mack, Nathan frowned at her. She frowned right back. "Remember that part about staying out of trouble and not going so that you didn't get into trouble again?" she asked him gently.

He nodded. "But I did it."

"Nope, you didn't," she argued cheerfully. "I'm not letting you go to jail a second time for a crime you didn't commit."

He glared at her.

"Isn't it bad enough that Annabelle is already dead? Let's not have you pay a price for somebody else again."

He got a stubborn look to his face and crossed his arms over his chest. "Nothing you can do about it. I already confessed."

"Sure, but considering you're wrong, it doesn't matter what you say. You're lying. That changes things."

"Not if I say I did it."

But she sensed the fear in him. She reached across the stainless steel table, picked up his hand, and whispered, "He didn't do it, you know?"

Nathan stared at her in shock. "What are you talking about?"

She squeezed his fingers, even as Thaddeus walked down her arm and looked at their entwined hands.

Nathan stared at the bird, shook his head, and said, "Jesus, how are you even in here."

"It's either here or the crazy ward," she muttered.

He nodded. "Crazy ward's about right." Nathan stared at her. "And what are you talking about? I did it. I already confessed. It's a done deal." He looked at Mack. "I want to go back to my cell."

"Too bad," she said, before Mack had a chance. "You're defending somebody you don't need to. Your father did not kill Kurt."

At that, dead silence filled the room.

He stared at her, and his bottom lip trembled.

She squeezed his hand again, and Thaddeus literally hopped from her arm over to his hand and wiped his head gently on his wrist. "Your father did not kill Kurt," she repeated.

He sank back. "Can you prove that?" he asked, his voice hoarse.

"Mack will prove it for you," she declared.

At that, Mack sighed. "I will?"

"Yep, you sure will," she repeated.

"Why would you think your father had done it?" Mack asked, looking over at Nathan.

Nathan remained silent, so Doreen answered Mack's question. "Because his father has always known what a bad influence Kurt Chandler has been on Nathan's life. His father knows that Kurt is the one who should have taken the fall over Annabelle's brother's death. And Nathan's father knows that his son has a weak spot and is unable often, hopefully not any longer, to deal with guys like Kurt, who seem to have this ability to make him do things that he doesn't know how to get out of."

"So his father was afraid of the influence Kurt had over Nathan here, so he came to the pool hall to kill Kurt?" Mack summarized.

"I'm pretty sure that's what Nathan here thinks."

Nathan looked over at Mack.

"But you don't know who killed Kurt, right?" Doreen asked Mack.

"We would have looked a little deeper," he stated, his voice hard, "if Nathan hadn't confessed to something he didn't do." He glared at Nathan.

"He didn't do it," she repeated sadly, "but he's already slipped back into that guilt complex, where he feels that it's all his fault because he knows how much his father hated Kurt and how much his father wanted Nathan to have nothing to do with him. And anything connected to Kurt was bad news. He never paid the price for his actions that ruined his son's life. So, in Nathan's mind, he's afraid that his dad killed Kurt." She looked over at Nathan. "Right?"

He nodded slowly. "But, if there's any way that it looks like he might be guilty, then I did it."

"And yet you didn't," she said, sagging back in her chair. She looked over at Mack. "Now maybe you can get some details out of him that will help."

Mack frowned, turned to Nathan. "Did you shoot Kurt last night?"

He shook his head. "I told you guys when you were there that somebody else shot him."

"And then you changed your story because why?"

"Because Nathan thought he recognized the shooter," she added. "But you'll find another man with another agenda, who also is about the same height as Mr. Landry. But the shooter moved with an awful lot of energy, didn't he?" she asked Nathan, looking over at him. "A lot more than you would expect from your dad."

Nathan frowned at that and then slowly nodded. "Actually, yeah. I didn't even think of that, but my dad's not moving very easily these days." He slowly let out a heavy breath. "You don't think Dad did it?" he asked, searching Doreen's gaze.

She shook her head. "No, Nathan, he didn't do it. And he'd be heartbroken to know that you're sitting here in jail again."

"So don't tell him," he said.

She laughed. "Oh, I'll leave that discussion to you." She smiled. "The bottom line is, as long as the world thinks you're guilty, this other guy thinks he's got off scot-free. So this is where you should stay, at least for the moment." She turned and looked at Mack. "Right?"

Mack just stared at her, and she felt not anger but some equally uncomfortable force.

She sighed. "Mack's angry at me too," she muttered, as she turned toward Nathan. "More about the circumstances because now they've lost whatever time frame they had to get the guy who really did these killings. Are you finally able to tell people that it wasn't you who shot Annabelle's brother?"

He jerked in surprise and then slowly nodded. "How did you know?"

"I got into Annabelle's emails. And again it's one more thing that you confessed to at the time because you were overwrought with guilt, but you really weren't the one who should have paid the price. You know he was going to kill you last night, right?"

"Who was?" Mack asked, struggling to follow the conversation.

"Keep up, Mack." She turned back to Nathan. "You know Kurt was going to take you out last night, right?"

"I wondered," Nathan replied, "but I got so angry at the end that I didn't even consider it, and I went out in the back alley with Kurt, so that we could settle our differences." He clenched his fists. "But we didn't even get a chance to get into it."

"Because the gunman was already there," she guessed. "You were supposed to get shot, not Kurt."

He stared at her. "I launched myself at Kurt in anger as we argued, and we ended up fighting, so it's quite possible the gunman was trying to shoot me," he noted. "But then, when Kurt went down so fast, I didn't even know what had happened. The cops were there, like in an instant."

"That's because I had asked Mack here to go there, to keep an eye on you, so that you wouldn't get into a situation like this," she pointed out.

He stared at her, frowned at Mack, and replied, "Well, it didn't work, did it?"

Mack snapped, "Because you were an idiot, and then you turned around and confessed to something you didn't do. *Again.*"

At that, Nathan's shoulders slumped.

"I get it," Doreen told Nathan. "You were trying to do the right thing at every turn."

"Sure," he agreed, "but somehow doing the right thing ended up always being the wrong thing."

She smiled. "The nice thing is, right now you'll get another chance to keep working on getting that right."

He shrugged. "And who will I do it for anymore? Annabelle was the person who I was trying to improve myself for, so I could keep her in my world. She was a beautiful person."

"Your dad doesn't deserve what you've just done here either, but, when he realizes why, it will warm his heart."

Nathan stared at her, and a tiny smile played at the corner of his mouth. "You mean, before or after he wants to take the belt to me?"

She smiled. "Your dad's been a hard man, but he's been in your corner every time. This time he knows that you were in his corner, and that will make a difference."

Nathan nodded slowly. "I hope so, but it all still feels so very wrong."

"What we aren't getting to is whoever killed Kurt," Mack reminded the room.

She nodded. "No, but I highly suspect that today"—she shrugged—"maybe tomorrow, I'll have a visitor."

Mack stiffened. "You want to clarify that?"

"How about you come spend the day at my place and maybe have an extra nap or two while you are there?"

At that, Nathan leaned forward. "I don't even know who could be the one you're after."

"Well, the less you know in this case is a good thing. I want you to stay here in jail, safe and sound, and Mack will come with me—and maybe somebody else." She reconsidered that. "I'm not sure. The gun was left onsite?"

Mack nodded. "In our possession now."

"Then the question is really about his methodology."

DALE MAYER

She groaned. "I'll go home now." She stood and, holding out her arm for Thaddeus, he walked along it and back up her shoulder. "Please take Nathan back to his cell and then come to my place."

Mack asked, "Are you going to explain?"

"I will," she whispered, "but I think it's much better if Nathan has no idea."

Mack nodded. "I'll be there in five."

And, with that, she walked outside, not looking left or right, and headed home again.

# Chapter 28

WHEN DOREEN OPENED her front door to Mack a little later, he stood there, hands on hips, glaring at her. She looked past him, happy to see that he had parked his vehicle out of sight.

"I really want an explanation, and I want a name."

"I can give you the name," she said, "but it's really been the same person the whole time."

He shrugged. "I don't get it."

"I know, and I'm not sure—unless we can talk to this guy—that we'll get the answers we need either."

He stared. "I sure hope you know what you're doing."

"Probably not, but I did phone him, and I did invite him over."

"You invited a killer here?"

"Sure," she admitted. And then she frowned. "What else was I supposed to do?"

"Oh, good God." Mack pinched the bridge of his nose. "Fine, and when's this person coming?"

"Soon. Very soon. So maybe you should go hide."

He stared at her. "Are you expecting to get attacked?"

"No, but I'm hoping we can get answers. Now, with the

current mess, a confession would be lovely to sort it out."

Mack shook his head. "That is entrapment."

"We're just talking in my house," she argued. "You've had a rough day, and you were having a nap, when you came down and heard it all."

He stared at her, and then he laughed. "What makes you think he'll talk to you?"

"Well, he has so far, but that doesn't mean he will continue to do so now."

Mack didn't even have a clue what to say.

She heard a vehicle, and she whispered, "Go, go, go."

Mack bolted upstairs, and she walked to the front door and opened it.

As soon as Joseph got out of his vehicle, he walked toward her and asked, "What did you want to talk about? I'm all packed up and ready to leave."

"Ah. Just a few things here and there. Did you talk to the cops?" she asked, motioning him inside. He really wanted to stay outside. She added in a lowered tone, "You don't want to be outside. My neighbor over there's very nosy."

A *harrumph* came from the other side of the fence.

She nodded at Joseph, as if to say, *I told you so.* He stared at the fence, shook his head, and declared, "God, you're weird." They both walked into her house.

"Thank you," she said cheerfully. "I know, for a lot of people, this is way more than they're used to."

"You're not kidding."

"So why are you leaving again?"

"I told you. I wanted to get out."

"Sure, but ..." She stopped, hesitated, then asked, "Did the cops ... are they okay with you leaving?"

"Why wouldn't they be?" he asked. "They've got their killer already."

"Right. I heard that Nathan had been picked up for killing somebody in town."

"What do you expect?" Joseph asked. "I mean, the guy does time, and the first thing he does when he gets out again is … he kills somebody." He laughed bitterly. "It's typical con behavior. They can't handle life outside, find it too hard, and do something so they can go back inside."

"Who would want to go back inside?" she asked.

"I don't know, but we hear about it all the time.'

Trouble was, she had heard of convicts doing things like that, so it was a pretty good reason. She smiled and asked, "Would you like some coffee? I was just going to put some on."

"Yeah, whatever," he mumbled. "I suppose you want some money for helping me before I leave," he noted, "but I don't have any."

"I didn't ask for any money in the beginning either." She walked into the kitchen. "Besides, you asked me to get you off the hook, yet you seem to think you're off the hook anyway."

"What do you mean, *seem to think* I'm off the hook?"

"I don't know if you heard, but the kid? … He didn't do it."

"What do you mean, he didn't do it?" he asked, staring at her in shock.

"Nathan Landry, … he didn't do it. I was down there talking to him this morning."

"You went to the police station and talked to him?"

"Sure." She turned to face Joseph. "How else will I get answers?"

He just shook his head slowly. "You are the strangest person I've ever met."

She winced. "Yeah, I'm starting to realize I'm a bit of an oddity."

"A bit?" he repeated, staring at her in shock. "You're a whole lot more than a bit of an oddity."

"Now be nice," she protested. She opened up the rear kitchen door wide and suggested, "We can sit outside, if you want."

"Sure, why not." Yet he seemed hesitant to go out.

"When you said you're all packed up, is like the car packed and everything?"

"Sure, I'm hitting the road now. I don't want to stay. Matter of fact, I'd just as soon leave."

And it was obvious he was getting antsy. "Okay, before you go, you want to answer a few questions for me?"

"What, more questions?" he cried out in frustration.

"Yeah. And the big one is, why did you shoot Annabelle?"

# Chapter 29

D OREEN KNEW SHE'D shocked Joseph to the core. He stared at her, but the anger was building on his face.

"You stupid ... idiot," he cried out. "I didn't kill her."

"You did," she argued. "I mean, besides the fact that they always look to the spouse and partner first, you also had an alibi, then you didn't have an alibi, *blah-blah-blah.* Then you came up with somebody who was a perfect patsy for you. And then there was the other issue with Kurt Chandler. Getting him involved was a stroke of genius."

He stared at her.

"After all, you heard from Annabelle how Kurt was the one who was actually guilty of the murder of Charlie. Getting Kurt all stoked up that Nathan would reopen the old murder case to make sure Kurt paid for his actions, well, that was just brilliant. But it all comes down to the fact that you couldn't be sure how it would play out, so you wanted to make sure that he died."

"Who?" Joseph asked. "Nathan or Kurt?"

"You were hoping that Kurt would kill Nathan. Instead you ended up shooting Kurt."

He stared at her in shock and shook his head. "You're

crazy, you know that?" He stood, walking over to the door. "I don't have to sit here and listen to this garbage."

"No, you don't," she agreed cheerfully. "Everything's already been recorded for the police."

"Recorded how?" he asked. "Nobody knows anything."

"Nathan does though," she shared. "He was pretty close to Annabelle."

"Too close," he said, with a sneer. "That was just a stupid distorted, nasty relationship. And she expected me to go along with it and to let this con into my space. No way I would do that."

"Right. So you had to kill him?"

He stared at her. "I didn't kill him."

"I know," she agreed, "but maybe that's who you were trying to kill. Maybe it wasn't Kurt you wanted to kill either. It was Nathan all along. Yet twice you tried and failed. Maybe you didn't see it as a failure, right? I mean, after all, kill one bad guy or another, what difference does it make? But it doesn't explain why you took out Annabelle. She was the beloved sweetheart of all."

He glared at her. "Yeah, she was, but she also had this sick obsession with helping him."

"With helping Nathan?"

He nodded. "It was more than that," he added in disgust. "She told me that she loved him, that she wanted to spend time with him, spend her life with him."

"Did she admit that to you?"

"She didn't have to. I could tell. Nobody does things like that for a con without feeling something, something that is disgusting and wrong."

"She was helping Nathan because Kurt accidentally killed her brother. She knew it wasn't Nathan. She knew about Nathan's involvement, and she knew about Kurt. Why would she *not* want to help Nathan?"

"I don't care why. I don't care anything about it," he yelled. "It's just wrong. He's a con, and he should have been in jail. Now he'll go exactly where he belongs."

"You think so? Because you just confessed to killing her."

"No, I didn't. Kurt killed her."

"Nope, Kurt didn't," she argued. "You did, and then you killed Kurt. I think the bottom line was, what you really wanted was, to make sure Nathan dies too. But, if you can't make that happen, you want him to spend another twenty-plus years in prison."

He stared at her, and his face twisted from being that stupid sappy bartender guy, who didn't give a shit in this world, to this mean ugly man who faced Annabelle down for the last time.

"Where'd you get the gun from?" Doreen asked.

He shrugged. "They're not hard to get."

She smiled. "Kurt by any chance?"

He glared at her. "You are a little too smart for your own good," he swore.

"Another reason to take out Kurt. I mean, after all, he could put the gun in your hand. Evidence Kurt could use against you."

He continued to glare at her, his fists clenching.

"All you wanted to do was leave, right?"

"Absolutely. Are you going to let me?"

She shrugged. "Maybe, but they will still find you."

"No." He shook his head. "I learned a lot from Kurt. Took a bit, believe me, but I got there eventually."

"Yeah? I mean you killed Kurt and set up Nathan and

killed your girlfriend. Not a bad streak so far, *huh?*"

He just smiled at her, like a cornered lion. "Now see? I take care of you, and I'm free and clear."

She smiled at him. "The thing is, people like to say things like that. However, it's just not so easy to do. How many guns did you pick up anyway?" She chuckled. "You've already lost two."

He glared at her. "So? Doesn't mean I don't know where to get a third one."

"You're a hot item right now," she noted. "I don't think anybody'll sell you a gun anytime soon. Yet I've been wrong before. I'm not exactly sure how that element always ends up surviving. Maybe for the right price, correct? And Annabelle had a bunch of money that you took from her, from your apartment, didn't you? Orders that she'd taken deposits on, money that she was saving and what for? To help Nathan go back to school and to get a start in life or whatever it was that he chose to do because she felt bad."

"Yeah, she felt bad all right," he confirmed, his face twisting. "It was sickening to watch her fawn all over him. They were making all these plans to meet but not with me, oh, no, no. I wasn't allowed to meet with him."

"Because you didn't approve of him." She turned to look at Joseph. "And they both knew it."

"Sure, but they didn't have to hide it all from me."

"So what? They did hide it, and you immediately thought the worst, didn't you? You thought that Annabelle was all about him."

"She was," he snapped.

"She was all about you, but was trying to right a wrong with Nathan," Doreen explained. "I feel sorry for her. She was trying to do right, but you were just so full of jealousy and rage that you couldn't let her."

"No, I wasn't," he yelled. "I was just done with it. I was just done with all of it. I didn't care anymore."

"If you hadn't cared, you wouldn't have killed her," she snapped. "But, having killed her, that just meant you had to cover your tracks."

"The old lady put this in motion. Annabelle had been on the phone, when Hannah knocked on the door, asking if she'd heard something odd. Only Annabelle was talking to Nathan, and Hannah overheard the conversation. She told Kurt. Kurt told me. And I just came home on my break. It happened way to easily."

"So once Kurt heard about it, then you knew Kurt was a problem, right?"

He swore. "Yeah, that guy will just wring everybody dry of money. He was blackmailing me. I didn't have any money, and he kept telling me that he would tell the cops all about Annabelle and Nathan, and then I would end up in jail, just like Nathan. No way I would do that." He glared at her. "And no way you'll stop me either."

And he lunged forward, grasped her by the neck, shoving her against the table. "I'll choke the life out of you," he cried out. "You're not stopping me from leaving."

She struggled to get a word out, to get a breath in, when he screamed in pain. She winced as his hand jerked free, and she backed up to the rear kitchen door.

Goliath's front claws dug into his shoulders, sliding in a slow skid down his back. Mugs had bit him and was still hanging off his butt. Thaddeus stared at him, eye to eye, screeching, "Thaddeus is here. Thaddeus is here," while beating him in the face with his wings.

But, if that weren't enough, her avenging angel, Mack,

stood in the kitchen, glaring at Joseph. He looked over at Doreen and said, "You want to call the troops back?"

She whistled and called off the animals. Mugs dropped to all fours and came racing to her, his tail wagging furiously. Thaddeus landed on Mack's shoulder, and Goliath, in a slow skid, jumped to the ground and sauntered toward her, his tail flicking in the air.

Joseph stared at her and her animals and cried out, "You're crazy. You're freaking crazy. So are they."

"Yelling at me, putting hands on me got them irate in the first place," she told him gently. "So maybe you shouldn't use that tone around me."

He looked over at Mack and pointed to her. "She's nuts. You know that, right? She's crazy."

Mack nodded. "She's a particular kind of crazy. Obviously not your kind." Mack pulled out a pair of handcuffs, twisted the younger man around, and snapped him up tight as he read him his rights. Mack looked over at Doreen. "You happy now?"

"Yes. Tell Nathan to go home and to give his dad a hug."

Mack chuckled. "Maybe, but you're in for a lot of paperwork."

"No, I don't want any more paperwork," she cried out, staring at him in horror.

"Too bad. So bring the animals and get them all down to the station right now."

She groaned and looked over at Joseph. "See what trouble you got me into?"

"Trouble?" he repeated. "Your animals attacked me. I'll file a complaint, and that's on you. You nasty woman ..."

"Self-defense," she said, with a shrug, between his profanities. "You attacked me. The animals were just trying to protect me. You are going to jail." And she lifted her blond hair off her throat so that Mack could see.

At that, a muscle working in his tight jaw, Mack faced the punk, roaring, "You did that? You tried to choke her?" he cried out.

Even Joseph had enough sense to shrink away from the irate tone in Mack's voice.

"You don't understand," he explained. "She's nuts. She needs to be put away, so the rest of the world's safe."

Mack shot her a dark look. "I won't argue that point with you. We're going down to the station."

"I need a hospital," Joseph cried out.

"You're not getting one," Mack declared. "We'll treat these few scratches down there."

"The dog bit me. That bird is a menace. He tired to poke my eyes out!" And Joseph was still hollering profanities as Mack led him outside.

She walked slowly to the front door and leaned against the doorjamb.

Once he had his prisoner in the vehicle, Mack turned and asked her, "Are you coming?"

She nodded. "I'll take my own vehicle."

"Then let's go," Mack said.

She smiled. "You're welcome."

He stared up at the sky and then nodded. "Yeah." And then he looked back at her. "You too."

She laughed. "See? We make a great pair."

"As long as you figured that out, it's all good."

With that, she slowly maneuvered the rest of her lot to her vehicle, where she loaded them all up and headed to the station. She could only hope that this would be a short visit.

The animals were getting way too used to her being there.

Besides, she just wanted to come home and to spend the afternoon, hopefully with Mack. But considering the amount of paperwork she had just given him, she didn't think that would likely happen. If she was lucky though, he might forgive her enough to come over and to cook dinner. She was still waiting on that beef stroganoff cooking lesson that he'd promised her a long time ago, not sure what all had canceled that earlier.

She walked into the station behind Mack and asked, "Are you still going to cook dinner for me tonight?" she muttered.

He looked over at her, and the corner of his lips quirked. "What's the matter? You afraid you're in my bad books?"

She shrugged. "Nope, you'll forgive me."

He asked, "What makes you think so?"

"You haven't killed me yet," she replied in a low whisper, "so you're not going to now." She shot him a mischievous look, "Besides, I have it on good authority that you like me."

He stopped, turned, and asked, "What?"

She nodded. "Yeah. In case you haven't talked to your mother or your brother, they're both matchmaking." He stared at her, and a bright red flush rolled up his cheeks. She chuckled, leaned closer, patted his cheek gently, and added, "Oh, yeah, you really should talk to them."

And, with that, she walked ahead of him into the station to take care of the paperwork. Then she called back, "You still haven't answered."

"Yeah, dinner tonight."

"Good," she said, with a beaming smile. "I've worked up quite an appetite."

He groaned. "Fine, I'm cooking though."

"Oh, good. At least that way we'll have something edible to eat."

And, with that, and the animals in tow, she flounced past their fascinated audience, watching them. She smiled at the captain. "Afternoon, Captain. We got this one sewn up."

His booming laugh spread out across the station. "Good Lord, Doreen, you are a force when unleashed."

"Yep, sure am," she agreed rubbing her hands together gleefully, "now… what's next?"

# Epilogue

S EVERAL DAYS LATER Doreen walked along the cemetery in Glenmore, Mack at her side, the animals roaming gently on leashes around them. Annabelle's funeral had been well attended by many of the locals. It did Doreen's heart good to see the large crowd, to see the people who loved Annabelle and who would miss her.

Doreen took a deep breath and stretched out her arms. "Life can be pretty good sometimes," she noted.

"At least you look a bit more relaxed, after taking a few days off from your bizarre hobby."

"I feel better too," she murmured, looking up at him with a bright smile. "That last one was a little scary."

"A little?" he quipped. "Remember how you weren't supposed to get attacked anymore?"

"Remember how you were supposed to jump in at the right time to save me?"

He sighed. "Yeah, believe me. I'm still not happy about that."

"What? The fact that you followed my instructions or the fact that we solved this one?"

"It's not even a matter of having solved it. We did get

the confession, on paper, and that makes it a heck of a lot easier for us," he noted, with a smile. "But just thinking about how crazy it was will give me nightmares for weeks."

"Right? And then Nathan, he needs some counseling."

"His dad's there for him," Mack noted. "I can't imagine what that conversation looked like."

"No, I'm sure it wasn't easy. I have heard from both of them since though, and they're doing better. They will be just fine."

He smiled, kissed her gently on the forehead, and said, "You're good people."

"I know I am. So are you."

He laughed. "Sometimes I wonder."

She looked over at the mausoleum full of tiny little locked drawers. "So these are full of those urns? I guess it's for people who have been cremated and who don't want to go in the ground."

He nodded. "People who don't want to be buried, and family members who want a place where they can come and visit their loved ones." He pointed to the beautiful plaques on the marble faces of each locked drawer.

She nodded. As they wandered up and down, she read off a bunch of the names. "Some of these are old."

"Sure," Mack said, "this practice is fairly common in a lot of places in the world."

"I haven't had a whole lot to do with death," she noted. "Outside of, you know ..."

He nodded. "I know." He gave her a smile.

She laughed. "Kelowna has been good for me."

"Yeah, it has been—and for me too. And, yes, I did talk to my brother and my mother," he shared, with an eye roll.

She chuckled. "At least we know that they have your

best interests at heart."

"Sure, but it's been a long time since I had to deal with my family checking in on my love life."

She smiled. "I never really had it at all, so I find it very cute."

"It's hardly cute," Mack argued. "Even my brother was in on this."

"I know, but just think. Maybe my ex will finally divorce me, and we can get free of him."

"Maybe." Mack studied her. "You keep telling everybody that, until you're free and clear, you won't take the next step."

"Nope, I won't. You know that."

"I do."

She hesitated, a little bit of uncertainty entering her voice as she asked, "Or are you changing your mind?"

He stopped and glared at her. "Do I look like I'm changing my mind? How many people do you know who wander cemeteries?"

"We were just here for Annabelle, so it's not all that unusual."

"Maybe." He sighed. "But no. I'm not changing my mind. I'm waiting. Patiently."

"Sometimes patiently." She chuckled.

"Fine. ... Impatiently."

She nodded. "And it's appreciated. I just don't feel that I can move forward until I take care of my past." He reached out, letting his hand slide down her arm to grasp her fingers in his. She gave a gentle squeeze back. "This is such a beautiful resting place," she murmured in quiet joy. "Just so much history." As she rounded the corner, she gasped. "Look."

And there, one of the tiles had been cracked open.

Mack frowned, as he dropped her hand and stepped forward. "Vandalism is another problem but not usually like this." He sighed.

"Yeah, but …" She stopped and looked into the opened-up area. "The urn's still here, or something is."

He opened up his phone and hit Flashlight and said, "Yeah, you can still see it there. Well, that's something."

Peering closer, she pointed. "Something else is beside it. I can't really see it clearly."

He put on a pair of gloves, and, moving some of the marble out of the way, he managed to open up enough that his flashlight shone into the dark space, and they could see what it was.

"It's black," she noted. "What is that?"

He muttered a curse word.

"We really have to work on your swearing."

He sighed. "Says you."

"What is it?" she queried.

He drew his phone closer and made a call.

She frowned at him. "What's the matter?"

He placed a finger against his lips, and he quickly answered the questions at the other end.

After he'd disconnected, she asked, "Uzi? Did you say an Uzi is in there?"

He glared at her. "No. No, I did not."

Her lips twitched. She'd heard him, and, once she'd heard him, there was no end to it. "In an urn," she cried out. "So there is … Wait for it, wait for it."

And he shook his head. "No, no, I'm not listening." And he clapped his hands over his ears.

"Doesn't matter," she declared grinning. "You can run,

but you can't hide. My next case is the *Uzi in the Urn*."

And she burst out laughing because she had another case, and it just rolled off her tongue. *Uzi in the Urn.*

This concludes Book 20 of Lovely Lethal Gardens:
Toes up in the Tulips.

Read about Uzi in the Urn: Lovely Lethal Gardens, Book 21

# Lovely Lethal Gardens: Uzi in the Urn (Book #21)

A new cozy mystery series from *USA Today* best-selling author Dale Mayer. Follow gardener and amateur sleuth Doreen Montgomery—and her amusing and mostly lovable cat, dog, and parrot—as they catch murderers and solve crimes in lovely Kelowna, British Columbia.

**Riches to rags. ... Hidden guns, ... old but not forgotten wounds, ... and a buried treasure!**

Finding an Uzi in the urn at the shattered mausoleum is exciting and frustrating. Yet Doreen can't delve into the case, and Mack has been firm about that. She struggles to focus on other cases from her journalist files, in particular the Bob Small file. Only her plan goes off the rails when Nan and her cronies show up at her door, with the Rosemoor bus, intent on heading to the excitement happening at the cemetery.

When a grave is opened to reveal its shocking contents, the city is on high alert, as gang members arrive, circling around, looking for a rumored buried treasure, all connected to a man who died six months ago. Between crooked lawyers, greedy family members, changes of heart, and everyone else out looking for a buried treasure, Corporal Mack Moreau is on his toes. Especially as Doreen and her animal cohorts are in the middle once again.

But no one could possibly envision where this case ends up—right back in the cemetery where it all started ...

Find Book 21 here!
To find out more visit Dale Mayer's website.
https://geni.us/DMUziUniversal

# Get Your Free Book Now!

Have you met Charmin Marvin?

If you're ready for a new world to explore, and love ill-mannered cats, I have a series that might be your next binge read. It's called Broken Protocols, and it's a series that takes you through time-travel, mysteries, romance… and a talking cat named Charmin Marvin.

Go here and tell me where to send it!
https://dl.bookfunnel.com/s3ds5a0w8n

# Author's Note

Thank you for reading Toes up in the Tulips: Lovely Lethal Gardens, Book 20! If you enjoyed the book, please take a moment and leave a short review.

Dear reader,

I love to hear from readers, and you can contact me at my website: www.dalemayer.com or at my Facebook author page. To be informed of new releases and special offers, sign up for my newsletter or follow me on BookBub. And if you are interested in joining Dale Mayer's Reader Group, here is the Facebook sign up page.
http://geni.us/DaleMayerFBGroup

Cheers,
Dale Mayer

# About the Author

Dale Mayer is a *USA Today* best-selling author, best known for her SEALs military romances, her Psychic Visions series, and her Lovely Lethal Garden cozy series. Her contemporary romances are raw and full of passion and emotion (Broken But ... Mending, Hathaway House series). Her thrillers will keep you guessing (Kate Morgan, By Death series), and her romantic comedies will keep you giggling (*It's a Dog's Life*, a stand-alone novella; and the Broken Protocols series, starring Charming Marvin, the cat).

Dale honors the stories that come to her—and some of them are crazy, break all the rules and cross multiple genres!

To go with her fiction, she also writes nonfiction in many different fields, with books available on résumé writing, companion gardening, and the US mortgage system. All her books are available in print and ebook format.

## Connect with Dale Mayer Online

*Dale's Website – www.dalemayer.com*
*Twitter – @DaleMayer*
*Facebook Page – geni.us/DaleMayerFBFanPage*
*Facebook Group – geni.us/DaleMayerFBGroup*
*BookBub – geni.us/DaleMayerBookbub*
*Instagram – geni.us/DaleMayerInstagram*
*Goodreads – geni.us/DaleMayerGoodreads*
*Newsletter – geni.us/DaleNews*

# Also by Dale Mayer

## Published Adult Books:

### Shadow Recon
Magnus, Book 1

### Bullard's Battle
Ryland's Reach, Book 1
Cain's Cross, Book 2
Eton's Escape, Book 3
Garret's Gambit, Book 4
Kano's Keep, Book 5
Fallon's Flaw, Book 6
Quinn's Quest, Book 7
Bullard's Beauty, Book 8
Bullard's Best, Book 9
Bullard's Battle, Books 1–2
Bullard's Battle, Books 3–4
Bullard's Battle, Books 5–6
Bullard's Battle, Books 7–8

### Terkel's Team
Damon's Deal, Book 1
Wade's War, Book 2
Gage's Goal, Book 3
Calum's Contact, Book 4
Rick's Road, Book 5

Scott's Summit, Book 6
Brody's Beast, Book 7
Terkel's Twist, Book 8
Terkel's Triumph, Book 9

## Terkel's Guardian
Radar, Book 1

## Kate Morgan
Simon Says... Hide, Book 1
Simon Says... Jump, Book 2
Simon Says... Ride, Book 3
Simon Says... Scream, Book 4
Simon Says... Run, Book 5
Simon Says... Walk, Book 6

## Hathaway House
Aaron, Book 1
Brock, Book 2
Cole, Book 3
Denton, Book 4
Elliot, Book 5
Finn, Book 6
Gregory, Book 7
Heath, Book 8
Iain, Book 9
Jaden, Book 10
Keith, Book 11
Lance, Book 12
Melissa, Book 13
Nash, Book 14
Owen, Book 15

Percy, Book 16
Quinton, Book 17
Ryatt, Book 18
Spencer, Book 19
Hathaway House, Books 1–3
Hathaway House, Books 4–6
Hathaway House, Books 7–9

## The K9 Files
Ethan, Book 1
Pierce, Book 2
Zane, Book 3
Blaze, Book 4
Lucas, Book 5
Parker, Book 6
Carter, Book 7
Weston, Book 8
Greyson, Book 9
Rowan, Book 10
Caleb, Book 11
Kurt, Book 12
Tucker, Book 13
Harley, Book 14
Kyron, Book 15
Jenner, Book 16
Rhys, Book 17
Landon, Book 18
Harper, Book 19
Kascius, Book 20
The K9 Files, Books 1–2
The K9 Files, Books 3–4
The K9 Files, Books 5–6

The K9 Files, Books 7–8
The K9 Files, Books 9–10
The K9 Files, Books 11–12

## Lovely Lethal Gardens

Arsenic in the Azaleas, Book 1
Bones in the Begonias, Book 2
Corpse in the Carnations, Book 3
Daggers in the Dahlias, Book 4
Evidence in the Echinacea, Book 5
Footprints in the Ferns, Book 6
Gun in the Gardenias, Book 7
Handcuffs in the Heather, Book 8
Ice Pick in the Ivy, Book 9
Jewels in the Juniper, Book 10
Killer in the Kiwis, Book 11
Lifeless in the Lilies, Book 12
Murder in the Marigolds, Book 13
Nabbed in the Nasturtiums, Book 14
Offed in the Orchids, Book 15
Poison in the Pansies, Book 16
Quarry in the Quince, Book 17
Revenge in the Roses, Book 18
Silenced in the Sunflowers, Book 19
Toes up in the Tulips, Book 20
Uzi in the Urn, Book 21
Lovely Lethal Gardens, Books 1–2
Lovely Lethal Gardens, Books 3–4
Lovely Lethal Gardens, Books 5–6
Lovely Lethal Gardens, Books 7–8
Lovely Lethal Gardens, Books 9–10

## Psychic Vision Series

Tuesday's Child
Hide 'n Go Seek
Maddy's Floor
Garden of Sorrow
Knock Knock...
Rare Find
Eyes to the Soul
Now You See Her
Shattered
Into the Abyss
Seeds of Malice
Eye of the Falcon
Itsy-Bitsy Spider
Unmasked
Deep Beneath
From the Ashes
Stroke of Death
Ice Maiden
Snap, Crackle...
What If...
Talking Bones
String of Tears
Inked Forever
Psychic Visions Books 1–3
Psychic Visions Books 4–6
Psychic Visions Books 7–9

## By Death Series

Touched by Death
Haunted by Death
Chilled by Death

By Death Books 1–3

## Broken Protocols – Romantic Comedy Series
Cat's Meow
Cat's Pajamas
Cat's Cradle
Cat's Claus
Broken Protocols 1-4

## Broken and... Mending
Skin
Scars
Scales (of Justice)
Broken but… Mending 1-3

## Glory
Genesis
Tori
Celeste
Glory Trilogy

## Biker Blues
Morgan: Biker Blues, Volume 1
Cash: Biker Blues, Volume 2

## SEALs of Honor
Mason: SEALs of Honor, Book 1
Hawk: SEALs of Honor, Book 2
Dane: SEALs of Honor, Book 3
Swede: SEALs of Honor, Book 4
Shadow: SEALs of Honor, Book 5
Cooper: SEALs of Honor, Book 6
Markus: SEALs of Honor, Book 7

Evan: SEALs of Honor, Book 8
Mason's Wish: SEALs of Honor, Book 9
Chase: SEALs of Honor, Book 10
Brett: SEALs of Honor, Book 11
Devlin: SEALs of Honor, Book 12
Easton: SEALs of Honor, Book 13
Ryder: SEALs of Honor, Book 14
Macklin: SEALs of Honor, Book 15
Corey: SEALs of Honor, Book 16
Warrick: SEALs of Honor, Book 17
Tanner: SEALs of Honor, Book 18
Jackson: SEALs of Honor, Book 19
Kanen: SEALs of Honor, Book 20
Nelson: SEALs of Honor, Book 21
Taylor: SEALs of Honor, Book 22
Colton: SEALs of Honor, Book 23
Troy: SEALs of Honor, Book 24
Axel: SEALs of Honor, Book 25
Baylor: SEALs of Honor, Book 26
Hudson: SEALs of Honor, Book 27
Lachlan: SEALs of Honor, Book 28
Paxton: SEALs of Honor, Book 29
Bronson: SEALs of Honor, Book 30
Hale: SEALs of Honor, Book 31
SEALs of Honor, Books 1–3
SEALs of Honor, Books 4–6
SEALs of Honor, Books 7–10
SEALs of Honor, Books 11–13
SEALs of Honor, Books 14–16
SEALs of Honor, Books 17–19
SEALs of Honor, Books 20–22
SEALs of Honor, Books 23–25

## Heroes for Hire

Heroes for Hire, Books 7–9
Heroes for Hire, Books 10–12
Heroes for Hire, Books 13–15
Heroes for Hire, Books 16–18
Heroes for Hire, Books 19–21
Heroes for Hire, Books 22–24

## SEALs of Steel
Badger: SEALs of Steel, Book 1
Erick: SEALs of Steel, Book 2
Cade: SEALs of Steel, Book 3
Talon: SEALs of Steel, Book 4
Laszlo: SEALs of Steel, Book 5
Geir: SEALs of Steel, Book 6
Jager: SEALs of Steel, Book 7
The Final Reveal: SEALs of Steel, Book 8
SEALs of Steel, Books 1–4
SEALs of Steel, Books 5–8
SEALs of Steel, Books 1–8

## The Mavericks
Kerrick, Book 1
Griffin, Book 2
Jax, Book 3
Beau, Book 4
Asher, Book 5
Ryker, Book 6
Miles, Book 7
Nico, Book 8
Keane, Book 9
Lennox, Book 10
Gavin, Book 11

Shane, Book 12
Diesel, Book 13
Jerricho, Book 14
Killian, Book 15
Hatch, Book 16
Corbin, Book 17
Aiden, Book 18
The Mavericks, Books 1–2
The Mavericks, Books 3–4
The Mavericks, Books 5–6
The Mavericks, Books 7–8
The Mavericks, Books 9–10
The Mavericks, Books 11–12

## Standalone Novellas
It's a Dog's Life
Riana's Revenge
Second Chances

# Published Young Adult Books:

## Family Blood Ties Series
Vampire in Denial
Vampire in Distress
Vampire in Design
Vampire in Deceit
Vampire in Defiance
Vampire in Conflict
Vampire in Chaos
Vampire in Crisis
Vampire in Control
Vampire in Charge

Family Blood Ties Set 1–3
Family Blood Ties Set 1–5
Family Blood Ties Set 4–6
Family Blood Ties Set 7–9
Sian's Solution, A Family Blood Ties Series Prequel
     Novelette

## Design series
Dangerous Designs
Deadly Designs
Darkest Designs
Design Series Trilogy

## Standalone
In Cassie's Corner
Gem Stone (a Gemma Stone Mystery)
Time Thieves

# Published Non-Fiction Books:

## Career Essentials
Career Essentials: The Résumé
Career Essentials: The Cover Letter
Career Essentials: The Interview
Career Essentials: 3 in 1